In a pirate's lair, nothing is as it seems . . .

Shipwrecked! When Royce Hastings is found washed up on the shore of a verdant tropical island, he tells the natives he is a merchant headed for Mozambique. The truth, however, is far more mercenary. Noble by birth, the once favored Royce has lost his fortune and family; now he is a hired henchman on the trail of an elusive pirate. His "shipwreck" was a fake. He'll stop at nothing to infiltrate the island and capture his prey. His mother and sisters' lives depend on it.

The last thing Royce expects is to be captured himself. But the lovely young woman who tends to his wounds in the tropics quickly takes hold of his heart. Simone is the island's healer, and her skilled ministrations not only awaken his soul but disturb his conscience. His path has been predetermined; his identity must remain concealed at all costs. Yet the passion he feels in Simone's sultry, loving arms cannot be denied. With his loyalties torn, Royce must make an agonizing, unthinkable choice . . ..

Visit us at www.kensingtonbooks.com

I0524980

Books by Tina Donahue

Dangerous Desires
Loving Lies
Wicked Whispers
Passionate Pursuit

Pirate's Prize
First Comes Desire
Days of Desire

Published by Kensington Publishing Corporation

Days of Desire

Pirate's Prize

Tina Donahue

LYRICAL PRESS
Kensington Publishing Corp.
www.kensingtonbooks.com

Lyrical Press books are published by
Kensington Publishing Corp. 119 West 40th Street New York, NY 10018

All Kensington titles, imprints, and distributed lines are available at special quantity discounts for bulk purchases for sales promotion, premiums, fund-raising, and educational or institutional use.

To the extent that the image or images on the cover of this book depict a person or persons, such person or persons are merely models, and are not intended to portray any character or characters featured in the book.

Special book excerpts or customized printings can also be created to fit specific needs. For details, write or phone the office of the Kensington Special Sales Manager:
Kensington Publishing Corp.
119 West 40th Street
New York, NY 10018
Attn. Special Sales Department. Phone: 1-800-221-2647.

Kensington and the K logo Reg. U.S. Pat. & TM Off.
LYRICAL PRESS Reg. U.S. Pat. & TM Off.
Lyrical Press and the L logo are trademarks of Kensington Publishing Corp.

First Electronic Edition: July 2017
eISBN-13: 978-1-5161-0063-7
eISBN-10: 1-5161-0063-8

First Print Edition: July 2017
ISBN-13: 978-1-5161-0066-8
ISBN-10: 1-5161-0066-2

Printed in the United States of America

To my fans. I couldn't have done this without you.

Author's Foreword

Several years ago, I watched The Bounty on cable. Mel Gibson was hard to resist as Fletcher Christian. His passion for Mauatua, a native woman, was pure romance. When I conceived Days of Desire, I wanted Royce and Simone's attraction to be as intense with the added complication of Royce's deadly secret that threatens their star-crossed relationship. The world I created for them isn't always easy but they fight for their future with intense passion and enduring love.

Acknowledgments

To the Internet and all the wonderful folks who've shared their knowledge. You've made research a joy rather than a trial.

Prologue

Mozambique—1717

"Diana Fletcher is mine." Benedict Bishop pinched snuff generously between his stout fingers. "You will make certain to deliver her."

In times past, Royce Hastings would have dismissed Bishop as the swine he was. Not now. Circumstances were not in Royce's favor, his loved ones' future in his hands. If he made a wrong move or didn't do everything Bishop demanded of him, his mother and sisters would pay with their freedom, virtue, and perhaps their lives.

Quelling his outrage, he simply listened and endured.

Bishop sniffed the tobacco. Face contorted, he sneezed explosively into a lace-edged handkerchief then blew his nose. The resultant honk mingled with the din outside the shadowed room. Horse hooves clopped, carriage wheels clattered, merchants hawked their wares. Slaves were among the items purchased.

A nude young woman, her skin as dark as night, fanned Bishop with ostrich feathers. The air she produced did naught to relieve the oppressive heat and humidity flowing through the open windows.

Sweat bathed Bishop's ruddy face and numerous chins. He blotted each.

Another female slave knelt on the polished stone floor, kneading his fleshy calves and naked feet.

He cleared his throat. "Tristan Kent will hang, of course, along with Diana's brother, Peter." His beady eyes gleamed. "That will teach her to try to get away from me."

Only a woman gone mad would willingly be at Bishop's side. Old and ugly, he stank of rose water, the scent heavy and cloying. "Have you considered Diana never joined you here because she and the others might be dead?"

"Impossible." He set his powered wig more firmly on his head. "Natives have heard of a white man and others on an island off Madagascar. From the description they provided, that man has to be Kent and his pirate crew. They also mentioned a white woman. Who else but Diana could be with them?"

"How can you be certain the natives spoke truthfully?"

"Woolding."

Nasty business that consisted of a rope wrapped around a victim's skull, then tightened until his eyes burst out. The perfect torture chosen by barely civilized men. "How many did you have questioned and killed?"

"Enough. Once my agents dispatched several, those remaining were eager to divulge everything. Except the island location, which they swore they didn't know. I believe them." He flicked a persistent fly from his brocade coat. "Even a witless savage wouldn't willingly die or risk his children's deaths to keep such a secret. The whereabouts are for you to discover. My crew will help you capture Diana, the others, and islanders, if there are any. The natives should bring a fair slave price, compensating me for losing the Lady Lark. However, if the vessel's about, you'll return it with everything else."

As easily as that. The man was either stupid or insane. "Have you any idea who Tristan Kent truly is? Not romantic rumors on how he treats his crew and captives, but fact. Mainly, what he's capable of."

"He's taken enough ships from me to prove he must hang. I will not rest until he does."

"If he's had Diana for as long as you say, she could be with child by now."

Bishop curled his upper lip. "Until I discard her, she belongs to me, no other man. If she's conceived, once she births the bastard I'll give it away or send it to a workhouse. Not my concern."

Even the Devil wasn't as foul. "Her reaction to your plan should worry you deeply. The moment you give her infant away and see her brother's neck broken, prepare for her to plot your end. I promise it won't be pleasant. Females are curious like that when it comes to their families. As far as Kent goes, you believe he'll be easy to fight and win against? A pirate no one has yet to catch?" Royce leaned up in his chair. "If he's alive, has an island, and Diana, he will protect both, especially if she's carrying his child. A frontal attack would be suicide. Should anyone escape death, he would hound them and you to the ends of the earth."

"You sound afraid."

"Sensible."

"I would expect daring from a man who is willing to engage in the foulest deeds for much-needed capital. It would seem your reversal of fortune has affected far more than your appearance."

Royce suppressed a retort at how common he must look to a windbag like Bishop. Wigs were for fools who had gone bald or cared what others thought, not him. In this clime, silks and velvets were a torment only a simpleton would suffer. Royce's wool breeches and linen shirt clung to him, providing enough discomfort. "Unlike some others, I value good sense."

"You should have thought of that before your—damnation." Bishop jerked his leg from the slave. "You scratched me." Rage tightened his features. "Filthy savage." He slammed his cane on her shoulder.

The crack and her shriek tore through the smallish space. Moans followed. Trembling, the slave drew her arms and legs into herself.

Royce gripped the walking stick before Bishop hit her again. "Beat her to death and you lose valuable merchandise." All that mattered to men like him.

"She deserves punishment." Bishop tugged his cane.

Royce held on to it. "You've succeeded in drawing blood and proving your superiority."

"I'll do far worse to her and to Diana. She's the one who should be naked and cowering at my feet, and she will be with your help."

Royce wrested the cane away, then hurled the thing. It struck the whitewashed wall and clacked against a table. He dropped to his chair. "Any woman will fight to her death if you threaten her child or family."

"Diana has no power. No female has.

"You." He threw his buckled shoe at the beaten slave. "See to your task and take care this time, lest I kill you." He stuck out his portly leg.

Tears slid down the young woman's ebony cheeks. She crawled to his side and stroked him.

He sighed noisily. "See what a strong hand does? It instills fear and obedience. No matter what you may believe, you have no control over this situation, any more than a slave, Diana, or Kent does. You will do as I demand or risk everything. Tell me, what would you do if harm came to your mother and sisters?"

Bile rose in Royce's throat. He swallowed the hideous taste. On Bishop's word, Royce's sisters and mother could be lost to him forever because he hadn't the funds to buy back their freedom. To bring them home.

His determination to succeed grew icy, his calculation cold. Having Bishop's neck in his hands was going to be heaven. A murder he promised himself once he had the money to rescue his family. "Care to find out?"

Fear registered in Bishop's dark eyes. He fiddled with his lacy collar. "You best see to your undertaking. If nothing else, Diana's enslavement, along with Kent and Peter's deaths will ensure your loved ones' well-being."

Chapter 1

Tristan Kent's island—several months later

Simone opened the bedchamber shutters. During the past week, the islanders had taken refuge in the stone house rather than their mud homes. Last night, the violent storm had done its worst, then finally passed, leaving toppled trees and uprooted bushes.

Water dripped from intact vegetation and tapped against windowsills. Sunlight streamed through fluffy clouds. Although the air was cooler and fresh, a metallic trace lingered.

"Simone!" Gavra, her friend and James Sullivan's woman, rushed into the bedchamber. "We need you. The children went outside before we could stop them. Henri cut his hand."

Simone grabbed her healing materials and ran after Gavra to the courtyard. Ruined palms and traveler's trees lay in a heap against the walls.

Henri's mother, Fantine, crouched at his side. Pain tightened his small face. He rocked in place on the muddy ground. "It hurts."

"Of course it does. Let me see." Carefully, Simone unfolded Henri's fingers. The superficial wound barely bled. "Not so bad. In no time, you'll be a strong boy again.

"Gavra." Simone tilted her face. "I need fresh water."

After bathing the wound, she wrapped several healing leaves around it, securing them with a linen strip. She brushed away Henri's tears and ruffled his dark hair. "You must be good now and take care not to harm yourself again or make your hand dirty. Can you promise me that?"

He buried his face in Fantine's shoulder, his chubby hand on her marriage collar.

Fantine patted Simone's arm. "*Merci.* I must warn you, though, the cloth will not stay clean."

Simone laughed softly. "I promise to fix whatever he does and heal each sickness he has." Tristan's books had taught her much about illnesses and treating wounds even though she couldn't read and the words were in a language he called Arabic, not the French she knew. He'd translated the passages for her, then wrote them down so Peter could relay the information whenever Simone needed it. Tristan's woman, Diana, had tried to do the same, but she wasn't yet skilled in French. "I used my last leaves on Henri. If anyone else needs me, tell them I have to gather more."

Today, many would bruise and cut themselves as they cleaned up here and at their own homes. Thus far, the men hadn't stirred. Few women were about. The evening had been like the others this past week, long with brutal winds and heavy rain keeping everyone frightened or alert.

Simone lifted her silk cloth above her ankles and stepped over puddles. Past the courtyard walls, snapped branches and overturned trunks partially obstructed the path leading to the point. An area where the island men stood guard in all weather, except foul, to make certain pirates or intruders didn't happen upon the beach.

The bushes she needed were at the edge. At her approach, bright green lizards skittered into brush. Lemurs watched from overhead branches. She brushed raindrops off her shoulders and pulled her windblown hair back.

Even after she'd collected leaves here, she'd yet to fill her bag. She padded closer to the path. In the distance, the sea stirred restlessly and glinted wildly beneath the sun. Wind hurried clouds away, vegetation lay scattered from the rocky point to the surf, and dead fish and birds littered the beach. Wood piled at one end. The material wasn't splintered trunks or branches but planks from a ship.

Not the Lady Lark. Tristan and the men had brought the vessel to safe ground before the storm broke.

She edged closer.

Two large wooden containers sank in the marshy sand near shore, canvas covering the bottoms. Close by, waves washed near a man lying face down, blood on his leg.

Simone raced over the path, dodging branches, trunks, insects, and snakes. On her knees at his side, she touched his mouth.

Warm breath glided out.

The gash on his thigh stained the sand bright red. She ripped a strip from her silk cloth, dampened the fabric, then tied it around his leg as tightly as she could to staunch the flow.

"Simone." Gavra looked down from the point. "What are you doing?" She hurried to the beach and slogged through wet sand, her long hair blowing off her shoulders. "Who is he?" She stopped at the man's side, then stepped back. "A pirate?"

Not like the ones who had once taken over this island or those who'd come here months ago. This man's linen shirt and woolen breeches were too fine. The same as Tristan wore when he'd returned from his voyages laden with jewels, gold, and silk. "If he is a pirate, he must be a captain like Tristan. They dress the same. Or he could be a merchant."

"Without shoes and stockings?"

"They were surely lost when his boat sank in last night's storm and he washed up here. Help me turn him over. We can ask him what happened once he wakes up."

"And have him harm us then? No."

"He can barely breathe. See how he bleeds? If we leave him on the beach, he may die."

"What is that noise? Chickens?"

Simone didn't hear anything except this foolish conversation. She gripped his broad shoulders and tugged but couldn't budge him. He was too tall and powerfully built. Panting, she grabbed Gavra's silk cloth before her friend could leave. "Help me. Then you can run."

Together, they rolled the man onto his back.

Sand clung to his face, bristly cheeks, and chin. Blood dotted a wound on his forehead. Despite his condition, his complexion was bronze not ashy, features virile and handsome. Given his powerful form and strong jaw, Simone guessed him to be Tristan and James's age. Like them, he looked English.

She smoothed his dark brown hair, the few dry locks wonderfully thick and silky.

Gavra slapped Simone's hand. "What are you doing?"

"Searching for wounds."

"On his mouth?"

She stopped stroking his bottom lip. "To check if he's still breathing."

"I can see he is from where I am."

His muscular chest rippled each time he exhaled. Short, dark hairs hugged his skin, his tiny brown nipples peeking through. Heat flooded Simone, the warmth surprisingly seductive and strangely welcomed.

She pushed his shirt open and touched his ribs.

Gavra made an impatient noise. "What are you searching for now?"

"A broken bone. He might have one."

"If he did, he would be screaming or dead."

Simone inched lower to his breeches. Dark hair swirled around his navel and dipped beneath his waistband to the promising bulge between his legs. She rested her hand on his thigh, its heat and strength evident through the fabric.

Gavra grabbed her arm. "Come. We need to tell *Capitaine* about this."

"You go." Simone twisted, freeing herself. "I have to tend his wound." The laceration was hideous but hopefully not deadly. "Bring the men back with you to carry him to the stone house."

Gavra stopped on the path and looked over. "Tristan may say otherwise."

No. He was a good man. He wouldn't let anyone die here, not even a pirate, and certainly not a stranger who appeared as civilized as Tristan was.

Simone dragged several palm fronds to the man's side. The leaves were large with flat surfaces that had collected rainwater. She ripped his breeches and drawers, cleansed his wound thoroughly, then covered it with her healing leaves.

What Tristan called periwinkle. Before pirates killed her grandmother, she'd taught Simone about the magic in this plant.

Using a wide strip from the stranger's linen shirt, she covered the leaves and wound as best she could. The bleeding had slowed considerably. However, he needed a poultice and potion to make certain he healed and didn't lose his leg.

She touched the silk knotted above his wound, reluctant to untie it yet.

Once she'd confirmed he had no other ghastly cuts on his legs, she straightened to examine his arms and scalp.

He stared at her naked breasts, the cloth tied about her hips, and then her eyes. His were as green as a new leaf, lushly lashed, and quite alert.

He clamped her wrist.

Her breath caught.

* * * *

Tristan Kent snuggled into Diana, his cock buried deep within her soft, heated sheath. His ears buzzed.

She purred throatily. "I thought you said you had tasks to get to."

"They can bloody well wait." Given the relative quiet, the other men were still asleep or enjoying their women. Time enough later to clean up the mess the cyclone had left. "Are you with me?"

She wrapped her legs around his hips and pushed her mound into him, taking more of his length inside. "Till my last breath."

A promise he could live with easily. For Tristan, making a happy and safe home for Diana, their children, and Peter was all he required. He'd once promised her that he'd never spill blood again and wouldn't. Didn't want to, unless someone threatened their peace.

He settled her legs on his shoulders so he could drive deeper and immediately reconsidered his outrageous move. Gulping air, he pressed his face to her velvety throat. "Will this harm the babe?"

"Our loving each other?"

"Me taking you like a madman, a savage, a blasted beast."

"I think not." She tightened her cunt around his cock, delivering more delight. "It's not yet been three months since I knew for certain I'd conceived. The babe is nestled securely within me. My belly's still far too flat."

The gentle roundness promised new life. Diana may not have seen the change in herself, but he did. Her complexion glowed. Her amazing eyes were a deeper violet. Even her hair was more lustrous, blacker than ever, making her flesh paler in comparison. "I best take care with the babe and you."

"Rubbish. Love me. Use me. Tame me."

Laughing, he thrust with abandon. Their mattress rustled and the bed frame creaked.

Diana clung to him as she had from the beginning when he'd captured her, spirited her to his island, took her as his bride, and loved her to exhaustion.

As he did now, succumbing to passion, spilling his seed within her.

"Capitaine! Capitaine!"

Gavra. Her hard, fast knocks pounded the door.

Gulping air, Tristan eased from Diana and grabbed his breeches.

She followed and pulled her silk gown off a chair. "Do you think one of the men is hurt?"

"How? Everyone spent the last week here. Even if they hadn't, Simone would be the one to heal them, not me." He called, "What is it, Gavra?"

"A man is on the beach."

Tristan's skin crawled. "Get James."

"I'm already in the hall, my friend, well aware of the situation, and waiting for you to get up."

"I'm here too."

Peter.

Tristan pulled on his brace of pistols. He snatched Diana's gown and tossed it on the bed. "Stay in here until I return."

"No. I want to know you're safe. You said no one would find us here. Is it Bishop?"

"If it is, he'll be dead the moment I see him. At that point, you can view the body before we toss it into the sea."

She made a face. "I never want to see that devil again. Call me after the fish consume him."

"Well said." He pecked her lips and opened the door a crack.

James and Peter slouched against the opposite wall, one yawning, the other stretching. Gavra tapped her foot. What Tristan would expect from a woman irritated by circumstances, rather than alarmed.

He crossed his arms. "Given how each of you looks, I trust we don't need the other men to mount an attack?"

James rubbed his eyes. "Adamo and Philippe went to the beach and used the glass. No ships anywhere. The one that did come close is in pieces now, the lone survivor on the sand."

"How near is he to dying?"

"Better ask Gavra. She saw Simone treating him and came here."

Gavra looked at them expectantly. They'd spoken English without thinking, rather than French the islanders understood. Tristan hated to ask the obvious but had to know the truth. "Is he a pirate?"

"Not like the others who came here. More a captain as you are, dressed as you were. At least, Simone believes so. She said he could also be a merchant."

Right now, he was trouble Tristan didn't need. He slipped into the hall. "Let's take a look."

Dressed, Diana left the chamber. "I'm coming too."

He cupped her elbow and led her away from the others. "Have you forgotten you're with child? My child?"

"Ours. How could I not remember as I'm carrying the infant? I promise to be careful. However, I'm not an invalid. Back in England, women still plow fields and do other demanding tasks even when they're about to give birth."

"That's there, not here. Thankfully, we're more civilized."

She kissed his knuckles. "If it makes you feel better, I won't go farther than the point, but I want to be there. I'm your wife, not a child."

"You're my life. If anything were to happen…"

"It won't." She eased into him. "I promise."

"You had better or I'll chain you to our bed and will never let you leave the bloody thing."

"I shall remember that promise and wait breathlessly for you to fulfill it."

She would not make him laugh. "Best you keep your tongue in addition to your distance. Your French is still too poor. The islanders won't know what you're going on about."

"I'll be as stiff and quiet as a statue."

Not in his bed she wouldn't.

Hand in hand, they followed the others down the hall to the outside.

* * * *

Of all the people to discover him, Royce hadn't expected such a beautiful young woman. Simone the other native had said.

She couldn't have been older than twenty. Her light brown skin complemented her dark hair. The ends grazed her waist. He detected a bit of European in her exotic features, and island custom in what little she wore. Simply a red silk cloth tied about her hips, those curves as lavish as her breasts. The mounds were full and lush, begging for a man's touch, her deep brown nipples quite tight. How a woman reacted when aroused or perhaps afraid.

Wary that she might scream, he'd released her quickly and had expected her to run.

She checked his arms, hands, and head. He supposed for injuries.

At last, she finished and peeked at him.

Cautiously, he pushed up, hoping she wouldn't bolt.

She sat back on her heels.

Needing an ally here, he tried a smile.

Hers was wondrous, broad and carefree, no deception or caution in her soft brown eyes.

His arrival would eventually change that. No better way to destroy a woman's trust and happiness than wresting her from an island Eden to imprisonment, lifelong slavery, repeated rape, and birthing children only to have them torn away.

Guilt and shame churned in his gut. Fear for his family competed with the other emotions. "Are you the only one here?" Besides Tristan, his crew, and the other island woman. Their conversation had mentioned Tristan, but not Diana or Peter.

Simone tilted her head. A tress fell across her breast. Confusion swept her lovely face.

Royce had deliberately spoken English so she wouldn't know he'd heard her speak French earlier when he'd feigned unconsciousness. He next tried Portuguese and received her same bewildered reaction. At last, he used her language.

Her eyes lit up. "My people live here. Once we have you in the stone house, I can see to your injury." She touched his thigh. "Does it hurt?"

Not as much as when he'd arrived on this shore. "My head is worse."

She brushed back his hair, her touch as light as an angel's.

Despite his callous intent here, and what prudence demanded, his lids slid down, his heart pounding as hard as it had when she'd stroked his ribs.

She explored his wound carefully. "I can make a potion to take your pain away. As soon as the men arrive I—"

Voices and footfalls interrupted.

Tristan led the way, his manner and appearance precisely as rumor had described: tall, golden skin, blond hair, and light eyes that offered naught except challenge and possibly death if anyone dared threatened him or those he loved. Following him was an equally tall man with long red hair, his face and chest freckled. Had to be James Sullivan, Tristan's friend and former quartermaster during their piracy.

An adolescent boy, fifteen or so, brought up the rear. Gangly, as youth were prone to be, he had long dark hair streaked with blond, his skin brown from days outdoors. Diana's brother, Peter. His features matched Bishop's depiction.

Tristan, James, Peter, and island men trained their pistols on Royce.

The land to their side jutted out, rocky and reddish as those found in Madagascar. A white woman stood there, wind whipping her dark hair and simple sheath-like gown in violet silk. Her slightly rounded belly didn't prove pregnancy, though Royce would have staked his life on it. She wore a choker about her throat, the diamonds glittering in the light.

Royce's pulse pounded. Diana was here, as Bishop had predicted. Along with too many armed men, as Royce had feared, though all islanders, not pirates.

He collapsed on the sand and tried to roll over, pretending to escape from so many weapons. Unable to, he reached to Simone for help, her face the only kind one here.

She curled her fingers around his.

He dropped his arm, feigning unconsciousness.

Chapter 2

"What are you doing?" Simone waved Tristan and the others back. "He can barely keep his eyes open, yet you threaten him with your pistols."

The men didn't lower their weapons. Staring at the stranger, they inched closer as they would when facing a dangerous bull.

Since the last pirate attack, everyone here had forgotten kindness again, acting with caution or suspicion instead.

Simone refused to behave the same even though she had cause. In an earlier raid, she'd lost everyone she loved and would have died if not for the surviving islanders protecting her. That didn't mean she'd turn her back on someone in need simply because he was white. This man posed no danger to those here, especially in his current condition.

"Do you see a weapon on him? Has he harmed you in any way?"

Peter made a derisive noise. "What makes you think he won't? No one invited him here. He's an intruder and probably English in the bargain. I say we tie him up before he can hurt anyone."

Tristan elbowed the boy.

Diana edged down the path, speaking English Simone didn't understand.

Tristan pointed at his wife, his English fast and firm, though not harsh.

Diana stopped and slumped. "*Très bien, mon...ah...pauvre français, il... sera si...cela signifie que je peux rester.*" Very well, my, ah, poor French it will be if that means I can stay. She breathed hard, struggling with the words. "*Qui...est-il?*" Who is he?

Simone called out, "A man who might die." She touched the ligature around his leg. "He needs healing. Far more than I can do here. We must bring him back to the stone house. Please."

Diana looked baffled.

The islanders exchanged troubled glances.

Tristan slipped the pistol into his brace and strode forward.

The men followed, everyone regarding the stranger's blood-soaked breeches, the cut on his forehead, his torn and soiled clothes.

Peter squatted near the man's legs. "How long before he dies?"

Simone pushed Peter's hand from the linen protecting the leg wound. "If I see to his injuries, I can save him. He needs a poultice and a potion to keep him from the fever or worse. He stopped bleeding but could start again unless I tend to his wound."

Tristan observed the sea. "James, you and Peter bring him to Canela's old room."

Peter shot to his feet. "Why me?"

"Because I said so." Tristan looked over. "The rest of you fan out and scour the island for anything amiss. Check for wreckage or other survivors."

The islanders ran up the path.

James scratched his chest. "Doubtful there would be many, or anyone at all, who could have lived through the storm that raged these last days. Only a stroke of luck or God's grace helped this fellow to our shore."

"That may be, but I want to be certain."

Diana shouted something in English and flapped her hands. "*Que se... passe-t-il?*" What is going on?

Peter snickered. He lifted his face to her and spoke French. "Your language skills are improving. In a year or two your French and island dialect should be as good as mine." He glanced at the others. "Care to wager she didn't understand what I said?"

Confusion swept her features.

Peter laughed.

Tristan bared his teeth at Peter. "Help James. Now."

Peter sobered. "Aye, Captain." He grabbed the stranger's feet, James his upper body.

Tristan spoke to Diana, his English words gentle and coaxing. She didn't look happy but finally nodded and left the scene.

Flapping noises and squawking sounded, both difficult to pinpoint, possibly the chickens Gavra had mentioned earlier.

Tristan pointed to the containers. "What's that?"

The man stirred and pulled from Peter, then fought James.

"Easy now." James lowered him to the ground. "We're not trying to hurt you."

Simone touched the man's arm. "Let them carry you to the stone house. There, I can tend to you."

Pain and fear flooded his eyes. "Don't let them kill the birds and fowl." He'd spoken French as the others had.

Tristan looked over. "That's what's inside the crates?"

"*Oui.* They're Edward's."

Tristan touched his pistol. "And who would that be?"

The stranger winced and gripped his leg above the wound.

"Take care or you'll bleed again." Simone eased his hand away. "Must we talk about this here, Capitaine?"

Tristan stared at the man. "Who's Edward?"

He panted. "The cabin boy. An eleven-year-old. The chickens and birds were his pets during the long journey. He came from a farm and wanted a taste of home. Before the ship sank, he begged me to see to the creatures' welfare. I promised I would, even though I intended to save him before anything else. A wave pulled him from the plank the crates were on, the same one we clung to. I tried my best to reach him, to direct the timber in that direction, but..." He squeezed his eyes shut, grief etched on his face.

Sympathy passed over Tristan's features, then disappeared beneath vigilance. "Who are you?"

"Royce Hastings, a merchant from London." He wiped his cheek on his shoulder. "I was on my way to Mozambique to trade. The captain thought the worst weather was over, but the storm doubled back on us and became too swift and severe to escape. Is the port near? Did the others survive?"

"How many were there?"

"I have no idea the exact number."

"The ship was yours, yet you don't know how many crew it held?"

"I don't own any ships. My best guess is seventy men, both crew and passengers. Do you think the others lived?"

"If they did, the islanders will find them. What area were you planning to trade in?"

"Damnation, my head aches. Everything keeps whirling."

Simone frowned at Tristan. "He needs healing, not questions."

Tristan focused on Royce. "Where were you headed, Mr. Hastings?"

He spoke three words or names Simone had never heard. "Then south to the other coastal ports. What is this place? What's it near? Who are you and these people?"

Tristan searched the water. "I'll see to Edward's pets."

"Wait a moment. I promised to keep them in sight always. I owe that to the boy."

"You can keep your word to him later. For now, Simone needs to tend your wounds."

"Hold on. I have questions."

Tristan lumbered across the drenched sand to the containers.

Royce gaped at Tristan's scarred back.

"Best we get on with this," James said. "You ready, Peter?"

"No, but I'll make do."

James grabbed Royce's arms. Peter faced away from them and lifted Royce's feet.

He stared at Peter's lashed back, then moaned and slumped, his head falling down, eyes closed.

The narrow path and steep incline weren't designed to carry a man. James and Peter panted hard. They tested their footing repeatedly, kept adjusting Royce's weight, and stepped around or over fallen vegetation. Once on the point, they lugged him through the storm-battered forest toward the stone house.

Simone cradled his hand.

He gripped hers tightly, roused again. "Will the captain keep his promise about Edward's pets? He won't have them cooked for food, will he?"

Peter chuckled.

Simone shot him a scolding look and ran her thumb over Royce's. "You can trust Tristan's words. Edward's creatures are safe with him before he returns them to you."

"When will that be?"

"Once you heal. Your room is ahead."

* * * *

Royce expected a crudely constructed home. A pirate's lair. Not this.

Within the clearing, a white structure stretched an impressive distance, its stone dazzling white beneath the sun.

Only during his family's glory days in England had he resided in a place as large and majestic. Fit for a king or a noble.

Bishop had no idea how well Tristan had fared. Diana too.

She'd obeyed Tristan with little pause, his gentle words and pleas doing more to gain her compliance than Bishop's violence ever could. However, kindness would ruin Bishop's fun in proving his supremacy, having her kneel at his feet, naked and defenseless, silent too, as she carried out every vile order he gave.

Royce had no doubt her tasks would quickly grow abominable, more than any woman could endure.

His chest tightened, shame threatening to overwhelm. For his mother and sisters' survival, he pushed sentimentality aside but couldn't meet Diana's gaze.

She stood near the wall that protected the interior structure. Once James and Peter carried Royce inside the ample courtyard, young women and small children paused in their work or play to stare. The boys and girls were nude, every adult female bare breasted, wearing naught but silk cloths about their hips. Those swollen with child also sported chokers on their throats. Brightly colored beads decorated the leather bands, rather than the diamonds Diana wore.

A young woman close to delivering plodded toward them. *"Qui est-ce?"* Who is that?

Peter blew out a breath. "Royce Hastings. An English merchant, he says. It appears he survived a shipwreck last night."

Disquiet raced through Royce, prickling his skin. He wasn't certain if Peter had spoken carelessly, as boys his age were wont to do, or had qualified his words because he didn't believe Royce was a merchant or that a shipwreck had actually occurred. Not that Peter's opinion mattered. Tristan's did. Unfortunately, he'd kept his thoughts to himself, his expression bloody unreadable, especially when they'd discussed the birds and when Tristan failed to answer where this island was or who he might be.

Best not to push him too far too quickly. Better that Royce keep his tongue and observe.

Children who appeared between three and five years old ran to him, their manner as guileless and open as Simone's. Women followed and pulled them back.

He squeezed Simone's hand.

"What is it?" She leaned down.

Her fresh, sweet scent filled him, stealing speech and thought. Her hair glided over his chest. Heat burst wherever those strands touched.

"Is your pain worse?"

Unruly desire swept through him, delight he hadn't known in too long, hadn't expected here, and shouldn't indulge in. "Should I tell your people not to fear me?"

"I will. You must rest." She stroked his neck.

His skin tingled.

She straightened. *"Monsieur* Hastings is our guest. The storm gave him terrible injuries. Tell him you want to see him well."

The children's sweet voices rose as one, wishing him a fast recovery.

Those innocents would be on the auction block too, after slavers tore them from their mothers' arms.

Nausea rolled over him.

Simone smiled at the tots. "Merci.

"Gavra, Fantine, please bring clean water and my healing materials to Canela's old room so I can see to our guest."

James and Peter tottered forward, straining for air.

Peter gripped Royce's ankles more firmly. "Someone should wish me good health. My shoulders and back ache. His legs are bloody heavy."

"Pierre!" A young woman ran up to Peter, her breasts bouncing, long neck unadorned, her age close to his. "What are you doing? Who is that?"

"A visitor who weighs too much."

"Let me help you."

"No. I'm man enough to handle this, Laure. Go to our room or do your tasks. I'll see you later, all right?"

"Are you certain?"

"Yes. Please do as I say."

She pecked his cheek and darted into a side room off the courtyard. Women streamed in and out.

Royce's group entered the main building, the ceilings high, halls shadowed, floors polished marble. After passing numerous doors, they entered a spacious chamber, its two arched windows facing the forest, an opening in the vegetation showing the sea. In here, a large mahogany bed dominated the space.

Peter and James lowered him to the mattress covered in a rose silk sheet.

James backed up and stretched. "I'm not as young as I used to be."

Peter sagged against the footboard. "You could always lie next to him. That way you can protect Simone while she works on his wounds."

"No. Tristan ordered me to do so."

The voice came from the unshuttered window. An island man stood framed there, his face oddly disfigured, left arm hanging limply at his side, a pistol in his right hand, pointed at Royce.

Tristan hadn't trusted the merchant story after all. Unless caution came naturally to him, a remnant from his pirate days.

James inclined his head to the native. "Merci, Adamo. We'll leave them in your care." He clamped Peter's shoulder. "Today you help me and Tristan with the cattle, pigs, horses, and whatever else needs tending."

"Anything to avoid books, but you best tell Diana or she'll rail at me."

"I'm certain Tristan's already had a word with her."

"Too bad we don't have storms every night." Peter grinned broadly. "Come morning, I'd never have to study."

"Right you are. Then you could tend the pigs and cattle all the time and never do anything else."

Peter made a face. "I didn't say I wanted that. Just not to do my lessons."

Shaking his head, James steered the boy from the chamber.

Royce tried not to react to the wealth and established community here, or what Peter had said about his schoolwork. None of this made sense for roving pirates.

Gavra and Fantine padded inside, arms laden with items Simone had requested.

"Fantine, over here." Simone directed the taller woman to put what she carried on the table near the bed.

"You left this on the beach where you shouldn't have been." Gavra held up a damp silk bag. Sand clung to it. She wore a beaded band about her neck. Her slightly rounded belly reminded Royce of Diana's. Being with child and not feeling well might explain Gavra's sour mood.

Simone took the bag. "Merci." She flicked her hand. "You can go now."

"We should watch."

"No."

"Yes."

Fantine regarded the battling women. "Why should we stay?"

Simone smiled stiffly. "Gavra is making a joke. I heal better without anyone watching me."

After shooing them away, Simone arranged her materials on the table. A blue silk bag dropped to the floor in back.

She crouched to reach it. Her cloth fell away from her leg, revealing a sleek, brown thigh marred by a brutal scar, horribly deep, the skin rutted and white.

Surprised, he reacted. "What happened?"

She flinched at Royce's question and hurriedly covered her leg, her cheeks flaming.

He hadn't meant to add to her distress and tipped his head to the window. "What happened to him...Adamo?" Royce kept his voice low. "His face and arm look odd."

She poured water into a shallow bowl. "The pirates beat him."

"Tristan and the redheaded man?"

"James? No. Never them. Both are kind and help my people. Their old crew came here to take Diana back to a cruel merchant."

Bishop. "Didn't the pirates live here too?"

"No. Only Tristan, Peter, and James. The other men never knew about this isle."

"How did they find it?" Royce had a bloody hard time locating this place. Its shallow waters made the land impossible for ships to approach.

"Canela brought them to our shore."

This was her old room. "Canela's a white woman who used to be wed to one of those men?"

"She was born here as I was, her parents islanders, the same as mine. Until she betrayed Adamo, she was his woman. Yellow Scarf nearly killed Adamo. Tristan banished him, the other men, and Canela to a distant island."

"Who lashed Tristan and Peter?" Their scarred backs had stunned Royce.

"Cruel capitaines. I must remove your clothes."

They barely covered him, both garments already shredded before he'd reached the beach.

She dropped his tattered shirt on the floor and focused on his breeches.

His cock lengthened and thickened, pushing against the fabric.

Her face flushed. "Does it hurt?" She traced the area around his wound.

Arousal, curiosity, and caution had blunted the pain, reducing his discomfort to a dull throb. "Not as much as before."

"It may pain you again before I finish. I should hurry." She ripped his breeches and drawers until she'd fully exposed his injured leg.

Her breath spilled out.

His balls tightened.

Cautiously, she untied the ligature. He lifted his head. To his relief, blood didn't gush from the wound.

She removed the soiled linen and leaves.

The gash was worse than he expected and more than he'd intended to do to himself. His intent had been to convince Tristan and the others a shipwreck had occurred. Wasn't likely they would have believed him if he'd merely flopped on the sand, fully intact.

Slashing his own flesh wasn't something he cared to remember, especially now.

Simone plucked another rock from the jagged skin.

Hurt shot down his spine. He winced and dropped back.

"I promise to take care."

A ghost couldn't have had a lighter touch. Even so, the laceration burned like bloody hell.

"This will sting." She uncorked a bottle and poured the red liquid over his wound.

Searing heat cut through him. He twisted the sheets. "Damnation."

"Forgive me." She blew hard on the area, chasing away the worst misery.

He panted. "Was that wine?" Looked and smelled like it.

"From the capitaine's stores. Once the poultice is on, it will ease your pain." She ground leaves into a bowl, mixed in ingredients he couldn't identify, then moistened the mess with water and smeared it on his thigh.

Although cool, its sharp prick proved as pleasant as a dog bite. He gritted his teeth.

After laying new leaves on his gash, she tore clean linen into strips and used them to bandage him. "Take care not to move too much."

Sweat rolled into his eyes, the sting hardly noticeable given his other agony. He nodded.

Simone mixed new ingredients in an earthen cup and sniffed her concoction.

Royce indulged in her fragrance, the most pleasant smell here. A rich, flowery scent that clung to her silky skin and hair.

She leaned over him toward the headboard, her nipples above his mouth, the dark halos tantalizingly close, mesmerizing in their female allure.

Pain vanished, replaced by hard lust.

Loud throat clearing sounded. Adamo. His crooked frown matched his lopsided mouth, distrust raging in his eyes. Whatever Canela had managed with the pirates, her actions had left Adamo a damaged man, possibly eager to kill anyone white or English.

Simone settled three pillows beneath Royce's head and shoulders, propping him up, then cupped his chin.

Her gentle touch did more than any medicine could. Pleasure and heat streamed in gentle waves, relaxing him.

"Drink."

He eased away from the cup. "What is it?"

"A potion to make you sleep."

Its earthy fragrance combined with the sweet wine she'd used. He sipped carefully, afraid the concoction would loosen his tongue, particularly during slumber. That would bring Tristan here, his pistol aimed, ready to fire.

Although parched, Royce pushed the remaining drink away.

"No. Finish every drop."

"In time. It hurts to swallow."

"The potion will help."

"I promise to finish it eventually."

Her lower lip jutted out, like a petulant little girl. Oddly enough, he found her displeasure charming and endearing.

"Very well." She placed the cup on the table. "Now I'll bathe you."

He sat up.

She pushed him back, tore off his breeches and drawers, and tossed them aside.

His cock jutted hard and eager from his hairy groin. His balls were tight to his body, so plump they hurt.

She regarded them and his shaft with interest, her color high, nipples constricted.

Royce could scarcely breathe.

"Do you feel shame?"

He started at her voice. She looked at him questioningly. "Am I ashamed by my nudity? No. Are you?"

She smiled. "What woman would regret looking at such a magnificent man?"

He puffed up without meaning to, his gratitude blending with quick unease. Her smile would soon turn to tears at his betrayal. Every lash she endured, each humiliation and heartache she survived, his fault alone.

It hadn't been enough that he'd failed to protect his mother, Nell, and Katie from their fates, struggling to get them back, to have the family whole again. Now, he'd have Simone's face haunting his sleep. Diana's too. And the children's. For them, there would be no big brother or son promising rescue.

He downed the potion and snatched the wine.

"What are you doing?" Simone took the bottle from him.

"I want more."

"Why? Is your pain so bad?"

What remained of his heart and soul would never stop aching. Peace wasn't something he expected any longer. Death would be a gift. "Drink helps me sleep."

She trailed her fingers over his jaw, delivering exquisite pleasure.

He wanted to drown in her goodness and warmth but turned away.

"Why do you have trouble sleeping?"

"A family curse." His bloody father the cause.

"You have a woman and children?"

"I have no one. Are you going to tell Adamo to shoot me if I imbibe the wine?"

Her slender eyebrows shot up. "Never." She frowned. "If you had refused to drink my potion, I would have shot you."

Royce laughed. "You're too bloody nice."

"For saying I would kill you?"

For teasing and making him happy. No matter how brief the moment, he didn't deserve her kindness. She should have left him on the beach and begged the others to put an end to his torment. Except then, no one would help his loved ones.

Weariness overwhelmed him. "One drink, please." Not enough to forget everything but to blunt his remorse.

She handed him the bottle.

He enjoyed a long draught, then fell back and prayed for darkness.

* * * *

Simone gestured Adamo away from the window where he hovered too close and saw too much.

He remained.

She mouthed, "Go. I will be all right."

He finally backed up but kept Royce and her in sight, his pistol at the ready.

He'd have to shoot her first before she'd let him harm Royce. He was already sick in his soul, unknown horror flaring in his eyes before he finished her potion.

Whatever his torment, she understood why he'd want wine to sleep. After what the pirates had done to her, Simone had needed Gavra's loving embrace to feel safe enough to close her eyes. Even then, trust and deep rest didn't return for years.

Royce's heartache must still be new.

She wrung out the sponge and bathed his face, then tended the cut on his forehead, using wine to cleanse the area.

He stiffened.

"Forgive me."

After smearing poultice on the wound, she blew on it. He relaxed and inhaled deeply.

She cleaned his hands, then his feet, liking his long fingers and toes. His muscular thighs and hair-roughened calves sparked excitement she'd never known before he arrived.

Lightheaded, she washed his dark, musky curls. Her sheath ached dully, too congested and wanting. His shaft enthralled. Hard yet smooth, long and thick, dominant but not frightening.

Although a cruel man could cause a woman great pain and sorrow, a good one would deliver astonishing pleasure.

At least according to Gavra who gushed about the heady nights she spent with James.

Simone had suitors but hadn't chosen a mate or given herself to anyone, not wanting a lover. Until now.

Moisture beaded on the slit in Royce's crown, proving a man's desire. The same as his firm sac, the skin lightly furred and ruddy.

She washed him thoroughly, hungry for his response.

He pretended to sleep.

His heightened breathing and stiffened rod betrayed him. She'd aroused him even though she was a simple islander. Too many English pirates had found her brown skin distasteful, calling her savage, an animal, wanting to rape not cherish.

Royce had taken care, pretending not to notice her scar.

She'd made him laugh. He'd reminded her of a young boy then, joy lighting his eyes, tenderness flooding his heart. The way a man and woman should be with each other.

She sponged his arms, the dark hair in his pits, and nicely furred chest.

A task she might have kept at for the rest of her days if not for Gavra slipping inside.

Gavra frowned. "What are you doing now?"

Enjoying herself as a woman should. "Use your eyes and see."

"You bathing him? Will that heal his wound?"

"What do you want? Why are you here?"

Gavra lifted her chin. "To make certain you do nothing to harm yourself."

Too late for caution. Simone craved Royce despite his white skin, English ways, and his life elsewhere.

He'd be here for no more than a few months before he found his way back home where he would forget her forever.

Not the future she hoped for. However, during his stay she intended to be at his side.

Chapter 3

Diana, Tristan, James, and Peter gathered at the library table, door closed. Diana presumed Tristan had herded the others in here, rather than tending the animals as he'd planned, because he wanted to discuss what to do about Royce.

It wasn't as though Royce could travel easily from here to Mozambique or England where he belonged. Even with the Lady Lark at Tristan's disposal, he, James, and Peter had a price on their heads for piracy they'd had no choice in. They didn't dare journey farther than the surrounding islands hidden from civilization. And the hangman's noose.

Currently, Royce's only option was to remain here as they did.

Tristan and James poured over charts unfurled across the table, their conversation low and at times animated. They discussed weather, currents, and other matters she didn't understand.

Peter didn't either, given his puzzled gaze. However, he nodded at everything they said, behaving as a knowledgeable mariner would even though he'd only been at sea for two years. First as a cabin boy, then an apprentice pirate before she'd rescued him from Tristan. Admittedly, she'd been wrong to want Tristan hanged and Peter returned to England. For that misstep, her brother had railed at her, insisting he was a man, while behaving more like a silly boy. As he had today, poking fun at her on the beach.

She was going to have a word with him concerning his rude behavior. First, though, she needed to know why Tristan had called this conference. "Is the door shut because you men fear Royce will hear you?"

Tristan rested his finger on the map and looked up. "No. He should be in bed swooning again or close to it, unless James and Peter forgot to put him there."

James stretched and grimaced. "My sore back says he's where he should be. How about you, Peter?"

"Mine hurts worse than yours." He mimicked how James kneaded his shoulders.

Diana resisted rolling her eyes. "Then why the closed door, lowered voices, and these charts?" Each bore incomprehensible swirls and notations. "Tristan, are you worried the islanders will see this or overhear what you say?"

"The latter, then repeating what we discuss. Innocently, of course."

"To Royce?"

"Who else?"

Goosebumps rose on her arms despite the steamy weather. "You don't believe he's who he says he is?"

"Right now, we're merely checking to see where his ship went down."

"Do you intend to go to the site and search for treasure?"

"I hadn't thought of it, but that's not a bad idea."

"Excellent, I would say." James pushed his hair off his shoulders. "We might find something we can use."

They weren't telling the whole truth. None could hold her gaze for long. "Why else would you need to know where his ship sank?"

Tristan exchanged a glance with the others. "Should we tell her?"

James shrugged. Peter shook his head.

She crossed her arms. "Am I only in here so you can make light of everything I say?"

"Of course not." Tristan slung his arm across her shoulders and shook her gently. "That's an added delight."

She elbowed him.

He rested his forehead against hers. "You're in here because you're my wife and I want no secrets between us, all right?"

She stroked the spot she'd jabbed. "Then explain, please."

"See this?" Tristan swept his finger over the swirls nearest her. "These are ocean currents. They tell us where Royce's ship had to have gone down for him to reach our shore."

James tapped another paper. "Once you consider wind patterns on the surface."

"And weather variations." Tristan pulled a sheaf closer. His writing filled the pages. "These are my observations over the years of fair and foul conditions and everything in between. By putting the information together, we can determine how likely it is that Royce would have landed on our beach rather than another island or at the bottom of the ocean."

Her uneasiness returned. "Are you saying he got here another way than what he said?" She feared asking why he'd do that.

"Merely double checking things." He patted her knee. "From what I can tell, his ship went down here." He touched the chart. "James thinks here." Tristan inched his finger north. "In either event, the current would have swept him to this island."

"That's never happened before, has it?"

"First time for everything."

"Then you believe his tale?"

He rubbed his chin. "I didn't say that. I've yet to question him fully, which I intend to do as soon as he's able to stay awake long enough."

Diana wished that were now. "Do you think the islanders will find anything? How long will it take them to check the land and return here?"

"Hours probably, even with them on horseback. The storm caused considerable damage, flooding paths, leaving debris they'll find difficult to traverse. Right now, all we can do is wait."

"While you're armed." None had put aside their weapons as they usually did in the mansion.

Tristan kissed her palm. "Everything will be all right and we'll have our answers as soon as our guest is well enough to speak."

* * * *

Unwilling to leave Royce, Simone rested in a chair at his side. At first, he pretended to sleep but gradually fell into a deep stupor. During the night, strangled cries burst from him, awakening her. He thrashed and moaned, his nightmare horrific, perhaps the moment he'd lost Edward to the storm.

He woke with a gasp and shivered violently. Sweat bathed his face and chest, dampening the sheet. Fresh blood rolled from beneath his bandage.

She lit another oil lamp and mixed a new poultice.

"What did I say while I slept?" He clutched her wrist as he had on the beach, his eyes wild. "Tell me."

"You only moaned, nothing else." She removed his bandage and the leaves. "Is your pain worse?"

He'd bitten his lip so hard blood dirtied it. Clear liquid and a partial scab covered his gash, the skin swollen but not infected, the bleeding a mere trickle.

He released her and fell back. "I'm fine."

"The sheet is wet. I can change it once I wrap new linen on your wound."

"No. You should go to your own room and sleep. Adamo should leave too."

"He did hours ago. Philippe took his place."

"Who takes your place?"

"No one. Keep still while I tend your leg."

He rested his arm over his face.

When she finished treating him, Simone doused the lamps, casting the room in shadows. Moonbeams washed away color and turned the outside a faint gray. Quietly, she regained her seat, not wanting to disturb.

Royce pushed up, eyes glittering in the scant light, his gaze on her, searching rather than irritated or unkind.

Her longing returned. She took his hand.

He sank to the pillows and cradled her fingers. "Since Philippe's out there, making certain I don't do anything wrong, why won't you leave?"

"I'd rather be here."

"In an uncomfortable chair?"

Even if she'd had to sit on the floor, she didn't mind being with him. She sensed he knew that, but wanted to ease his worry about her. "The storm destroyed my home and many others where my people live. I have no place else to stay but here."

"I had no idea. I'm sorry."

"Others have it worse. In time, the men will build another house for me."

He loosened his hold. "Did your people find anything…other survivors or more of the shipwreck?"

"No. Only what was on the beach with you."

He released her hand. "What of Edward's pets?"

She buried her fingers in her silk cloth. "Peter saw to the creatures. Three chickens and one bird died before he could do anything to save them. The rest are well."

"I should take a look at them."

"Later. Not now. You need to rest."

His stomach growled.

She stood. "And eat."

"I'm not hungry."

"Your belly says otherwise."

"I'd like more wine."

"Water is best to help you heal." Earlier, Gavra had brought a pitcher in, delivering it and Simone's meal with a new frown. Simone filled a cup and helped him sit. "Drink this. When you finish, I want you to have two more at least."

He guzzled the liquid, quickly downing three additional cups, then ran his hand over his mouth.

"Now for bread and broth. Perhaps some meat."

He cuffed her wrist. "I'll eat in the morning. I'm too tired for anything now except sleep. You should be too after sitting in that chair all day. The bed's big enough for both of us. You can use the other side. I promise not to hurt you."

Coming to harm didn't worry her. She craved intimacy between them. The worse thing would be if he never touched her as a man should. "I have no need for your word. I trust you."

His grip tightened, then fell away. "You shouldn't."

"Why?"

"You don't know me. I'm a bloody stranger. For the love of God, what in the hell is the matter with you?"

She went cold, then hot. "I can never be perfect like an Englishwoman. I will always be a simple islander."

"What are you talking about? You're as fine as or finer than any Englishwoman."

She knelt beside him, ashamed she'd doubted his good heart. "I have never met any man as wonderful as you."

"You don't mean that. You're too honest and trusting. The world isn't filled with good people."

"It is on this island."

He shoved his hair back. "Pirates have raided here. Remember you telling me so? What makes you think it won't happen again? Or that everything will always remain as you want, rather than something ghastly happening?"

"Why are you angry with me? What have I done?"

His features slackened. He hung his head. "Nothing. Forgive me. I had no right to rail at you. I should leave. I can sleep on the floor or in the hall so you can have the bed."

"You will not."

He got up anyway. She did too and shoved him on the mattress. He sat hard. The frame creaked.

"Simone, what's going on in there?"

She looked over at Philippe. "Nothing."

He glanced past her to Royce. "What are you doing?"

"Tending his bloody wound. What else? I could use your help to remove the pus and to smear the poultice on."

Philippe's mouth turned down. "I would only make him worse. He could die. Go on, do what you must." He backed up quickly and sagged against a trunk, moonlight drizzling on him through thin clouds and leaves.

Simone leaned into Royce, her knee touching his, her nipple against his shoulder.

He swallowed. The ridge in his throat bobbed.

She kept her voice low. "Do as I say, unless you want me to shoot you."

"You mean Phillipe, don't you?"

Royce's skin warmed her as nothing else could. "No. Me. Lie down and stay there, unless you want to keep me from sleeping because I have to change your bandage again."

"Sorry." He stretched out, motionless as the dead. "Share the mattress with me. Please. We'll never touch." He arranged the pillows to his side, then went stiff. "See? This will separate us and keep you from concern."

His cock was so hard it lay on his belly, the crown pointing at his chin. He covered himself.

To slap his hands away would be a joy. Slipping his meaty shaft between her lips, then tasting his balls was the only nourishment she needed. She might have given into her urge if not for Philippe outside and Royce refusing desire. He wanted her carnally but his proper English ways prevented him from acting on his passion.

His restraint would kill them, his breathing ragged, the same as hers.

Frustrated, she dragged to the other side and settled on the mattress.

Royce had already turned away, his back to her, his injured leg tucked beneath the other despite her warning to take care.

* * * *

Come morning, Simone piled rice bread, bananas, bacon, and cheese on a tray, poured milk into a pitcher, and gathered several napkins under Gavra's watchful gaze.

Gavra leaned against the kitchen table, lengthy enough to serve twenty. The equally spacious room smelled wonderful. Bread baked, food sizzled and fried. Pepper, ginger, and cinnamon scented the air. "Do you plan to wait on the Englishman the entire time he stays here?"

"Not this morning." Simone pushed the tray to Gavra. "Today, you serve him breakfast. If he prefers tea rather than milk, please make some for him."

"Why me and not you?"

"I have other things to keep me busy."

She filled a pitcher with water and left it in an unoccupied bedchamber, then hurried outside. In the courtyard, sun rained light through gauzy clouds. The broken trees and branches were gone, looms and potter's wheels set up where they should be. She smiled at the boisterous children and slipped past an opening in the walls to gather more healing leaves.

With her bag full, she picked white flowers Tristan called jasmine. Their intoxicating sweetness delighted her.

She washed in the chamber and rubbed the blossoms over her damp skin, transferring their perfume to her neck, wrists, beneath her arms and breasts, and between her legs. Wearing her soiled and torn cloth wouldn't do. She chose one in deep green, the shade similar to Royce's eyes, and tied the knot quickly to hide her scar. Several strokes with a brush made her hair shine.

In the hall, Diana approached, her eyes widening. *"Bonjour. Ah, comment belle vous regardez."* How lovely you look.

"Merci. You do too. Capitaine is a lucky man to have such a fine woman at his side for all time."

Diana nodded slowly and offered a hesitant smile.

For once, Simone was grateful Diana wasn't skilled in French. Her shortcomings with the language made it easy to escape whatever questions she had about Royce and what happened in his chamber.

Quietly, Simone slipped inside the room. Philippe wasn't outside, nor was Adamo. Either Tristan had said a watch wasn't necessary any longer or the current guard had fallen asleep on the forest floor.

Bacon hung from Royce's mouth. He regarded Simone's breasts, new cloth, and brushed hair. His shaft blossomed. He didn't cover it.

She padded to him, pulse racing. His bed-mussed hair showed her how he'd look once he enjoyed her. She fought her urge to smooth back the strands. "Bonjour."

He made a noise that sounded aroused.

Her heart beat faster. "Finish your bacon, please. While you eat, I should change the sheet."

He chewed quickly, swallowed, and lifted his face, his lips nearly grazing her nipple.

She couldn't imagine anything more pleasant than his mouth on her. "You can sit in the chair while I tend the bed. Let me help you to it." She slipped her arm around his middle.

He favored his uninjured leg, brow furrowing, breath coming hard and fast.

She stroked his bandaged thigh. "Does it hurt?"

"Bloody right it does."

He pressed her against the wall, imprisoning her wrists, his length molded to hers, cock snug to her mound. "You're driving me mad. I can't take any more of this. I won't."

He slanted his mouth over hers.

She surrendered willingly, joyously, accepting his tongue, melting into him.

His savage growl told her all she needed to know. He desired her.

She'd never been more alive.

His touch branded her soul, claiming it, marking her forever. She twisted free from his hold and wreathed her arms around his shoulders, her fingers buried in his silken hair to keep him near.

Their greedy and wild kiss turned tender and slow.

She ground her hips into his, needing to be closer.

He held her so tightly nothing could come between them. Boldly, he cupped her breast and thumbed her nipple.

Pleasure sped from every direction, filling her.

Forever wouldn't have been long enough to enjoy him. He tasted salty from the bacon and glorious from a flavor that was his alone. His bristly cheeks rasped hers, the mild sting encouraging her to yield further. She longed to wake up each morning to him and this.

They only had now.

Whatever the future brought, Simone refused to dwell on loss. She'd willingly belong to him for a moment rather than have no time at all. In two or three months, she'd say good-bye. Not today.

A fist pounded on the door.

She flinched.

Royce tore his mouth free and limped to the footboard, too far away from her.

"Simone." James knocked. "Are you in there?"

"Oui."

"Is Royce awake?"

"Yes, I'm up."

"Good. Tristan wants to see you as soon as you dress. I brought a clean shirt and breeches for you."

Simone put out her hand, stopping Royce from crossing the room. "Stay where you are. Rest your leg." She smoothed her hair and opened the door.

James handed the clothes over. "Once Royce is dressed, I'll escort him to the dining room."

"He needs to finish his food first. I have to put a new poultice and bandage on him."

"No rush." He crossed his arms and leaned against the opposite wall. "I'll wait."

She slammed the door.

Royce washed at the basin. Water clung to his long lashes and chest hair. He scratched his throat.

"I should shave you."

"Tristan's not going to wait for that. I have to get dressed."

"Not before I change your bandage."

"It's fine. Do you have a towel?"

She clasped the clothes to her breasts and kept her voice low. "I enjoyed our kiss, did you?"

He glanced around, then dried his face on the bedsheet. "What happened shouldn't have."

"Why not? I want you and you want me."

"Give me the clothes."

She twisted, keeping them from him. "Are you worried that someday you'll leave? I know you will. We can enjoy each other until then."

"No."

Her stomach cramped. "Why not?"

"There's no point, no future. You deserve better than me." He pulled the clothes from her. "I'd appreciate if you'd make more poultices while I'm gone. Leave them and the bandages. I'll take care of my wound from now on."

Tears stung her eyes. "You hate me so much you no longer want me to touch you? After one kiss?"

He turned away, dressed, and hobbled from the room.

* * * *

If Royce could have run, he would have. Each time he put weight on his injured leg, white-hot pain shot to his teeth, keeping him at a great-grandfather's pace. Having James at his side and armed didn't help. The moment Royce dared shuffle away, James would shoot him.

Tristan couldn't want this meeting to exchange pleasantries. Something had happened and it hadn't been good.

Unfortunately, James kept his peace and Royce had no stomach to ask questions. Kissing Simone had been madness enough. An insane act he couldn't shake.

Lust sluiced through him, refusing to depart, weakening his knees. She'd smelled better than paradise could, her flowery scent captivating, her underlying musk far better, while her ungodly softness and heat...

He craved more, everything she had to give, them naked and joined on the bed, floor, ground.

Until Bishop sold her to the highest bidder or destroyed Royce's sisters and mother because he hadn't accomplished his mission.

He clenched his jaw.

"Here we are." James led the way into a dining area, the mahogany table large enough to accommodate thirty.

Diana and Tristan sat at the far end near bowls heaped with grapes, bananas, pineapples, and rice bread. Trays bore sizzling fish and bacon.

Two pistols rested between the couple, one for each.

"Good morning." Tristan gestured Royce to a chair near him. Sun poured through tall windows and an opening in the roof, the rays glinting on the table and weapons. "Allow me to introduce my wife, Diana."

She inclined her head slightly. A stray tress glided across her creamy cheek tinted a soft rose, the same as her silk gown.

Seeing her at a distance hadn't prepared Royce for her exquisite features and coloring. No wonder Bishop wanted her. "A pleasure to meet you."

"That's James of course." Tristan gestured to him. "Our friend."

"Yes, we've already met."

"That's right." Tristan regarded Royce. "He and Peter carried you to the chamber because you kept swooning. Do you know who I am? Did Simone tell you?"

"Only your first name and that you're a captain or were a captain."

"I'm a pirate with a price on my head." He smiled. "Make of that what you will. Would you care for tea?"

Royce wanted wine or spirits to calm his sprinting pulse. Forced civility charged the air, menace bristling beneath it. The fare he'd had in the chamber might be his last meal if this talk didn't go as he hoped. "If it's no bother."

"Not at all." Tristan looked over. "Gavra, *s'il vous plait, un peu de thé.*"

She carried a silver tea service, shot Royce a withering look, and filled his cup.

At least she wasn't armed except for her foul attitude. He tried a smile. "Merci."

She bumped James's arm and left.

James pulled out his chair on the other side, next to Diana. Both stared.

Tristan broke his bread. "How's the leg?"

Royce's heart proved the greater worry, beating so fiercely he had trouble speaking and standing, his legs watery. He sank to his seat. "Hurts, but it stopped bleeding."

"Good. I trust you find our accommodations adequate."

Tristan lived better than many nobles Royce knew. "Did you build this house?"

"My husband killed the pirate who owned it." Diana touched his hand. "Didn't you, love?"

"Indeed I did. Sadly, a necessity as he planned to kill me first."

James placed his pistol on the table, muzzle pointed at Royce, and smiled. "That wouldn't do."

"No." Tristan leaned back. "I value safety. I'm sure you agree, Royce." He nodded.

"Good. What's the name of your ship that sank?"

He couldn't think. "The ship?"

"That's what I asked."

"It wasn't mine." He sipped his tea. Scalding. He suppressed a wince. "It was called Sea Sprite."

"Never heard of it." Tristan glanced at James. "Have you?"

"No."

Tristen faced him. "Are you certain that's the name?"

Bishop had sworn he owned the vessel. Royce wasn't a neophyte at deception, especially against a worthy opponent like Tristan. "I'm quite sure. Why? Did the logbook from another ship or other materials wash ashore? Was there a second tragedy?"

"Did the Sea Sprite belong to Benedict Bishop?"

The hairs on Royce's neck rose. "I have no idea. The vessel was either his, Jenkins, Gaspar, or any others who provide transport. My greatest concern was booking passage on a ship that would take me where I needed to go."

"What did you say the name of your company is?"

He hadn't, unless he'd spoken in his sleep about the beast who'd put his mother and sisters at risk. Perspiration rolled down Royce's back. "I do business under my own name. I'm a merchant who serves as a broker for others, dealing with them rather than the public. The man I worked for this time is Quentin Wister." A boyhood friend who didn't travel in the same circles as Tristan. Those in Parliament were more Quentin's style. "I merely roam the world and make deals to bring him and others the finest merchandise for their customers."

"How fortunate for Mr. Wister." Tristan's neutral expression gave nothing away. "What exactly do you deal in?"

Royce recited the information he'd committed to memory before coming here.

"No slaves?"

His throat constricted. "Mr. Wister has no market for them."

Diana's teacup clinked against the saucer. "How well do you know Bishop?"

"Not at all. I do know of him, though. Most everyone in business does. Why do you ask?"

"I loathe the devil."

Royce feigned surprise. "Why?"

"He tried to trap me once but will never do so again. I have unfinished business with him or anyone who dares try to harm my husband, our children, and my brother. If Bishop were ever foolish enough to come here or send an agent, I would shoot him and that man on the spot. No regret. Then I would go after their families. Hurt mine, and theirs will not live."

Determination flared in her eyes.

Tristan kissed her thumb. "Diana was magnificent against the pirates who attacked here. She outwitted them, ensuring their capture. Peter wanted them hanged. We don't do that here. Of course, I would make an exception for Bishop."

"And his agent," she said.

Tristan smiled softly at her. "Quite right. For them, we would have no compassion. Lucky you haven't anything to do with this foul business, Royce." Tristan's easy manner faded, replaced by hard distrust. "You don't, do you?"

His blood ran cold. "No. I can assure you, I do not."

"Then you'll live to see another day."

Chapter 4

Later in the morning, Simone rapped lightly on the open library door.

Diana and Tristan stopped their quiet conversation, their broad smiles greeting her. He stood and gestured to a chair. "Come in, please, and sit."

The books with healing magic weren't on the table. Rolled up papers lay to the side. Gavra had told Simone that Tristan and Diana wanted to see her, not what they'd say.

Reluctantly, she accepted the chair he'd offered.

He closed the door and returned. "While we speak, I'll have to explain to Diana what we've said. I hope you don't mind. I wanted her here as she cares for your well-being, as I do."

Simone's face warmed. They shouldn't be concerned for her. She'd done nothing wrong. "Do you want me to talk slowly?" Sometimes that helped Diana to understand.

"No need. I can communicate whatever you tell me." He spoke English to Diana.

She smiled gently at Simone. "Ah...*soyez vous-même*." Just be yourself.

Simone nodded.

Tristan took his seat. "How are Royce's injuries coming along? With your excellent care, I trust he's recovering."

"His wound still pains him, but I see no illness inside. I change his poultice and bandage more than he wants."

Tristan smiled. "I can imagine." He conveyed the information to Diana. "Gavra said you spent the night in his room."

Simone bristled. "I had to. I feared for his good health."

"Of course. Philippe said he saw Royce put his hands on you."

She stood. "He did not. I shoved Royce back on the bed. He wanted to leave."

"You mean escape?"

Diana waved her hands, her words hurried yet halting. "*Que ce...passe-ti-il? Qu'est-ce que...vous...avez dit?*" What's happening? What did you say?

He spoke to her. At the word "escape", her eyes widened.

Simone squeezed her fists to keep from shouting. "Royce told me to take the bed. He said he would sleep in the hall so I could be comfortable. I told him no. I pushed him. Philippe saw nothing bad or wrong."

"Of course not," Tristan said. "I wasn't accusing you. Philippe wasn't either. Please sit."

She perched on the edge of the chair.

Tristan spoke hurriedly to Diana. She flushed and said something in return.

Simone didn't like this. "What did she say?"

"That we mean no harm. We don't know Royce and worry about anything untoward happening to anyone here. Has he mentioned where he hails from or who his people are?"

"He said he has no one."

"Have you ever heard him say the name Benedict Bishop?"

"No."

"Has he talked in his sleep about anything?"

Simone tensed. "You think he wants to hurt us? No. He was kind to me, worried for my comfort. He has terrible nightmares that make him moan and break my heart. I have never known a finer man. He reminds me of you."

Diana looked from her to Tristan.

He translated and turned back. "Did he tell you what his nightmares are about?"

"They must be of losing Edward in the storm."

"But he didn't say?"

"No. His soul is sick, his pain as great as mine when I lost my family. I already told you, he has no one. He and I are both alone. I understand his sadness."

Diana patted Tristan's arm.

He held up a finger as he always did when needing a moment. "Do you want to continue treating him, Simone? You don't have to if he reminds you of your loss. I can ask Gavra to take your place."

"No. Gavra isn't a healer. She could harm or kill him. I see how she frowns."

"Very well, tend to him as you have been. However, I want you take care, please. Royce seems like a good man, but we don't know him fully yet. Diana and I would never forgive ourselves if anything bad happened to you."

It already had. She hungered for Royce and he'd turned her away, wasting precious time they didn't have. "Are you going to keep him prisoner here?"

Tristan sagged in his chair. "No one is that on this island. However, he has to stay until he heals and we find a means to return him to his land."

Her heart sank. "How long will it be before you do?"

"I can't say. James and I will try to come up with a plan to help Royce. Please don't tell him that. I wouldn't want him disappointed if we fail."

She wasn't certain whether to be happy for herself or sad for Royce if he could never return to his people. "Forgive me for being angry at you. I promise to take care. May I leave now?"

"Of course. If anything unusual happens with him, you will tell us?"

"I would never hurt our safety and peace. How could I when Adamo, Philippe, or another islander is always outside Royce's room, watching everything we do?"

Tristan tapped the table. "I intend to keep a man there, at least for the time being. Not because I don't trust you. I worry."

"You have nothing to fear. Royce will do nothing to me."

He'd as much said their one kiss would not happen again. Anything more between them was certainly out of the question.

* * * *

A native Royce had never seen before stood sentinel in the forest, pistol in hand, his full attention on this room.

Royce's already perilous situation had worsened into a nightmare he wasn't certain he'd escape.

During the planning stages for this operation, he'd never underestimated how difficult success would be, or what he'd have to do to outwit his opponent. He'd dismissed rumors that Tristan acted fairly, wasn't prone to violent rages or killing sprees like most pirates. When a situation involved family and love, a saint would turn to murder.

Royce had prepared well, informing Bishop that once he'd located the isle, he'd pretend to be shipwrecked, gain Tristan and the other pirates' trust, then find a way to get Diana alone to spirit her away to a skiff and finally Bishop's waiting ship. Royce had created Edward, the cabin boy, as a reasonable explanation for his worry about the carrier pigeons. Using them, he'd send messages to Bishop and his men in Mozambique, telling them when to set sail for this locale and where to hide to await him. Once Diana was in Bishop's hands, the other men could do whatever they pleased whether storming the island or burning it to the ground. Particulars hadn't mattered to Royce. He'd believed his only remorse would be taking Diana and her unborn child, if she proved pregnant. After Bishop paid Royce for his work and he killed the swine, Diana would be free to do whatever she wanted. A pleasant outcome for everyone involved, except for Bishop.

Pity, Royce's idea hadn't worked as simply as that. He hadn't anticipated so many island men, each armed. Nor had he considered Tristan would be suspicious so soon that the shipwreck might be Bishop's doing. No way for Tristan to know for certain, of course, but his distrust would make life difficult.

Then there were the innocents. Women and children Royce hadn't expected to meet firsthand, foolishly hoping there would only be men here, except for Diana. Bad enough to ruin her life, but the others too?

He held his head, not wanting to think about them and especially Simone. A sweet, trusting soul, lush as Botticelli's Venus, seductive as sin, ripe for a rapist and master's cruel acts.

If Royce executed his plan, she and her people would suffer greatly. Halting the scheme was impossible. His mother and sisters would never return home. The horrors they already faced would intensify once Bishop exacted his revenge.

Even the devil wasn't as vile.

There had to be a way out of this to spare everyone, including Royce's family, Simone, and Diana. If only he knew what.

Royce's shoulders and arms ached. His head throbbed from too many competing thoughts, none feasible. If he did nothing, everyone on the island would be safe. Bishop might actually believe Royce had perished in the fake shipwreck.

That would spare all here but not his mother, Nell, and Katie. Katie was only twelve, a little girl who should be laughing not struggling for food and shelter.

He wanted to scream. Anguish tightened his throat, not letting him breathe. If he could have moved without pain, he would have paced until he'd worn a path in the marble. For what seemed an eternity, he considered options, discarding each, beginning anew, going in circles.

The door swung open.

Gavra. Wearing another frown, she carried in bread, meat, cheese, fruit, and a teacup on a tray. Sun slanted across the fare, rays brightening the room. Hours gone without him realizing it.

Royce stood. Pain ripped through his leg ruthlessly. He clutched the chair. "Is it time for the midday meal?" The sun wasn't at its highest point.

He hoped Gavra hadn't drugged the food, inducing him to sleep and talk.

She placed the tray on the table and pivoted.

"Wait." He followed unsteadily. "Where's Simone?"

Gavra glared. "Not here."

"I can see that. Where is she?"

"Not here."

His belly clenched. "You mean on the island? She left? How? To go where?"

"You leave her alone." She poked his chest.

He teetered back, favoring his good leg. "I haven't done anything to her. I simply want to know if she's all right. Is she?"

"As long as she stays away from here and you."

"Is she on the blasted island?"

Gavra looked down her nose at him. "Peter had other tasks to do so he left the chickens and birds to Simone. I told her not to bother. If they belong to you, they should die. You will bring us nothing but trouble like Canela did."

His face burned. "I don't want anyone here getting hurt." More truth than he'd ever spoken. "I want everyone to be all right."

"Then leave. Now." She flung out her arm. "Go."

If not for his family, he would have. To behave as cowardly as his father had wasn't something Royce could allow. He'd die first. "Where are my pets?"

"I will never tell you." She slammed the door in his face.

Undeterred, he followed.

The islander guarding his room shouted. "*Arrêtez!*" Stop.

Royce moved as quickly as he could.

Halfway down the hall James blocked him, hand on the pistol in his belt. "Sure you should be up and trying to walk?"

Royce sagged against the wall, breath hitching. "Gavra said Simone's caring for Edward's chickens and birds. I wanted to see the creatures. That's all. I promised Edward I'd do so."

"Been having nightmares about not saving him?"

Royce pressed against the stone to steady himself. He didn't want to consider how he'd behaved during sleep or what Simone had told the others. "I'll never forgive myself for his death. Simone said Peter couldn't save every chicken or bird. I don't want to lose any more. I'm sure she has other tasks to see to. She shouldn't be troubling herself with the creatures."

"You're right. She should have seen to you. You're bleeding again."

A doubloon-sized stain dirtied his breeches. "I can tend it later. Take me to her first. Please."

James tapped his pistol. "I'll have to ask Tristan."

"Do so now. I'm not going anywhere." His leg felt twice its normal size. He yielded to the fiery pain and slid to the floor. Sweat soaked his shirt, the damp linen clinging to his chest.

James left.

The islander who'd shouted stood in the chamber doorway, pistol raised.

Royce nearly laughed at the absurdity of this. "Shoot me if you must. I can't move from here."

"*Assurez-vous que vous ne.*" See that you don't.

Diana entered the hall and halted yards from Royce. Although she carried no weapon, her hard frown kept him cautious. "What are you doing out here?"

"Waiting for James. He's asking Tristan if I can see Edward's pets."

She hurried in the same direction James had.

Two young women strolled by, eyeing him curiously. He tipped his head in greeting.

They dissolved into giggles and ran away.

A chicken squawked, head bobbing as it explored the hall and floor. He hoped to God Gavra hadn't let his birds loose. If he didn't contact Bishop eventually, the bloody bastard might send another agent here who'd have no trouble destroying these people.

Two children darted into the hall, pursuing the hen. It flapped its wings furiously, evading its captors. The boys won out and carried the chicken away, possibly to the kitchen for roasting.

Royce rubbed his temple.

James finally returned, carrying a crudely constructed crutch. "This might help you walk."

"Did you just make it?"

"Belonged to Philippe's grandfather before the pirates killed him."

"The ones Diana outwitted?"

"Those before Tristan took over the isle. Here." He offered his hand. "Be certain to thank Philippe for his kindness. He was reluctant to help at first."

Royce tested the device. Not as good as two sturdy legs but better than limping. "I promise to show my gratitude the next time I see him. Thank you for thinking of this."

James looked past him to the islander. "You can leave. I'll watch him now."

The man strode past.

James regarded Royce. "Tristan said you can see your pets. As long as you're here, you'll have to make yourself useful. Once your injuries have healed, we'll put you to work with the pigs or in the fields."

"I promise to pull my weight." He followed James down the hall, past numerous bedchambers. "The women don't have to work at those hard physical tasks, do they?"

James glanced over. "If you mean Simone, she heals and helps with the children. The others spin cloth, sew, make pottery, clean, cook, and do whatever else is necessary to thrive. No one is idle here."

"On Tristan's orders."

"By custom. The islanders work now as they always have. The only thing Tristan has done is use his knowledge to improve their crops and animals."

Royce stopped outside a room. So many books filled the space he couldn't count them. Volumes stretched from floor to ceiling, many stacked on chairs and the floor. There were charts too that would prove most valuable. "Are those Tristan's?"

"They are. He can read, write, and speak seven languages. Knows more than most nobles, possibly even the king."

Alarm raced through Royce. Before coming here, he'd learned as much as he could about Tristan, finding nothing from his past. He seemed born, fully grown, on the ship where he turned to piracy. "Are you saying he's a peer?"

That would be the worst possible thing.

James laughter rang through the hall. "God, no. Tristan taught himself everything he knows. He's better than any bloody noble. Come on, I haven't all day to escort you."

In the kitchen, Gavra and two other women stopped chopping, mixing, and stirring the food.

"Ladies." James tipped his head and winked at Gavra.

She blushed prettily. The others smiled. None glanced at Royce.

Children scampered in the courtyard. Women worked the looms and potter's wheels. Some washed clothing. Sun shone from a flawless sky. Simone's scent wafted past, floating on the mild breeze.

"Your creatures are in here, but only for the time being." James stopped at a room off the courtyard, the door closed, shutters drawn. Faint cackles sounded within.

"I'll gladly keep them in my chamber."

"Tristan doesn't allow anything but humans in the house."

"Why does he want the birds moved from here?"

"It's a birthing room for the women. Peter planned to keep the cages in the courtyard. Simone worried the children might open them accidentally, letting the birds escape, and had him move the lot in here. The ladies will need this space in a few weeks. Careful when you go in. I'm not sure if Simone let the creatures loose or not."

Royce couldn't risk losing another bird. Not if he planned to stay in contact with Bishop, since another reasonable choice hadn't presented itself.

Clumsily, he squeezed past the door into the shadowed space. Simone's fragrance surrounded him, the musky undertones muddying his brain.

She sat on the floor in the corner, grains, seeds, and berries to her side, spread out for the pigeons. They poked their heads through the metal slats in their cage and ate like gluttons. Chickens strutted freely, pecking their food.

Simone stood. The hens scattered. "Are you all right?"

Exhausted and aroused. "Fine."

"You're bleeding again."

"Not much. You shouldn't be doing this."

Her chin trembled. "What? Speaking to you? Asking questions? You want me to be silent and unseen?"

He longed to be in her arms, comforted and warmed. Anchored to all the good he'd never really known. Her words proved true. This island had wonderful people. The best life had to offer. Nothing he deserved. "You're a healer, not someone who tends chickens and birds. Peter should be doing this. Is he a lazy boy?"

She lowered her face, hiding her smile. "A surly one. He thinks he knows everything. Too many times, Diana has promised to thrash him."

"Good for her. A proper man needs manners. Let me help you." Eager to reach her, he strode recklessly.

A hen flapped its wings, going right and left to escape his crutch, its squawk ear-piercing. The other chickens scattered, many getting in his way. He twisted to keep from falling.

"Take care." Simone slipped her arm around his waist, her precious breast pressed to his side.

Surrendering to loneliness and enchantment, he leaned in, his face to her hair. The English countryside couldn't compete with her blessed scent. Nature had met its equal in her. He nuzzled her glossy tresses. No matter how wrong and irrational his desire, for some reason he'd found home at her side.

Pity he'd managed that too late.

He should have moved away but hadn't the will.

She guided him to a bed nearly as large as the one in his chamber. This lavish room, like his, boasted a marble floor and whitewashed walls. A lovely place for a new life to take its first breath.

She laid his crutch to the side. "Sit before you fall." Gently, she pushed him on the silk-covered mattress.

He made a show of falling down.

Her laughter pealed through the room.

Royce feigned insult. "Are you making light of me?"

"Oui."

His laugh produced happy tears. "Have you no pity for a poor cripple?"

"I have never seen a stronger man." She held her hands behind her, breasts thrust out, and swayed her hips slowly.

Aphrodite in the flesh. "Is that what you think of me?"

"What I know. You survived a storm that nearly tore our isle from the earth and flung it into the sky. You are no mere man. You are close to a god."

He was a liar when honor demanded he do nothing to ruin anything here. He was a besotted fool when duty required he see to his family. His mother and sisters had no power to liberate themselves. Without his help, Katie, especially, would know nothing except a life spent in hard labor, cowering at harsh words, dreading the next beating or something equally horrible.

Simone cupped his face. "What is it? Is the pain bad again?"

The worse a man could face. Having to choose between angels: the one in here now with him, or those in his family who he'd been trying to save. "I'm fine."

"No. I see hurt and sadness. I need to make it better. Stay on the bed until I return."

He captured her wrist, his breath catching at her achingly soft skin. "Don't let me cause you any trouble. Ignore me, please."

"Never." She brushed her lips over his. "Argue with me and I will shoot you."

He laughed heartily, fearing if he didn't he would cry.

She blew him a kiss and slipped outside.

Royce missed her instantly. Horribly. He pounded his fists into the mattress and muttered every oath he knew. He wanted to rip off his bandage and claw his ruined flesh, digging deep enough to reach a vessel, glorying in the spurting blood, his life slipping away.

He didn't deserve to live. He had no bloody right to die.

The door flew open.

Royce lifted his face.

Peter growled. "Damnation." He bolted after a chicken that escaped, tossed it back in the room, and ran down another. With it cradled in his arm, he sidled inside and slammed the door, trapping the rest.

Thankfully, Peter's foul mood and mouth were his only weapons.

Royce relaxed somewhat. "What are you doing in here?"

"Simone ordered me to cage your blasted hens and to clean up the mess she made."

"I'll do it. Go on, you can leave."

"Not bloody likely. You have no idea what she'll do if I defy her."

"Shoot you?"

He wrinkled his nose. "She'll tell Diana I enjoyed Laure when I should have studied. Once my nosy sister informs Tristan, he'll make certain I never leave the library until I'm old like him and you."

"I'm hardly ancient."

"I'm a man." Peter bounced on his heels, fists tight, face red. "Why can't anyone here see that?"

"They should, in time, when you're as old as I am."

"I hardly want to wait that long." Working quickly, he herded the chickens into their cage, snarling obscenities the entire time. He left briefly and returned, broom and cloths in one hand, a bucket in the other.

He attacked his cleaning with more fervor than a dervish did a religious dance. His hard sweeping worked up dust clouds.

Royce coughed.

Peter scrubbed and dried the floor, leaving no dirt, debris, or water. "She'd better be satisfied with this." He hauled the cages outside.

"Wait a moment. Where are you going with Edward's pets?"

"A room off the kitchen where we keep supplies."

"Take care with them, please."

"What else? Simone would have my head if I hurt the precious things." He tossed his cleaning tools outside and slammed the door behind himself.

Children's voices rose. Excited shrieks and laughter punctuated their words.

"No, these aren't for you to fool with," Peter said. "They belong to someone else. Plenty of hens in the courtyard. Chase and pet them."

The din moved away from this area.

Simone returned carrying a large silk sack. She regarded the room. "Did you help Peter?"

"Not at all. I never budged from this spot."

She grinned. "Threatening him with Laure always works, and probably will until he slips the marriage collar around her throat. Then, even a gun to his head will be useless. Once she belongs to him, Diana will have no say in what they do."

"Marriage collar? You mean the leather ones with beads and the diamonds Diana wears?"

"Oui. On this island, the collar shows a woman belongs to a man." She sank to her knees beside him. "Remove your breeches."

Each breath she took made her breasts tremble. Her rich skin radiated heat warmer than the day. "Take them off completely?" His pulse pounded hard in his temples and throat. "Why?"

"If I rip these, as I did your other ones, the women will have to make a new pair."

"I meant I can slip out of one leg so you can treat my wound."

"Oui, but your blood stained them. They need a good wash. Take them off and I can give them to Fantine." Simone patted her sack. "I brought another pair with me."

He undressed.

She regarded his cock, as erect as it had ever been. Perhaps more so. His skin felt close to splitting.

"Sit." She stroked his thigh.

Riotous heat and pleasure billowed through him. He dropped to the mattress.

She hurried to the door.

"Should you open it now?"

"Only to get the pitcher."

She brought the water inside and mixed a potion. "Drink."

"What's in it?"

"Herbs to lessen your pain."

He tasted the brew and held back a gag. "This is dreadful."

"No. Healing magic. While you were in your room, I asked Tristan to find a potion that would take away your hurt. He read it to me from his book."

Royce's stomach rolled. "Are you certain it isn't poison?" If Tristan had learned the shipwreck was a masquerade, death wouldn't be far behind.

She frowned. "We use the herbs to cook. They never make anyone sick."

"Excellent." He drained the cup.

She cleaned his wound. Surprisingly, it didn't look as bad as he'd feared, the blood minimal, the scab larger. Her new poultice was a different color than the last, more brown than green. "Did you use the same ingredients?"

"Today, I tried something different." She placed leaves over the mess and wrapped a new bandage around his leg. "Is the pain still bad?"

"Stings and throbs a bit."

She washed and wiped her hands. "I have something to make you forget the hurt."

"Another potion?" He smiled weakly. "One that tastes sweet?"

"No. This."

She buried her face in his thatch, one hand on his cock, the other, his balls.

Chapter 5

Royce dropped his cup. The world spun. Heat like nothing he'd experienced journeyed to his thighs and chest.

Simone inhaled deeply, her resultant sigh followed by a throaty moan. Gently, she squeezed his sac, her touch firmer on his rod, strokes quick.

He fell back, helpless as a newborn, unwilling and unable to stop her. His limbs were too weak, his need far beyond intense. She smelled of life. Her touch held hope he didn't know existed.

She licked his curls, then tugged them with her teeth.

Joy bubbled inside him. He wanted to shout and carry on like a man gone mad. He could scarcely breathe, not caring if he ever drew a full breath again. She'd mentioned magic that healed. Of everything the world offered, nothing proved more miraculous than a woman honoring a man as she did him.

She licked his crown and explored the bumpy skin on the back.

Pleasure raged. The room lurched. He gripped the sheet.

Her mouth was exquisitely hot, delightfully wet.

She took his shaft inside.

Rapture burst, then rolled in waves, too mighty for him to contain. He cupped her head and wrapped his legs around her, needing them to be close.

Her lips slid down his length, her tongue bathing and teasing him as she descended.

He was so hard his skin stung. Pain didn't result, only immeasurable satisfaction.

Her nose touched his pelt, his cock sheltered fully inside her mouth, her breath skipping over him.

He struggled for control. This had to last an eternity. He wouldn't settle for anything less.

She released him in small measures, then glided down, imprisoning him.

Each stroke tested his resolve to stall his release, her sweeping tongue impossible to resist.

He ground his teeth and battled his crushing need. Her alluring fragrance washed over him, mocking his meager struggle.

She caressed his sac and trapped his crown between her lips, suckling, licking, damning him to follow her lead. Her power greater than any he possessed.

His passion broke, hurling him to a place he never wanted to leave, his seed spurting into her mouth before he could stop it and spare her.

She swallowed his offering, accepting who he was. A man reduced to an animal state, stripped of civilization, unmasking his basest nature. She'd given him the greatest gift she could by not turning away.

Euphoria engulfed him, his need to indulge in his primitive nature boundless. To hell with being proper and English. Nature had always intended this for her creatures and more. Heaving chests, sweaty bodies, tangled limbs, lids too heavy to lift.

He dropped his hands.

Simone licked his rod clean, then rested her chin on his uninjured thigh. "Have you forgotten the pain?"

He laughed loudly, unmindful of those outside, though he should take care. To have the women or Tristan come in here now would be disaster. He quelled his outburst and kept his voice low. "I can't feel anything except my cock and balls. Pure magic."

She laughed softly. "I tended you well?"

"You're a miracle worker. Never has there been a healer like you."

"I have yet to finish."

He strove to lift himself and failed, his weakened state keeping him from looking at her. "What do you mean? What's left to do?"

She eased his right ball into her mouth.

His head nearly blew off. "Oh my dear God." He gasped and choked, too much pleasure threatening to do him in. "Stop."

She released his testicle. "Why? This hurts?" She lapped his sac.

He shuddered, wanting more, unable to bear it so soon after gaining relief. Each time she touched him increased his sensitivity to everything she did. "In a manner of speaking, yes, it bloody well hurts."

"What do you mean?"

"It's discomforting in a good way."

"Then you like this."

"What else? But—"

She tongued his ball back inside and suckled gently.

He writhed, wanting to get away, desperate to be closer.

Simone leaned on his leg. Her confining weight settled the matter.

She played with him at will. Her carnal torture stunned and seemed endless, yet also too brief. He knew heaven a second time.

She licked his seed eagerly. "Are you tired?"

He might never function normally again. A small price to pay for ecstasy. "Not at all."

"Why are you yawning?"

Royce stopped, not wanting her to think him frail. "Simply a habit I have. Truth is I have never been more...more..."

"What?"

He couldn't capture the word, fatigue overtaking him. "Give me a moment."

"For what?"

"To answer. Alert. That's it." He grinned in relief. "I have never been more alert than I am now."

"Put your legs on the bed."

Movement wasn't conceivable any longer. Perhaps tomorrow he'd be able to do as she asked. "Why?"

"So I can get on too."

What a swine he was, not considering her comfort. Twice, he tried to hoist his legs and failed.

"I should help you."

"No, I can do this."

He finally managed, too exhausted to do anything except sprawl.

She lifted her cloth and straddled him. Her cunt nestled against his cock. She released the silk.

It skimmed his thighs. His rod twitched with renewed life. "What are you doing?"

"Pleasuring you."

"No. Wait."

She pushed to one knee and directed his crown to her slit.

Royce grabbed her arms and forcibly rolled them over to put her beneath him. The mattress shook.

Her eyes rounded. "What are you doing?"

"Stopping you." If they were to couple, he'd risk filling her with his child. Then what? Have her and his son or daughter ripped away, both sold into slavery to another man if he couldn't prevent it because Bishop had outwitted him? "What were you thinking? What in the bloody hell is the matter with you?"

She blinked. "I want you. You want me. I proved that with your happiness." She slipped her arms around his neck. "This is what lovers do."

He grabbed her wrists and held them to the bed. "And what happens then? You and I cannot create new life."

Hurt flared in her eyes. She turned away. "You would hate a child that looked like me?"

He loosened his hold, pained that she'd think him heartless enough to worry about skin color or culture. In everything that counted, she beat him soundly. Her acceptance inexhaustible, manner genuine, affection pure. "Have you even been with a man before?"

She shrugged.

"Is that a no?"

"Do you dislike virgins?"

He'd guessed correctly about her state and loathed himself for allowing their situation to come this far, sending the wrong signals that his desire for her could ever be acceptable. His only sensible option meant leaving this bed and room, then keeping far away from her.

He wasn't able to manage a first step. He lowered his head. "I don't want to cause you any distress."

"Gavra said the pain only lasts a moment before pleasure replaces it, with the right man."

He'd forgotten about Gavra. If she saw this, she'd shoot him. He still couldn't leave. Simone's scent and heat bound him to her more easily than the strongest chains and shackles. "That's not what I meant. No man should mount a woman unless he can remain at her side for a lifetime."

She opened her mouth, then closed it and averted her gaze.

He tilted her chin so she couldn't avoid him or the truth. "You know I must leave this isle."

"What does it matter what may happen? As long as a woman and a man's hearts are one, they are together even when they part."

He fought laughter and sorrow. "What am I to do with you?"

"Give me joy. I saw to yours. You have not seen to mine."

She should be in Parliament. Her skillful arguments would trounce the fools there.

A prudent man would have turned his back on this scene and left. He pushed to his knees.

She reached for him. "What are you doing? You should lie down. Your wound."

"To hell with it." He untied her cloth and pushed the silk aside.

Crimson patches colored her cheeks and throat. She pressed her hands on her scar, unable to cover it. The jagged mark looked worse than the previous glimpse he'd had.

He lay down and eased her into his arms. "What happened? Who did that to you? Please tell me."

She gripped his shoulders. "A pirate."

"When?"

"I had just turned twelve."

Still a child. My God. "Was he from the group that lived here before Tristan arrived?"

"Oui." She snatched a breath. "They came to our shores one day and killed everyone who was old, sick, or lame, and those who fought them. My family died then. My grandmother was teaching me to heal. Pirates broke into our house. They shot my grandfather. When my mother cried out, they shot her too. I tried to protect my grandmother. A pirate slashed my leg with his dagger. I felt nothing and refused to let him near her. He stabbed me again, twisted the blade, and laughed. I couldn't fight any longer. He cut my grandmother's throat. As she died, he and another man dragged me to the bed. I must have screamed. My father and brothers burst inside to save me. They died too, falling next to my mother and grandparents."

Royce couldn't find words to comfort. He held her close, praying that would suffice.

Her breath skipped over his skin. "Should I be quiet now?"

"Only if that would be easier for you."

"I can never forget. I want you to know everything."

"I promise to listen." Although the world had always been an appalling place, he would never understand brutality and wasted lives.

She pressed her face to his neck. "The pirates fought over who would mount me first. They were hitting each other when island men stormed in. After they killed the pirates, they hid me in the forest and warned that I should be quiet and still like an insect hunted by a lizard. I lost so much blood I was dizzy, and bound my leg as I did yours on the beach. I knew enough to put the healing leaves on me from the nearby bushes. I stayed behind them all day and night. There were horrible screams and laughter where my people lived. I thought I would die in my hiding place. I was too afraid to come out."

She trembled and caught more air. "Gavra found me the next morning, an Englishman at her side. By then, our families were gone, the pirate captain owning everything we once called ours. Because of my wound, none of the white men bothered me. There were other women to rape. Some killed themselves to keep from lying beneath an Englishman. Canela offered herself willingly to the capitaine. He had a white woman and pushed Canela away. He used us to build the stone house and see to everyone's food and drink. We were their slaves. When the infants came from what the pirates did, they left the newborns in the forest to die because they were brown like the islanders, not white like them. None knew who fathered which child. All of them used the women repeatedly. They promised to kill the mothers if they tried to save their children."

He wanted to be sick. "I'm so sorry."

She hugged him. "My people survived. With Tristan's help, we made the isle what it was before the raid. Not all Englishmen are bad. Even Gavra knows that. Although the pirates used her as they did the others, she loves James. You are as fine as him and Capitaine."

"You're wrong. I'm not worthy of you."

"How can you say such a thing?" She pressed close. "You worry about my sadness and comfort even if you refuse to pleasure me."

He smiled. "I've hardly refused. I want nothing more. I hope you know that."

"I did before you untied my cloth. Does my ruined leg sicken you?"

"Of course not." He kissed the uneven skin. "Never."

She cradled his face. "What had you planned to do before I told you about the pirates?"

Something he shouldn't. That was his downfall here, following his heart and lust rather than hard reason. "I was going to bring you great joy without taking your virginity."

"How? Is it too late for that now?"

It had been even before they met. He eased back. "Stay where you are."

She grabbed his arm. "Will you leave now?"

"Not this bed or you until we finish. But you must promise to remain beneath me. I expect your full obedience."

"Even if you tell me to stop breathing, I will."

He tapped her nose playfully. "Not that. But you must be quiet lest the others hear."

Short of the door, women conversed and laughed, children shrieked, hens cackled.

Simone sighed. "I'll keep my tongue so you may take me as you will, for as long as you desire."

For him, their lifetimes wouldn't be enough.

* * * *

Simone had hoped he'd make her his for all time. She had his desire. She needed his heart. Her hunger for their shared lives was so great she'd nearly confessed what Tristan had said about failing to find a way for Royce to leave the island.

She feared making him sad, ruining their moment.

He eased the cloth from beneath her, dropped it on the floor, then sat on his heels and took her in.

Her cheeks and throat got hot. "You stare."

"Any sane man would. Do you have any idea how beautiful you are?"

"My skin is brown."

"Oui, wonderfully rich."

"My eyes will never be like the English, more colorful than rainbows."

"Your shade is far warmer, the loveliest I've ever seen."

She stroked his knee. "I like your green color better."

He grinned, crinkling the corners of his eyes. "We'll call it a tie then."

"A what?"

"Never mind. Time for pleasure." He fitted his mouth to hers, his hand on her breast.

She gave him her all, her length pressed to his, their hearts beating as one. Tasting him chased away sadness and doubt. He squeezed her breast as a lover should, proving she already belonged to him.

She always would.

On each strained breath, their chests tapped. His musk perfumed the air, mingling with her scent, creating a fragrance that belonged to them, no one else.

She eased his tongue aside and slipped hers into his mouth. He smiled. So did she, their lips still joined. Their searching kiss healed her soul, pushing away the bad she'd known, making her impatient for happiness. He matched her eager desire, then exceeded it, his grunts and growls wonderfully primitive, delightfully male, proving his strength. His whiskers bit into her cheeks and chin, another reminder of the man he was.

She softened beneath him, moisture dampening her slit, preparing her for his passion.

He tore his mouth free, slid down, and latched on to her nipple.

A rare thrill whisked through Simone, weakening and arousing her further. He lapped and teased her tip, his suckling gentle, then firm.

She loved both.

He settled on her other breast, his hair sliding across her arm, his mouth and tongue worshipping her flesh. She'd lived too long without knowing this and would die when it ended, already aching at the coming loss. "Never leave."

At her whisper, he lifted his head. "What?"

"Why did you stop?"

"You said something I didn't hear."

"Only praise. Go on."

"Gladly. See that you don't interrupt me again, unless it's with more praise."

"Always."

He winked and trailed kisses down her torso and belly, his stubble tickling her.

She giggled.

"Shh." He pressed his face to her mound and moaned lustily, though not loud enough for the others to hear.

His pleasure delighted Simone as nothing had. He wanted her as a person, not only as a woman who could satisfy his craving. She mattered to him.

Loving him was easy. Repeatedly, he'd proved he was a good man, worrying about her pleasure and future as much as his own. After so many trials, good fortune had come to her at last.

She lifted her hips, offering herself to him. Being with a man wasn't something to fear any longer. Royce would never hurt her.

He licked her cleft.

His intimacy opened her heart and freed her soul. Hope, joy, excitement, and lust rushed to the surface. Emotions she'd locked away for too long. Willingly, she submitted to her restive feelings, allowing them and him to guide her.

He tongued her opening and eased her nub between his teeth, imprisoning it gently. Her pulse jumped. His firm hold on her hip restrained her further. She held her breath. He slid his hand between her buttocks and stroked her tightest opening.

Air poured from her.

He suckled and licked, fast and firm.

Outrageous desire coiled within, filling her so quickly she feared she might burst and fly apart. The feeling overwhelmed and grew breathtaking.

She spun and soared. Pleasure deep within her channel broke free, a pulse inside beating rhythmically and hard. Her legs fell over. She fought to breathe.

Royce looked up. "Shh."

She covered her mouth unaware she'd made a sound.

He wagged his finger and lapped her nub.

Simone bucked. "No." The pleasure was too much to endure. "I may die if you lick me again."

"Trust me, you won't."

"Please." She gripped his hair. "The feeling is too…"

"What?"

"There is no word."

"Then your release was bad?"

"No. Wondrous. Glorious. Miraculous."

"That's several words. How about this—it was magic."

"The best kind." She pulled him onto her and kissed him deeply, her legs wrapped around his lean hips. She tried to roll them over to be on top to let his wound rest.

He was too big and heavy, kissing her at his leisure, with a male's right. One she'd given him.

They broke free, laughing softly and gulping air.

He touched his nose to hers. "I take it you enjoyed that."

"I never want to do anything else."

His humor faded, replaced by a troubled look.

She touched his mouth. "Was I wrong to say what I did?"

"What? No. Pity the world doesn't let one do whatever they want for as long as they wish. James told me that in a few weeks, the women are going to need this room. I'm afraid they will run us out."

"We can use this until they do, then go to your bedchamber."

"Not with a guard outside the window."

She'd forgotten about that. "We can go to my chamber."

"And risk having Gavra, Tristan, or Diana see us and rail at you? I think not."

Simone clung to him. "What they say means nothing. I do want I want. What we did today isn't wrong."

"Not for us, but the world doesn't consist of this room."

"It should. Please stay in here with me today until we have to go. Being alone is too sad."

He held her to him and stroked her hair. "Of course, I'll stay. I'm sorry you lost everyone you loved."

"You did too. Tell me about your family. Why you have no one."

His hand paused on her hair. "Shouldn't you be sleeping? Aren't you tired after your release?"

She dreaded closing her eyes, fearing he'd disappear and she'd never see him again. "I can sleep later. Talk to me. Tell me your past."

He eased them to the mattress. "Not much to tell. I wanted to grow up like my father, as a boy usually does, until I realized he wasn't an honest man. His desires came before anyone else's, especially his wife and family. You said your brothers and father gave their lives to protect you. That's what men do. Why God made them, to protect and cherish women. I have no doubt if my mother and sisters had been in the same situation, my father would have run in the opposite direction, with no thought except to save himself."

"He sounds like the pirates. Oh no." She covered her mouth. "Forgive me for my words."

"No need. You're quite right. He always was a coward."

"You had sisters?"

Grief tightened his features. "I try not to think of them. It's too hard."

"Now I made you sad."

"Not you. The situation. My father took everything our family had and left us impoverished. England, unlike this isle, isn't populated solely by kind people who will aid you in hard times, especially if they believe you deserved what happened. If you can't pay for things, you go without, even if that means shelter and food. Anyone without employment or money either begs, which is a criminal act, or ends up in the workhouse, forced to toil long hours in order to eat. Many succumb to starvation or illness. Those who have unpaid debts languish in prison until they can pay what they owe along with the price required for their stay in those hellholes. Any man who would put his family through that is a bloody beast who deserves to die."

"How did you survive?"

"By any work I could get, no matter how loathsome. That didn't save my mother and sisters from their fates."

She cupped his face. "Your nightmares are about them."

"They're always close to me. They're why I've become what I am."

"A merchant who sails on ships."

He lowered his face. "Among other things."

Simone wanted to ask more, but dreaded making him sadder. Today they'd share joy and hope, not a past no one could change.

She kissed his lids and drew him into her. "Sleep. When you wake, I will tend to your wound and your passion."

"As far as I'm concerned, we can forget about everything except pleasure."

"In this room we'll have nothing else. When the others run us away, I promise to find another place where we can be alone. No one will keep us apart."

"Tristan will have something to say about that."

"He does not own me. No one does."

Royce stared at her.

She'd never seen him so intense and dismayed. "What?"

"Nothing." He rested his head against her shoulder and closed his eyes.

Chapter 6

Trading Simone's freedom for his mother and sisters' future wasn't possible for Royce. Never had been. There had to be a way to spare everyone.

First, though, he had to prove to Bishop he'd arrived and was working on the plan before Bishop contacted a cold, calculating rogue to get the job done.

To locate the isle, Royce had spoken to natives who'd suggested the possible location. They'd do so for others too, given enough incentive. A surprise attack would be imminent, no matter the precautions Tristan took, the outcome worse than what Simone had already lived through.

Royce had to secure paper and pen for his note to Bishop, then get to the damn birds alone.

For days, Peter escorted Royce to the creatures and always remained nearby, sighing loudly from boredom or anger, muttering about wanting to be elsewhere.

Royce finally had enough of this nonsense too. He wasn't armed and couldn't fly off the island to escape. "Why not move these cages outside my bedchamber? The creatures would have fresh air they surely need and I could reach them from the windowsill." With the ever-present armed guard nearby.

Of course, the islanders weren't always as watchful as they should be. Some fought sleep or had to relieve themselves. During those scant minutes of diverted attention, he could release a bird and pretend the creature had escaped when he'd opened the cage. Wasn't likely the men would shoot and hit the thing, ruining his plan. "If Tristan agrees, I wouldn't need to bother you or anyone else to bring me here to take care of them."

Peter shrugged. "I can ask."

Days passed without an answer. Tristan had no time to consider the trivial matter, spending his efforts tending animals, surveying ruined crops, or helping the others rebuild their homes.

Simone's visits to Royce's bedchamber grew less frequent. His healing wound didn't require new bandages as often. During the cleanup after the storm, the others had cut or scraped themselves and needed Simone to look after their injuries. When she finished with those tasks, expectant mothers wanted potions to ensure their coming infants' good health. Children needed care.

Royce suspected Tristan, Diana, and Gavra were behind the full schedule Simone had mentioned to him.

No longer able to wait for Tristan's answer, Royce woke early and lingered in his chamber until Gavra delivered his morning meal. Once she had enough time to return to the kitchen, he opened his door.

The hall was empty.

Movement sounded from behind Royce.

Unfortunately, it wasn't only the wind and rain. Last night, he'd closed his shutters against the new storm.

Adamo rattled the barrier now, then shoved it open rather than peer through a slit in the wood as he'd done for hours. "What are you doing?"

Royce strode down the hall, a crutch no longer necessary, his pain gone and gash fully scabbed.

Adamo's feet slapped the marble floor, his pursuit as relentless as a London banker running down a defaulting creditor. *"Arrêter, sauf si vous voulez que je vous tire."* Stop, unless you want me to shoot you.

Royce held up his hands, walked backward, and spoke French. "I'm unarmed. What trouble can I cause? If you must kill me, you'll have to shoot me in the back." He resumed his march through the building, stopping at the dining area.

Tristan, Diana, James, and Peter stared at him as they might an unholy apparition. Rain slashed the closed shutters. Wind rattled them. The roof opening sported glass that kept the room dry but horribly stuffy.

Everyone wore a dour expression. Oil lamps added little warmth to the dreary mood and day.

Tristan, James, and Peter's pistols lay on the table at their sides, the muzzles glinting in the yellowish light. Only Diana had arrived unarmed.

Adamo clamped Royce's shoulder.

He put out his hands to Tristan in surrender. "I need a word. Please. I have been trying for days to speak with you. This morning seemed the perfect time as you can hardly build or tend anything in this rain."

Tristan glanced past him to Adamo. *"Tu peux rejoindre les autres dans la cuisine."* You can join the others in the kitchen.

Conversation and laughter from a sizeable crowd flowed into this room. Tristan smiled. *"Profitez de ce que les femmes ont fait."* Enjoy what the women made.

Adamo remained. The cowhide covering his head and shoulders dripped water, puddling at his bare feet. "Should I come back here when I finish?"

"I'll call when you're needed. You did a fine job in guarding our visitor. Merci."

Adamo nodded and left.

Tristan told Diana what they'd said, then faced Royce. "Go on, sit." He gestured him to a chair. "A word of warning. Do not roam about on your own. If Adamo doesn't shoot you, one of us may."

"I'm unarmed. What threat do I pose?"

"You tell me."

If only Royce could. That would make the situation easier and would result in his immediate death, leaving his family no protection or hope. "I deal in exotic merchandise, not danger or murder. I would leave here in a moment if I could."

Gavra carried the silver tea service into the room, her eyes on James. *"Qu'a dit l'Anglais?"* What did the Englishman say?

Royce told her before James could.

Simone leaned against the kitchen doorway, humiliation and sorrow in her eyes.

Of all the things for her to overhear, Royce wouldn't have chosen his last words. However, he had to keep up his performance or risk worse than her bruised feelings. He spoke French. "Am I your prisoner here, Captain? Is this to be my fate for the rest of my days?"

Gavra filled James and Tristan's teacups.

"Merci." Tristan pulled the saucer close. "Please bring one for our visitor." He regarded Royce and spoke English. "Have you eaten?"

"Gavra brought ample food as she always does. I came here instead, wanting to speak."

Tristan looked over. *"S'il vous plaît lui apporter une assiette et des ustensiles pour qu'il puisse nous rejoindre."* Please bring him a plate and utensils so he can join us. Tristan leaned back and switched to English. "As a guest, not a prisoner. Have you seen Newgate or heard of it? Trust me the accommodations here are far better."

"I didn't mean to be impolite. However, I'm going mad spending each day in my room, having to wait for Peter to escort me to Edward's pets so I can tend to them."

Peter snorted. "If you think I like it any better than you, then you'd be wrong."

Diana gave her brother a look as cool as her pale blue gown. "We know how taxing you find your obligations here. However, you will continue with them."

He hunched over his food, muttering beneath his breath.

"Enough, Peter." Tristan waited until Gavra delivered the plate, fork, and spoon before he spoke to Royce in English. "You best follow our rules as you're going to be with us awhile. Mozambique is quite a distance from here. We can't risk taking you there."

"I understand that. Small craft would never make the journey. Even a longboat would probably have difficulty reaching the Mozambique shore."

"That's not what I meant."

Royce didn't have to feign surprise. "You have a larger vessel?" Surely, the Lady Lark.

"Whether we do or not, James, Peter, and I have prices on our heads. We can't risk escorting you to civilization. James has already asked the islanders if they'd care to see to the task."

"They said no." James flicked something from his freckled chest. "They want nothing to do with the English, except for us, of course. Given their experience with the last pirate who ruled, one can hardly blame them."

Tristan put down his cup. "That means you're here until the islanders we trade with arrive. Perhaps they can help. That said, we won't be able to ask them for some months. Wisely, they don't travel during cyclone season. Your bedchamber may seem like a prison to you, but it's far better than what most in this world have."

"I'm not complaining about that. Admittedly, you've been gracious. But I want to make myself useful. James said everyone here works."

"They do." Diana shot Peter a look. "Whether they want to or not."

"Then make use of me." Royce pled with Tristan. "Allow me to care for Edward's pets without pulling Peter from his tasks. I can put the cages outside my room. When the hens and birds need tending, I can climb over the windowsill and do what I must. If I travel farther than that, surely an islander can shoot me."

Peter snickered.

Tristan cut his fish. "That's seeing to your needs, not those on the isle."

"I could also assist Simone in her daily tasks."

Diana's fork clattered against her plate. "Absolutely not. You will not spend your days with Simone."

She pattered into the room. "*Que dites-vous à propos de moi?*" What do you say about me?

Peter told her.

She frowned. "No one here owns me. I can do as I please."

Peter translated for Diana.

Tristan put out his hands. "Of course, Simone. But this is your home, not Royce's. Healing is your task, not his."

"If I may say something." Royce waited for Tristan's attention and switched to English. "I could read her the passages from your medical books, recording those she needs on another sheet for future use." That would give him access to paper and pen.

Tristan arched one eyebrow. "You can read Arabic?"

"French, English, Latin, and Greek. However, if I have the Arabic alphabet at hand, with its translation into the languages I do know, I can piece things together and learn to read it. Until then, I can use your other books to tell her what she needs to know, sparing you, Peter, or Diana the task so you can return to your regular work. I could also teach Simone to read."

She touched his arm and asked what they'd said about her.

Royce told her.

Simone's face lit up. "You would do that for me?"

"If you want to learn, of course and gladly. Though it's up to you." Royce spoke English to the others. "Everyone here should learn to read and write so they have access to the knowledge in the library. It's a sorry waste if they don't."

Tristan tapped his chin. "Diana's already had an idea to teach the islanders."

Peter chuckled.

Tristan glared. "What's so amusing?"

"Nothing." He sobered. "It's just that she'd have to learn the languages Royce knows, and fluently too, before she could teach anyone else anything. The infants could have their own children by then."

Royce sensed a fight brewing that might steer everyone from the course he'd set them on. "I don't want to intrude if the matter's been settled."

Diana's cheeks flamed. "It hasn't. I have no objection to you teaching them what they need to know. I want them to learn and thrive."

"As do I." Royce chanced a smile. "You're more than welcome in my classroom too. I'm a fair teacher and will have you speaking and writing the languages as promptly as I can."

"No thank you. My husband sees to my lessons."

"As you wish. What about the fields and pigs?"

Tristan looked at him blankly. "What about them?"

"James said I'd be working there when my leg mended. It has. Will I be outside during daylight and in the library after dark?"

Tristan worked his mouth, fighting a smile. "I think we can let you forgo the physical labor. You seem more suited for the library."

"I can pull my weight in any endeavor and shall."

Simone touched his shoulder. "What did you and Tristan say?"

He told her.

"Please stay in the library. I need your help with my healing."

"That settles it." Tristan tossed his napkin on the table. "You two can begin today." He told Diana what he'd said, then spoke to Royce in English. "Once the rain stops, Peter will put your cages outside your window. They'll have to go back to the storage room when the storms start up again."

"Agreed." Royce stood.

"Wait." Diana laid her hand on Tristan's. "Peter and I use the library to study. It's hard enough getting through the lessons without others in there reading aloud or speaking and causing endless distractions."

Simone glanced at everyone. "*Ce qui se passe?*" What goes on?

Royce told her.

She spoke to Tristan. "Royce and I could use the birthing room. No one needs it today, tomorrow, or the next. When they do, we can find another place. Either my bedchamber or his."

A crash sounded.

Gavra. She picked up the tray she'd either dropped or thrown down.

Diana looked confused. "What just happened?"

Tristan explained, then spoke to Simone. "Not the bedchambers. Use the birthing room for now. You can bring the books you need in there. I'll translate the Arabic alphabet into English for Royce."

He nodded. "What about Adamo and Philippe?"

"What have they to do with this?"

"While they're guarding me in the birthing room, they should have a chair, unless it's acceptable for them to sit on the bed. It's not fair to ask them to stand the entire time. Or worse, wait outside in the rain. The damp heat would be terrible for them."

Tristan didn't react.

Royce stared him down.

"Simone." Tristan looked at her. "*As-tu confiance en* Royce?" Do you trust Royce?

"Oui. He only wants to teach me what I should know so I can help everyone here. How is that dangerous? How does that cause harm?"

"Very well. No more guards…if my lovely wife feels the same." Tristan stroked her fingers and explained what they'd discussed. "Do you agree? I trust your opinion on this."

Diana slumped. "We're not in England any longer. I keep forgetting that."

Peter kept his head down. Given where he sat, he managed to hide his smirk from Tristan and her.

Diana glanced up. "Yes, I agree with my husband. Ah, *bien apprendre, Simone*." Learn well, Simone. *"Lecture et…l'écriture va ouvir un monde que…vous ignoriez…l'existence."* Reading and writing will open up a world you never knew existed.

She clapped her hands. "Merci. We should begin now."

"Oui. Off with you." Tristan gestured them away. "Wait. Royce, you can start taking your meals in here with us. Saves Gavra the trouble of serving you."

"I can eat in the kitchen like Simone and the others."

"They're only here until we rebuild their homes."

"Then I'll dine with them until they leave for their own places. If you don't mind."

"Have it your way. Though we will want you to take the evening meal with us so you can provide an update on your day and progress."

"Of course."

Simone laced her fingers through his. "Are we leaving now?"

"Oui."

She tugged him toward the kitchen. "We can see to Edward's pets first, then prepare the birthing room with what we need."

* * * *

Animated conversation streamed from the kitchen. Silence followed, then muted but heated words. If Tristan had to guess, he'd say Simone had made an announcement about her and Royce's new plans and Gavra didn't take the news well.

A pot clanged.

Diana looked over and leaned into Tristan, her mouth on his ear. "Do you trust him?"

He couldn't say no, but wasn't certain he should say yes. Royce was a paradox. Slick as could be in presenting his arguments that were hard to refute, but also strangely vulnerable around Simone. With her, he seemed genuine, having no hidden agenda, truly wanting to help.

Tristan considered how he'd respond if he found himself in Royce's place. Stranded on an isle in the middle of nowhere and surrounded by armed strangers. He probably would have behaved the same. "He has no weapon, nor means of leaving and telling anyone anything. Even if the other islanders agree to take him to Mozambique, which may be doubtful, they'd blindfold him so he couldn't reveal where this island or the others are. He's not a mariner who knows the route the captain took. For good measure, we could threaten to run him down if he ever opens his mouth about us being here. He doesn't strike me as a man who's had experience besting pirates. We can cow and confuse him easily."

The din in the kitchen quieted.

Diana crossed her arms over the table. "So you don't trust him completely? What about you, James?"

"I'm staying out of this."

Tristan laughed. "That's no answer."

"Very well. Gavra doesn't like him."

"With good reason, given what the pirates did to her. That said, she's not you." Tristan slumped in his chair. "What are your thoughts?"

"I have no complaints about the man. He's eager to work and did bring up what I'd said earlier about him toiling in the fields or tending the pigs. He didn't have to tell you that. I sure as hell wouldn't have even though I'm no stranger to hard labor."

"That's probably why you'd react differently than he had." Tristan wiggled his eyebrows. "I can't picture him wrestling a pig."

Peter laughed. "Want to know what I think?"

Tristan leveled his gaze on him, tired of Peter repeatedly goading Diana. "You should be in the library by now doing your lessons. And I do mean schoolwork, not running off to enjoy Laure. Don't make me tell you again."

Peter's face and throat colored. "No, sir." Shoulders slumped, he dragged from the room.

Diana sighed. "Will he ever grow up?"

"In time. Everyone does. We'll have to muddle through with him as we'll eventually do when our babes come. Why don't you trust Royce?"

"I… It's not that I don't. I worry about Simone. You saw how she looks at him."

"And he at her."

"They're going to use the birthing room for far more than her healing and his lessons. What happens when he leaves?"

"He may not."

"Then what happens when he's forced to stay here but wants to return home? I see nothing but tragedy in this for them."

Tristan pressed her palm to his cheek. "That's the risk one takes when attraction overrules good sense."

"Unless love blossoms."

"Yes, there is that."

* * * *

Royce hated that Gavra's unpleasant comments had ruined Simone's good mood. However, he couldn't argue with Gavra's assessment of the man he was or her logic in wanting to keep Simone far from him. Simone had no business spending time at his side, hoping for something that couldn't be.

If he got her and the others out of this mess, along with rescuing his mother and sisters, he'd disappear next. Didn't matter to where, as long as he posed no threat to anyone ever again.

Simone scuffed her foot over the storage room floor, the kitchen close enough for muffled conversation to drift in here. Gavra spoke louder than the others did, though low enough to mask her words.

Simone glanced over, head cocked.

He hunkered near his birds. They strutted to and fro endlessly, as he would if caged. He eyed the sturdiest and the runt. "Oh no."

Simone joined him on the floor. "What is it?"

"The largest one to the right. It doesn't seem as well as the last time I saw it."

"How can you tell? They all look sturdy to me."

They were. He had no choice except to lie. "It wobbled a second ago. I noticed one of the other birds doing that on the Sea Sprite. It perished before the storm hit."

"Do you think what we find in Tristan's books will help this one get better?"

"Doubtful. That's for people, not creatures. It may die." That would provide an excellent explanation as to why he had one less bird, and might prove more convincing to Tristan than the thing having flown away.

Which it would once he slipped his message in one of the tubes Bishop had provided for this scheme. Royce had brought them here for the bird's leg. He'd put the cylinders in a pouch and buried it on the beach long before Simone had discovered him. All he had to do was get to them.

Another hurdle to surmount.

She poked her finger through the cage. "We should give it more to eat and extra water. Maybe the poor thing is simply weak."

"Perhaps, but please don't get your hopes up. We can only do the best we can."

He fed the creatures and hens quickly, then transferred them to another container so he could clean their cages.

Finished, he rubbed his hands on his breeches. "Before we get the books, I'd like you to show me the bushes where you gather the healing leaves and the other items for your poultices." With any luck, they were close to the beach.

She made a face. "In the rain? We should wait."

"The weather might not improve for days. We can use cowhide like Adamo did to stay dry." He pressed his mouth to her ear. "We can also be alone there, even more so than in the birthing room."

She slipped her arms around him. "Oui."

"Wait a moment. We can't."

"Why not?"

"If Adamo and the others guard my room, surely they do the same with the beach. Tristan seems quite worried about anyone coming to the isle."

"He is, and the men do watch, but not in this weather. James told Gavra only a fool would sail in fog with so much wind and rain. How would they see?"

"They couldn't." This opportunity was too good to miss. All he had to do was convince Simone to go to the beach.

He hated deceiving her. However, with her eventual freedom at stake, he had little choice. "Where do they keep the cowhides?"

"We have pig skins too. Much smaller and they weigh less." She gathered two in light brown and handed him one.

He stroked her cheek. "Let's make this fun, shall we?"

"After I show you the bushes?"

"Oui."

"Are we going to the birthing room then?"

"I have another place in mind. A surprise." He placed the skin over her head, did the same with his, and took her hand.

Wind whipped his shirt and her cloth, rain lashing in great sheets, the temperature mild and sticky. Thankfully, it wasn't lightning. He pulled her close, protecting her from the worst of the shower.

They dashed into the nearby forest, the heavy vegetation serving as a protective canopy.

Sodden hair clung to her shoulders and breasts, the silk to her luscious legs. Laughing, she tossed the pigskin aside. "That did no good keeping me dry."

"You're lovely wet."

"You are too." She sagged against him and suckled his throat.

Her tongue warmed him better than spirits ever had and stoked his desire.

"You need another shave." She touched his cheek. "You should let me see to the task. While I do, you can rest for your other work."

"What say we try that in the birthing room when no one's watching?"

"With our clothes off?"

"Is there any other way?"

Giggling, she broke free and ran ahead. He caught up easily, his arm around her waist.

"Here." She pointed at the bushes in front.

"What is that?"

"Healing leaves. Periwinkle." She swung her arm to the side. "Over there are other plants I use." She indicated another direction. "And those are special herbs."

Royce padded to the periwinkle. Despite heavy fog, he could see faint outlines below, indicating the point and beach. Beneath the rain patter and wind, the surf churned. "Is this where you were when you first saw me?"

"Oui. I was gathering new leaves after I tended to Henri's hand."

Royce turned into Simone and cupped her face. Raindrops clung to her lashes and rolled down her smooth cheeks. She regarded him with such trust and affection, he lost his resolve, wanting to confess everything, yet terrified to do so. His plan to put Bishop off for the time being had to work. "Were you afraid when you saw me?"

"I worried for you. I feared you had died or might."

"We should go down there now."

"Why?"

"To show nature I survived when she wanted me dead." He pressed his face to Simone's hair. Her scent filled him, a seductive mixture boasting sweet flowers, fresh air, and cooling rain. "To celebrate you rescuing me. Come on."

He pulled her to the point and down the path. The surf broke higher than when she discovered him here, but posed no danger. Shielding her, he chose an area close to where he buried the tubes, the forest sufficiently thick to give them cover.

Panting, she sagged against a trunk.

Royce untied her drenched cloth and peeled it from her.

She smiled wantonly. "Is this the fun you spoke of?"

"Not yet...not until I have you exactly as I want."

"How is that?"

"As my prisoner, captive for my use."

She looked at her cloth.

He rolled it to resemble a rope. "Put out your hands, wrists together."

Chapter 7

Simone smiled, liking this. "Are you going to tie my hands?"

"Oui. Then I'll secure them to a branch to keep you from moving until I allow it."

Warmth gathered in her belly and dipped to her cleft. "You need to do that to keep me close to you? You have no faith in my desire?"

"I wonder about your resolve to submit to what I have planned."

Her skin burned from excitement, not shame. "And what is that?"

"Obey me now and you'll see."

She offered her hands and her entire being to him, thrilled at this game.

He tied the silk around her wrists, loose enough to be comfortable, though tight, too, to keep her from pulling free. She wouldn't, eager to be his prisoner, naked and helpless for him to use as he desired.

Her nipples puckered, the tips hard enough to hurt. A lovely feeling.

Royce eased into her, their hips joined, his shaft hard and long against her thigh.

She pressed closer. "When are you going to take off your shirt and breeches?"

"Your nudity is all I need." He lifted her arms and bound the cloth to a branch.

Finished, he stepped back, hands on his hips, strong legs parted. A conqueror's stance. Leisurely, he raked his gaze over her, taking in her breasts, belly, and mound. What he had owned from the moment they'd met.

For him, she didn't mind being a slave to passion. They'd been born for each other and this. No one could tell her otherwise. What he'd said in the stone house about wanting to leave wasn't true. His eyes had shown her the truth in his heart. "You stare."

"As is my right. Part your legs."

She pushed her feet over the spongy ground.

"Wider."

Air licked the dampness between her legs, her sheath glutted and pining for his touch.

Fog swirled, enclosing them within its gauzy embrace. Behind him, rain poured steadily, adding another barrier to the outside world, making this moment and place theirs alone.

Royce dropped to one knee, hands heavy and hot on her hips. He looked up.

Hair clung to his forehead and cheeks. Lust burned in his eyes. "I intend to indulge in your womanly charms for as long as I wish. Your soft folds and cunt are mine to master and own. You will not allow yourself release. You'll endure until I grant you completion. Each time you come close to relief, I'll stop and will begin anew until you can't bear the wait any longer. Do you understand?"

Her need was already too much. One touch from him and she'd soar as she had the last time. She had no chance to win against his rules, yet if she did, she'd experience an even greater prize.

He stroked her cleft.

Delight sped through her. She pushed to her toes and trembled.

"Say you understand, Simone."

"I do."

"And you'll obey?"

"Oui. Touch me again where you should. I beg you."

"In time." He pressed his face to her curls and stroked the furrow between her cheeks.

Pleasure crept close.

He circled her tightest opening.

Tingles raced to her sheath, leaving it heavy and wanting. She clenched her teeth to fight her response. Ignoring her soaring need wasn't possible.

Gently, he probed her anus and licked her nub.

Heat shot to her face. Craving consumed her. She tugged on her bounds.

Royce stopped, face to her cleft, his breath grazing her.

Simone dug her nails into her palms. "You must continue."

"No. I told you my rules and you broke them."

"I was far from relief. Too far."

"You tried to get free. That's not allowed. Now, you have to wait for more pleasure." He tongued her slit, missing the most sensitive part. He tugged her hair with his teeth, giving her no contentment, only a smile. He sniffed repeatedly, pulling in her scent.

Not once did he lick her nub or touch her other opening. Instead, he squeezed her buttocks.

Frustrated, she pushed close, forcing him to stroke and tongue the parts that mattered most.

He pulled back. "Again, you defy me. Very well. I'll wait until you obey." He speared his tongue into her navel.

She laughed and squirmed. "That tickles."

"I suppose that's allowed." He licked her belly.

She bounced. "Between my legs, please. I promise to be good."

"I never said I wanted that." He latched on to her nub, spread her cheeks, and stroked her anus.

Her knees sagged, but she also endured as he'd commanded. For a little while.

True to his word, each time she stiffened, preparing for release, he stopped and rubbed his face to her furry mound or kissed her scar. The moment she settled, he resumed his unending torment, never licking her more than a few times before pausing. Drawing her release close, letting it slip away.

Perspiration coated her face, throat, and chest, soaking her more than the rain. Her musk scented the air, her hunger for relief intolerable. She couldn't breathe enough to satisfy her craving.

He stopped and rested his face against her belly.

Drained and defeated, she sagged against the trunk.

Royce held her tightly and dipped to her slit, enjoying her as the slave she was to his passion and love.

His tender licks and gentle strokes undid her, the pressure between her legs mounting, searching for escape.

She fought it, resolved to do what he wished.

He increased his pace, then slowed, keeping her from knowing what his next move would be.

She dug her toes in the ground but remained open and helpless to him.

He breathed as hard as she did, their sounds drowning out the rain and surf.

One lick became two, three, a countless number she couldn't keep up with. Release slammed into her. She shuddered but didn't beg him to stop as she had the last time. Submissively, she endured his intimate moves.

Royce worked her tirelessly, the bliss he created far too intense.

Her head fell down, knees buckled.

He stood, his arm supporting her, mouth on her nipple, each lick too acute.

New pleasure battered Simone, settling into a gentle hum that relieved and warmed. She was too limp to stand, too eager for more to deny him anything.

He used her breasts and nipples well, then sank to his knees and reclaimed her mound.

* * * *

If Royce tasted her every day, hour, and minute through eternity, it would never be enough. Her scent was in his blood, her labored breathing and deep moans the only music he wanted to hear.

She could barely remain on her feet and still he couldn't stop. If not for the blasted tubes, he would have savored her until darkness fell.

On his feet, he untied her bounds. She collapsed into his arms.

He wished he could always be there to catch her and bring her to this point. "What's this? You seem tired."

"No. Now, I pleasure you."

"First, you rest." He eased her to the tree and pulled off his clothes. They were wet, but clean. He spread out his breeches for her to lie on. Once she'd curled on her side, her back to him, he draped his shirt over her and stroked her ear. "Sleep."

Her lips moved but no words sounded.

He didn't dare glance away lest she wake and see what he did. On all fours, he crawled backward, running into bushes and a trunk before reaching the spot he needed.

Her shoulders rose and fell with her gentle breathing.

Rain needled his face. He dug in the loam, hitting roots and rocks, not his small pouch. His chest tightened. Surely, Tristan or the others hadn't found the tubes. If they had, Tristan would have known what the birds were for and Royce would be dead.

Desperately, he clawed mud and sand, terrified what failure would mean. His next chance to come here might not be for weeks, making Bishop restless for action from another man. Sending an uncovered message to Bishop was unthinkable. Moisture or rain would ruin the ink. The binding might come loose, and the bird lose the paper during flight.

Royce dug deeper and had to take time to cover the spot before moving on. Simone would surely want to know why there were now holes in the ground where they hadn't been before. He edged to the right and tried there. Nothing. The same on the left. In front, he touched something soft yet solid.

The pouch.

He lowered his face and sucked air. Now, all he had to do was hide the thing on him...once he had access to his clothes and without Simone seeing what he did.

He slid the pouch beneath a bush, washed his hands in the rain, then sank next to her.

She stirred. "Did I sleep?"

"You did." He kissed her ear. "You deserved rest as you obeyed me beautifully."

She turned into him and cradled his cock. "Now I tend to you."

Royce wanted nothing more, but needed to get the tubes back to his bedchamber and hide them. He had no idea where that might be or who would traipse in and out of the room during his absence. "We should get back to the mansion or the birthing room." Perhaps he'd find a place to use in there or the library. "It's dry."

"I like being wet with you." She rolled away and pushed to her elbows. Head down, she presented her buttocks, her skin a soft brown, cleft and anus deep pink.

Flesh should never be so plush or inviting, her beauty a bloody crime against a man as weak as him. If sin existed, what raged within Royce for Simone met the qualification, tempting him to take, use, love her.

He wouldn't allow himself to do so.

She looked over. "My other passage is safe."

"What?"

"The women here have always used their second opening when food was scarce so no infants would come. Mount me. We can have pleasure without worry."

"I…" He didn't know what to say. She offered more than any lady had given him or would have allowed. Only a doxy, paid to deliver whatever men required, had permitted unlimited pleasure.

Simone gave herself freely.

"Have I said something wrong?" She searched his face. "Could you never like this?"

"No. That is, I'm honored. You give too much."

"Only what I want. For you, everything. Why do you wait?"

He couldn't any longer, but feared harming her. "Can you relax so it doesn't hurt?"

"I know what to do. The other women talk. I listen."

Royce laughed. "Thank God for that."

"Become a part of me. Make us one. Please."

He should be the one begging her. With great care, he used the moisture on her folds to lubricate her opening.

She squeezed the ring. "I like how that feels."

He worked his index finger inside, giving her a small taste of what would come. Her incredible heat stirred him, her muscles relaxing around his finger. What an apt pupil she'd become when it came to lovemaking.

If she applied herself like this to languages, she'd soon speak and write better than he did. "Still feel good?"

"Oui."

He prepared her as well as he could. For himself, he had to control his desire and not plow inside, rending her. "If this hurts, let me know and I'll stop."

"I trust you."

She shouldn't.

That didn't stop him. He guided his crown into her opening. Her heat and tightness stole his breath.

Simone pushed against him. "More."

"In time. We need to go slowly."

"You do."

They both did. From the start, their situation had veered out of control. Now they careened toward further disaster. Taking her like this wouldn't satisfy him for long, his hunger to have her in every way destroying what restraint he managed.

Her sleek passage held him spellbound. Pleasure beckoned. His crown slipped completely inside. He couldn't swallow or breathe. This was too fine. Spectacular warmth. Soft woman. "You all right?"

"I want more."

He laughed weakly. "What am I to do with you?"

"Love me."

He would and did. An utterly foolish reaction that went beyond the physical act. Simone was the soul he'd lost, what he'd been before everything turned to ashes. The future he'd once hoped for and would never have again.

Reality should have stopped him.

He tunneled slowly, as deeply as a man could go. Their bodies touched. Royce knew paradise yet would always require more with her. He leaned down and kissed her back. "Tell me if you're in pain."

"Only because you worry too much."

Someone had to. She trusted too easily. His adoration for her deepened.

"Use me as you will." She pushed her buttocks into him and squeezed her opening. "I promise not to break."

He grinned, liking her playfulness. "When did you become so saucy?"

"Does that mean wanting you? I did the moment you grabbed my wrist on this beach."

Seemed like a lifetime ago, nothing else existing now except this isle and these moments.

Indulgence prodded him, fueling his need to engage in an act as old as time. He pumped into her, carefully at first.

She made an impatient noise. "More. Faster. All you have to give."

"For a slave, you're most demanding."

"Should I hold my tongue?"

"Would you?"

"As long as I could."

He roared with laughter. "I wager that would be a minute, perhaps less. What say I distract you from speaking?" He stroked her nub and pumped.

She moaned indecently, captive to desire. Exactly what he wanted. His shaft's slow slide pulled love sounds from her and brought him to another plane that belonged to them alone. Their thighs tapped merrily, his balls swung free. Her nub couldn't have been harder, slit wetter.

Their mutual desire unmistakable and futile.

He'd recall these days till his last breath and would always yearn for a chance to do it again.

Saving the others and her had to be enough. The same as Simone's carnal release and his. Possibly the last one they'd know together.

She came first and cried out. Her joy filled him with pride and melancholy. When relief arrived for him, he pressed his face to her back to keep from making a sound, not wanting to share what they had with anyone or anything, including the rain and wind.

They quieted but he didn't pull out, unwilling to face the world without her. He needed a few additional moments, months, years, decades with Simone at his side. Selfishly, he took her again, this release more stunning than the last.

When they separated, she fell over onto sodden leaves, her back to him.

Remaining awake was a bloody effort, but he grabbed the pouch, tied its strings to the top button on his breeches, and hid it beneath his shirt.

He leaned over Simone. Her lids were down. "Are you asleep?"

"I may never wake."

"Are you saying I did you in?"

"You made me happy. Lie down and hold me."

A siren's call, him the too willing mariner. However, he didn't yield to her. She reached for him blindly.

He kissed her palm, then laid her arm on her side. Her hand fell to the ground.

Royce backed away, washed in the rain, and dressed, the pouch against his belly, his shirt masking the faint bulge it made.

Lightning flashed. Seconds later, thunder rumbled some distance away.

She lifted her head. "What was that?"

"The storm's grown dangerous. We must return to the mansion."

"Not the birthing room?"

"Later." He needed to find a hiding place in his chamber first. If none proved likely, he'd try the other spots. "Let me help you."

Her cloth refused to unfurl easily. A stronger bolt lit the sky, the resultant boom coming faster and louder. He worked hurriedly on the knot. Though dressed, they were wet, mud on their clothing and legs, his hair a bloody mess, hers tangled.

He kissed her hard and rested his forehead against hers. "You're beautiful."

"You are too. Will we do this again?"

"Not today. We must run."

He tugged her up the path and tore through the forest to the mansion, then pulled her aside before she could enter the door. "Wait."

Her nipples poked his chest. Their breaths caught. "Why?"

Royce tugged her to a spout on the roof, water streaming down. They bathed within the flow, washing away dirt and sand.

Simone looked at the silk clinging to her legs. "Should we go to the birthing room first to get dry before we see the others in the stone house?"

"You go. I'll bring my towel to keep Gavra from complaining about your state. I know you don't want her being cross with you."

"She has no right. I thought she was my friend."

He touched his nose to hers. "She is. That's why she's giving you so much trouble. She worries about you."

"I do what I want."

"Do as I ask, please." He eased back. "Go to the birthing room. I'll be there as soon as I can."

She clutched his arm. "It takes so long to get your towel?"

"One of the women might have taken mine to wash. I'll have to find something else."

"More towels are in the closet three doors from your chamber. Not far at all. I can wait here for you."

"No. I should get books first to cover the towels. That way Gavra won't see anything and fret about what we've been doing. Go on, please. I'll meet you shortly."

She screwed up her mouth. "I need to talk with Gavra as Tristan does to Peter. Come back to me soon."

White streaks cut across the sky. A violent roar followed.

She pecked his cheek and dashed to the room.

He waited for her to get safely inside, then ran around the mansion to his bedchamber. Ordinarily, he would have had trouble finding the correct room, but Adamo hadn't closed the shutter when he'd barged in, leading Royce straight to it. He pushed the covering tight against the window to keep out the wind and more rain. Large puddles had collected on the floor.

He rubbed his towel over his face and hair, mopped up the water, then scrubbed his feet.

Nothing in here served as a good hiding place. The women who tidied up might check beneath the sheets or pillows.

He dropped the chair cushion into its proper place, afraid to leave his pouch under it. Someone might discover the tubes while dusting the wood or brushing the silk…or whatever one did to fabric.

There weren't any cabinets or drawers around. No hidden crevices. He felt beneath the mattress and slipped his pouch between it and a slat. Far enough from the side frame to go unnoticed should anyone grope about.

When he stood, the pouch wasn't noticeable from any angle or distance. He dropped to the floor. Even prone, only a small bump gave him away. Perfect.

Unless Tristan ordered him to another room.

He had to get his message out the moment the rain stopped. Royce hoped the storm would clear by tonight or tomorrow, at the latest, so the bird would have clear weather for its journey.

After shaking water from his shirt and breeches, he washed at the basin, combed his hair, and got dressed.

Outside his door, he stopped abruptly and reared back before colliding with Peter. "What are you doing here?"

"Walking during my study break, if it's any of your business. What happened to you?"

"What do you mean?"

"You're wet. Haven't you noticed?"

"Adamo unhinged the shutter in my chamber when he came in. That was before we both ended up in the dining area with his gun at my back. You recall that, correct? I tried to fix the hinge from inside but it wouldn't work. I went out the window next and managed from there." He gestured to himself. "Thus my wet clothes."

"You will never survive on this isle unless you use the brains God gave you." Peter shook his head and ambled down the hall.

Royce found the closet Simone had mentioned and snatched two towels. Cautiously, he approached the library. The door was open, no sounds inside from Diana. She might be reading.

If she asked about his state, he'd tell her the broken shutter story and that the towels were to protect the books from getting wet. No reasonable person would argue with that explanation.

She wasn't inside.

The charts were, rolled up and out of the way.

Knowing Tristan's intelligence, Royce suspected those maps were as accurate as ones could be, despite longitudinal problems, and surely showed the island in relation to Mozambique.

To view them would give him enough information to guide Bishop here or send him on a chase with no reward at the end. Mariners frequently shipwrecked and died due to errors in navigation.

Bishop could be one, delightfully dead at last, his money unreachable. That would leave Royce's family no better off than when he began this scheme.

He ached to look at the maps, but didn't dare with people up and about. Perhaps some evening while everyone slept...

Not knowing how Tristan had organized his volumes, Royce rushed through countless titles, finally determined the system, and selected medical tomes in French and Latin. Tristan's Arabic-to-English alphabet lay on the table along with quills, ink bottles, and paper. Some sheets were as fine as those Royce had once used in London. The others crudely constructed, possibly made here.

He slipped several within the top book and gathered everything else, anxious to leave.

Diana watched him from the doorway.

He couldn't guess how long she'd been there. Hopefully, he hadn't looked guilty while staring at the charts or collecting the items. "I hope you don't mind me taking the towels. I wanted to cover the books so they won't get wet on my way to the birthing room."

She glanced away from his damp shirt and breeches. "Peter told me about your problem with the shutter."

"I fixed it as well as I could."

"I'll send an islander in there to see to it."

"No, please. No need to bother them with such an insignificant problem. I'm sure they have more important work to do."

"Not in the rain. Nothing in Tristan's and my home is insignificant. I'm not speaking of its beauty. Though wonderful, I could easily live without it as long as I have my husband, brother, and the fine people here beside me. I worry about safety from storms and outsiders."

"Yes, of course. I didn't mean... I believe I fixed it properly." He didn't want anyone roaming the chamber. "No rain or wind is coming in. Would you care to see? It will only take a moment."

She led the way and examined the thing. "It seems the same as the others."

"I promise not to disturb anything. I'm grateful for your hospitality and saving my life."

"Take care with Simone."

He gripped the books. "I intend to."

"The islanders are precious to Tristan and me. They're our friends as we are to them. They've been through too much already."

"I know. Simone told me about her family. She's a remarkable young woman."

Diana crossed her arms. "She needs to be with a man who can give her his all till death separates them."

"I agree. She and I are merely friends. Forgive me for being indelicate, but she will never be with child from me. I'm fully aware of my circumstances here and hers."

"What if the situation changes and you have to stay?"

His heart soared. Reality and despair rushed in quickly, spoiling the moment. "That can never be. If I must, I'll leave with the islanders Tristan trades with, and will eventually work my way back to where I belong without his kind help. I give you my word never to tell anyone, ever, about who he is or this island's location. I owe you too much to ever betray you."

Chapter 8

Simone wished she could chase the storms from the isle and bring back the sun. Each gloomy day added to Royce's sadness. He stared at the sky. White light streaked it. Thunder rumbled. He troubled over Edward's pets, especially the birds, even though the one he'd pointed out hadn't died.

She offered him the choicest food Gavra and the other women prepared, serving it in his bedchamber. The few times he'd joined her and the islanders in the kitchen had proved uncomfortable. No matter where he dined, he ate little. She asked James if Royce had his fill during the evening meals with him and Tristan.

James smiled sweetly. "Don't worry. He'll eat when he's hungry."

Perhaps for food. She worried Royce's craving might have returned for his home, away from this muddy isle, but didn't want to ask.

Today, rain pounded on the birthing room. Gusts slammed the walls. An oil lamp lit his side of the floor, another near her, the healing materials, papers, and books spread around them.

Intense light flickered behind the shutter. A horrific boom followed.

He stopped reading a passage aloud and looked over. "Does it ever bloody end?"

"In time." She wished she knew how to make things better. "It always does."

"When?"

"Each year is different. Some worse than others."

He rubbed his forehead.

"Please have more bacon. I brought you the best Gavra made." Simone pushed the plate closer.

"I'm not hungry. It's so blasted stifling in here." He stood and opened the door. Rain and wind burst inside. Papers flew.

Simone tried to catch them.

He pushed the door closed and sagged against it. "Sorry, that was idiotic."

"What does that mean?"

"Foolish. Thoughtless."

"You were warm and wanted air. I do too."

"I messed everything up." He swiped papers from the walls they'd blown against and pulled several from beneath the bed. "I've made a bloody wreck of everything."

"The papers blew away. You did nothing to hurt them. What you wrote is still there."

He dropped the stack on the books and paced, going nowhere. No different from his birds in their cages, trapped here as they were.

Simone didn't want to face the truth, but she couldn't ignore how he suffered. "Is something making you sad besides the storms? Do you long for home?"

He rested his fist against the door, head lowered. "I yearn for an end to trouble."

She pushed to her knees. "What kind? Tell me. I can help."

He laughed wearily. "There's not a thing on God's good earth you could do."

"I could listen. I will. Talk as much as you want."

"Wouldn't change anything."

"You mean you being here with no way to leave the island?"

He looked over, heartache in his eyes, the same that she'd know at losing him.

Royce hid his feelings quickly. "No, I didn't mean that at all." He joined her on the floor and took her hands. "I'm sorry. My intent wasn't to make you unhappy. The damn weather is driving me mad."

She sat on her heels. "The ale I brought will make you smile. It does for the men during our birthing celebrations, even when the new babe is a daughter instead of a son."

"That's rubbish. Forgive me for saying so, but it is. No man should complain about having a girl. It's not right."

"Do your people want female children? Was your father happy your mother gave him daughters?"

Royce released her hands and slumped against the bed. "I'm sure he didn't want any of us. Well, perhaps, my mother at first because of her wealth. Eventually, we got in the way of his frivolous activities. Spending money as fast as he could on women, drink, wagers. Not necessarily in that order. Gambling was his favorite pastime. Thanks to my mother's inheritance, he was able to indulge far longer than most, losing her resources and his own, every residence and farthing. That's when he started swindling his friends and family acquaintances. Poor fools couldn't see what he was doing until they'd lost nearly everything they owned. My mother, sisters, and I were no better. We had no idea what he was up to until everything came crashing down. Where is that ale?"

Simone poured him a cup from the pitcher.

He downed it quickly and ran his hand over his mouth.

She didn't understand much of what he'd said. The same as the last time he'd spoken about his father. She did know what losing everything meant. She gave him more ale. "After what your father did, your mother and sisters had no food and died?"

"What? No." He swallowed the drink and squeezed the cup, his face reddened. "They're still alive."

"How can that be? You said you had no one."

"In England, where they should be. My father ended up in Newgate. Do you know what that is?"

"No."

"It's a prison. I mentioned that word when we last spoke about him. I can't blame you for not knowing what I meant. You have nothing like that here."

"What is this prison?"

"A cage for people like what I have for Edward's pets. Those in charge keep men and women locked up until they hang them. Many die from disease you've never seen here or perish because they simply don't have enough to eat. The lucky ones finally pay back their debts and gain release." He poured himself another ale and drained the cup. "No one believed my mother, sisters, and I didn't know about my father's crimes. We were aware he drank to excess at times, but he kept his other activities well hidden from everyone. I lost my position as a barrister and couldn't find employment anywhere, not even as a solicitor. Those are jobs men in my position, or I should say my old position, work in. I sold everything I had to support my mother and sisters, but the money soon ran out. Restoring our family's good name was impossible. Too much had happened. As I've said, I took whatever work I could find, mainly physical labor that didn't pay enough for me to manage everyone's needs."

He ground his hand into his forehead. "My mother and sisters hadn't a place to live in London. No one would house them at any price because of my father's scandal. I thought we could move to the countryside. Life there was far less expensive but it takes time to find shelter and work. When I returned from a village with news about a room for them and field labor for me, they weren't at the charity house where we'd parted. My fault. I hadn't found a solution quickly enough. During my absence, they had to leave the institution. There wasn't room for them any longer. I reasoned they'd gone to a workhouse, but learned a rich plantation owner had an agent nearby, advertising for laborers in the Colonies. My mother and sisters indentured themselves to that man."

"Indentured?"

"They're his slaves, Simone. Much like you and the islanders were to the other pirate captain. They're across the ocean in a continent called America, a land that's a thousand times the size of this isle. They work in the fields or his house, doing whatever he demands. He has a right to starve or beat them as he sees fit. I'm sure rape isn't out of the question. Katie, my youngest sister, is only twelve, your age when the pirates attacked here. A little girl. Before Father ruined everything, Katie's only problems were which frock she should wear or if she'd had a falling out with a friend. Nell, my other sister, hoped to make a good match, have a happy marriage, a house filled with children. After my father's arrest, none of the young men who'd once courted Nell would look her way. Mother was raised a lady. She wasn't prepared to earn a living or fend for herself and her children. To think of her in a field doing backbreaking labor at her age is more than I can bear. I became what I am to buy them back, return them to their rightful home, spare them the hell their lives must be like now."

Sorrow flooded Simone. Shame too. She'd been selfish, thinking only of her loss, not his. She cupped his face. "You must leave here to see to your family."

He pulled her into him. "I shouldn't have told you. You've given me the only happiness I've known. I want you so much I can't breathe or think." He kissed her temple, cheek, and captured her mouth.

She tasted his love and her tears.

They sank to the floor, clasping each other, their passion as fierce as the raging storm, certain loss fueling their desire.

She tore at his shirt and breeches. He unknotted her cloth. Naked, they kissed and embraced, rolling across the floor, bumping into their materials, attempting to get closer.

Being a part of his heart and soul wouldn't have been enough for Simone. To lose his touch, never hear his voice again, or not witness his smile would kill her hope. She'd thought the world had ended when her family died. It would when he left, sailing from sight, distance taking away his last wave to her, his final glance.

She pressed her mouth to his so forcefully, her teeth cut into her bottom lip. She suffered the pain gladly, his impassioned kiss making everything worthwhile. Yet this act only touched upon what she required. Beneath him now, she parted her legs fully.

He tore his mouth free.

His gaze held her. The same as this moment. She hadn't lied when she told him a woman and man's hearts were still together after they parted. "I will miss you until my last breath. Even after that. And I will never forget you."

An anguished sound poured from him. He kissed her deeper than previous times, his shaft hot and hard against her cleft. Moisture bathed her entry, welcoming him inside, begging him to make them one. She wanted his child. A lasting reminder from these days of desire.

She pulled back her legs, encouraging his passion.

In one strong thrust, he entered her fully, breaking through her virginal barrier.

Her torn flesh burned. She gripped his shoulders.

Royce lifted his face, mouth rounded in horror.

"I want this." Tears slipped down her cheeks. "Love me, please. As much as you can before you have to go."

His eyes filled.

Simone touched his lips. "In the days ahead, we can think of this and smile." She eased his mouth to hers.

They kissed, their shared sorrow making them tender, then insatiable for what they could claim now and everything they'd miss. His rigid shaft stretched and filled her more than she dreamed, the pain from her lost virginity already gone. She tightened her sheath around his thickness, adding to the friction, dazed by the enchanting pressure.

He pulled his mouth free and groaned. "What you're doing is bloody wonderful. Don't stop."

"Not even if someone shoots me."

Laughing, he stroked her nub.

Delight erupted from deep within. She gripped his arms. "I like that."

"Then I must continue."

He rubbed and pumped. His sac slapped against her buttocks, adding a wicked touch to the incomparable act. Their feelings true, hearts joined. No man and woman had ever loved each other more.

Whatever they faced in the coming days, there wasn't anyone who could take this from them.

Simone didn't try to delay pleasure, greeting the crest, riding the waves.

Royce grunted, his complexion darker than before. Jaw clenched, he kept thrusting. Hair bobbed on his shoulders and around his face. He panted. "You must have another go at it. I won't allow myself release until you do."

"You have to. Your face is red. You keep forgetting to breathe."

"I don't care." He stroked her.

Unimaginable delight filled Simone.

"Squeeze me." He thrust into her. "Make your opening as tight as can be."
Nothing else would do.

He worked her hard. She did the same to him. Their gazes locked.
She surrendered first, as she had the last time, the tension impossible to
withstand, the rolling heat irresistible.

Breathless and limp, she settled, her hands sliding down his damp arms.

He threw back his head and bellowed, louder than the storm. Silvery
light lit the shutter. Wind howled, rain drummed, thunder crashed.

She giggled.

Royce sank to his elbows, gasping and smiling. "What's so funny?"

"You were noisier than the storm, making it want to compete."

"You do that to me." He brushed his lips over hers.

She embraced him, holding on as hard as she could. "Rest. Then eat.
Then we can do this again."

He fell to the side, pulling her with him. Once he'd settled her on top,
his shaft still inside, he smoothed her hair. "Are you all right? Do you
have any pain?"

Only in her heart for what the coming days would bring. "No." She
kissed his chin. "You brought me joy. I will never forget it."

"I shouldn't have told you my problems."

"Why? I want to know about your worry and sadness. How sorry I am
for your mother, Katie, and Nell."

He clasped her to him. "Please don't tell anyone what I said about them.
I'm too ashamed for others to know how I failed."

"I'll never say anything. But you have no reason to hate yourself. You
tried to help them and you'll do so again."

"You're too good."

"Some would say I was bad." She tightened her muscles, squeezing his
rod. "I want to be that and more, as soon as you rest."

He looked at her as he hadn't before, more wonder on his face, far less
misery. "I need to work."

"Now? Wait."

He rolled over, separating them, and grabbed his materials. "I have no
time to waste."

She pushed to one elbow. "Did you think of a way to help your family?"

His quill tip flew over the paper, words appearing swiftly on the page.
He read what he'd written, scratched it out, and started anew.

She touched his knee. "What are you writing?"

He tapped the black feather against his cheek, then scrawled more words.

* * * *

Taking Simone's virginity should have sent Royce into deep despair. Oddly enough, loving her energized him. He had to fix this escalating crisis or die trying, possibly his best choice once he'd settled everything.

She scooted next to him and ran a damp cloth over his cock.

He jerked. His pen skidded across the page. "What are you doing?"

"Cleaning you and me." She turned the cloth over and washed her slit.

The blood was scant but distressed him. "Are you certain you're all right?"

"Oui. No broken bones."

He chuckled and rested his hand on her mound. "Any aching here?"

"Much. You must fill me again to take it away."

They were doomed, wanting each other too badly. That sorry truth didn't erase his smile. "Perhaps later."

"Only perhaps?"

He couldn't talk himself out of having her again. "No. Surely later."

Beaming, she poured ale and offered him the cup.

"Thank you, but no. I'm not thirsty."

"Are you sure?"

His throat was so dry he could scarcely swallow. However, to imbibe more than he had might mean leaking additional secrets, speaking Bishop's name, and telling her about the original plan. If she forgave him, he'd lose himself between her legs until they created a son or daughter.

Madness. His father had nothing on him.

"Do you want this?" She eased the plate beneath his nose.

Bacon and honey scents wafted up. His mouth watered, his appetite returned when he'd settled nothing for her, anyone else on this isle, or his family. "Half. You take the rest."

"We can feed each other." She slipped one end into her mouth and brought the other to his lips.

No lady in England had ever been as playful or entrancing. Pity the poor bastards who'd never known joy as he'd found with Simone.

They ate their respective ends, attention focused on each other, lips joined at last.

She drooped against him, her tongue in his mouth.

Royce had never had any food or drink that tasted better than she did. If he wasn't careful, he'd think of little else except taking Simone and wouldn't accomplish anything.

Fear for her future snapped Royce from his randy fog. He broke free and held up his quill. "I must work. You should too."

She offered him more bacon, and took a slice for herself. "What did you write?"

His first message to Bishop, or rather his initial attempt at writing it. Difficult to do when he had yet to access the charts for the isle's location, and hadn't come up with the perfect words to not only delay but also please Bishop, so he'd willingly wait for more news. Once Royce solved those complications, the bird would deliver his communication as soon as the bloody weather cleared.

Nature seemed intent on mocking him and taking out her rage on this land, the rain harder, wind stronger, thunder unending.

Simone tapped his leg. "Tell me what your words say."

"I wrote a passage I recalled from the Latin medical text."

She leaned against him, her breast pressed to his arm, and touched the parts he'd inked through. "Why did you do this? Did you remember it wrong?"

The words he'd written were too honest, then obviously deceptive. Bishop would take action on both, decimating everything in his path. "I thought I had, but maybe I didn't. You spoke of *tambavy*. That's what you use for men's coughs."

"No. Tambavy is to treat children." She ran her finger along the words he'd inked through. "Tell me which one says tambavy."

He pointed to Tristan's name.

Simone grinned. "I like how it looks. Write it for me on another paper so I can remember it and learn."

"I will later, with other passages from the books. Now, I need to compose something else."

"Compose?"

"Write. A lesson plan for you to follow. Like Diana and Peter have from Tristan."

Simone poured water, took a sip, then offered the cup to him. "Not so hard as theirs. Peter mutters in the library. Diana scowls. What they have to do must be terrible."

"I promise not to make your studies that bad."

"Read me the passage again about the potion for stomach sickness. Adamo's face was pale this morning. He refused food. This might help him. While I mix what I need, you can write your lesson plan."

Royce prayed the correct words would come, buying him time with Bishop.

He found the passage and read the ingredients. All had scientific names Simone didn't understand. Even nobles would've had difficulty. Royce described how the plants should look and showed her the illustrations. She studied them, lining up her leaves and herbs to match. Some were quite close, others merely similar.

Mixing the incorrect materials might result in a poisonous elixir. He didn't want Adamo dying unexpectedly. Tristan and the others barely trusted Royce now. The moment he had a death on his hands, they'd kill him or lock him in his chamber for good. During that time, Bishop's men might storm the shore. "Do you test your potions before you give them to the islanders?"

"Test?"

"Try them out to make certain they're safe. That they won't cause more sickness."

"Why would they? I told you, we always use these plants."

"Mixed together as the book potion states?"

She looked at her materials. "No. How would I do this test?"

"Perhaps on an animal." If the creature didn't die, a human probably wouldn't.

"Which one? We have pigs, cattle, hens, horses—"

"Fowl would be best." Few would miss a chicken. "The younger the better." If a chick survived, anything could.

"How would I get the potion in a chick?"

"Does Tristan have a medicine dropper?"

"What is that?"

"A tube you fill to give a child or an animal liquid."

"I can ask if he does and get a chick too, then come back here."

"Wait." He circled her wrist. "Not in the storm." The rain wasn't falling as hard, the lightning and thunder subsiding. With any luck, fair weather might be here soon. "Things should be quieter in a few minutes. You can use the time to mix your potion."

She set to work.

He did too, not writing anything yet, planning first. He'd begin with the truth, that he'd found the island, Tristan, and Diana. Lies formed next, as to who populated the isle so Bishop wouldn't insist on a head-on maneuver that would kill everyone.

Of course, he and his men would want to know the correct location first or their preparations would be for naught. Tristan's charts held the key to truth and deception...as soon as Royce could get to them.

His spirits rose. Perhaps he could draw this out until he found the perfect solution. If one existed. In any event, as long as he kept in reasonable contact with Bishop, he had a chance at success.

Simone slid her hand up his thigh.

He smiled. "What is it?"

"The storm is quiet, my potion mixed. I should leave now for the chick and medicine stop."

"Medical stopper. You can tell Tristan we want to try your potion on the creature to make certain the mixture is safe for people."

"I will." She kissed him deeply. "Work hard until I return so we can enjoy other things later and definitely."

He laughed. "I will. Promise."

She draped a pigskin over her head and hurried outside.

Royce slapped wind-blown papers down, then filled his sheet with false starts and phrases he crossed out. He grabbed another paper and selected each word carefully before writing it, wanting to convey an optimistic yet cautious mood, while also keeping the message short enough to fit in the tube.

Not once did he offer an apology for taking so long to respond. Bishop crushed those he could cow, responding best to men he feared.

Before Royce and Bishop's relationship ended, the swine would be sorry he'd hatched this plan.

With a rough outline of what he had to say, Royce perfected the words repeatedly, filling this sheet and another.

His fingers cramped. He read what he'd written:

B. B.

Arrived. T and D here as suspected. Pirate hideaway. 80 plus armed men. No natives. Shore watched constantly. Head-on attack impossible. Stealth best. Exact location unknown. Pin-pointed isle proved incorrect. Storm swept me to correct one. T's charts hard to access. Will send location when possible.

R. H.

Chapter 9

The weather cleared that evening, moon heavy and bright, stars twinkling by the hundreds.

Royce grinned hard enough to make his cheeks hurt, but didn't trust his good luck. For hours, he sat on the windowsill, alert to any change, dreading even the wispiest cloud. Islanders' voices floated through the trees, fading as the men said their farewells to each other. A cough sounded close to the mansion. Foliage rustled farther away, that individual striding to the point, most likely to keep watch. Simone had said Tristan gave the men his glass to check the distant sea for intruders.

Given Tristan's vigilance, it was a miracle no one guarded Royce any longer, and he wasn't about to waste his chance.

He closed the shutter, casting the room in deeper shadows. Silvery light spilled through the seams but wasn't enough to help. Once he'd groped his way to the bed, he retrieved his pouch from beneath it, then his message that he'd slipped between the mattress and another slat. After some difficulty, he rolled the paper tightly enough to slip into the container, returned the others to their hiding place, and kept the prepared missive under his pillow.

Despite his fatigue, sleep didn't come easily, too many possible complications besieging him. The air was still close and muggy.

He tossed for what seemed hours and woke with a start, surprised he'd drifted off.

Faint light at the windows told him the morning had barely begun or the damn clouds and rain had returned. He yanked back the shutter and sagged against the sill. Dawn broke, golden light streaking the blessedly clear sky, the wind mild. Hurriedly, he washed, combed his hair, and secured the tube to loose threads inside his waistband. His shirt hid the thing further.

Naked feet slapped the floor outside his room. Simone burst inside, her smile as bright as her yellow cloth. "Did you see the sky?"

"I did."

She threw herself into his arms and kissed him breathless. He did the same to her, his joy and hope unsurpassed. This had to be a new beginning where loving her and succeeding in his family's rescue proved equally possible.

Simone had become his future. He couldn't imagine spending a day without her smiles, sweet voice, heat, and scent. He had no idea how he'd stay here, or return to her if he left, but he had to try.

She hugged him, then bounced like an excited child. "The sky is a good omen. Baylee's infant waited till now to come so the sun could bring good fortune."

"Then what are you doing here, wasting time with me? You must hurry to the birthing room to make certain all is well."

"I have my materials ready." Her brow furrowed. "I never waste my time with you." She stroked his cock.

He leaned into her. "No, you do not."

"We have other trouble."

"Gavra?" He prayed the problem couldn't be worse than her disapproval.

"Not her…well maybe. Has she said something to you?"

"I only see her when I go through the kitchen."

Simone wagged her finger. "Never go in there again. Climb out the window in here to get to the courtyard. The new trouble is the priest should be here for the birth. Tristan warned him not to visit the other isles. Our infants need him to bless them. The weather has kept him away."

"And will bring him back once it remains fair long enough for his journey. Until then, the *bébé* will have you to see to its good health. Won't it?"

"Of course. I have to go." She kissed him soundly. "I'll miss you while I tend to Baylee. Today, we have a celebration of new life. You must be there too."

"At your side, the moment you're through."

Her luminous smile lightened his mood further. She tore from the room.

Royce checked the ground outside his window. Slimy muck. The hall was coolish, clean, and deserted. Close to the dining area, he held his breath, praying Tristan and the others weren't there yet. Their expected conversation would keep him from his plan.

No one was about. Dishes and food absent.

In the kitchen, Gavra stopped kneading dough. The other women glanced at him, then looked away.

Royce inclined his head. "Bonjour. I need to tend Edward's pets. Have a lovely day." He strode through the room to the storage area. Children giggled and shrieked in the courtyard, men laughed, women chattered, none close to here.

Alert to possible intruders, he turned away from the door, broke the thread around the metal tube, and quickly selected the largest bird.

It writhed, trying to free itself.

Royce's pulse raced. He stroked its feathers. "Easy. Didn't mean to hold you so tightly."

After a seeming eternity, the creature settled, allowing him to slip the tube on its leg and to hold it to his chest, his hand hiding the cylinder. He edged outside. Islanders gathered in the courtyard. Men hauled out long tables and benches. Children jumped in puddles. Women scolded gently.

He sprinted past an opening in the courtyard walls to the forest, deliberately choosing the opposite direction from the beach and the man who guarded it. Royce put a fair distance between himself and the mansion, its white façade barely visible through the heavy foliage.

The sun broke free of the earth and spilled through the trees.

Breathing hard, he turned from the light and lifted the bird. "Please get there. Do not fail me."

There'd be no way to know, of course, if it had completed the journey. Royce could only hope.

Icy dread filled him. He pushed the emotion away and released the creature.

It took wing instantly, drenched in the brilliant rays, and flew west, as it must, to return to its proper home.

No birds of prey followed.

He shaded his face. Against the brightening sky, the creature became a speck, then faded from sight. Relief washed over him, followed by renewed worry. He remained longer than he should, fearful the thing would return here and force him to do this again or choose another bird.

His prolonged wait merely made him a curious object for the lizards to skitter around. He returned the same way he'd come and stopped abruptly.

James and Tristan stood at the storage room entrance, peering inside.

Good God, they couldn't have seen anything. They would have run after him and shot.

Braced for the worst, Royce forced himself to join them. Neither man wore a shirt but each had a pistol beneath his belt.

Tristan looked over. "Where have you been?"

His stomach clenched. "There." He pointed at the trees behind him. "Relieving myself. Isn't that allowed here?" He feigned surprise.

James's expression remained as unreadable as Tristan's. "We have chamber pots for that."

"Yes, I know. But since I was tending Edward's pets, the forest was closer than my bedchamber."

Tristan glanced at the courtyard. "We need you to help the men set up tables and such for the celebration. Think you can handle that?"

"I'm used to hard labor. In fact, I welcome it."

James smiled. "You are an odd one, aren't you?"

"Simply trying to get along and be civilized."

"Ah, a word my wife adores." Tristan arched an eyebrow. "Make certain you never do anything vulgar to displease her. She's had enough trouble refining me."

James clamped Tristan's shoulder. "Which she hasn't come close to doing, my friend."

"True. She actually prefers me as I am. Not you two, though. Watch your step or I'll let her thrash you soundly."

Royce chuckled, pleased to be included in the banter. When Tristan and James let down their guard, they were easy men to like. To become their friend was a worthy goal and seemingly possible on such a splendid day.

He matched the islanders' jovial spirits, helping where needed. Most accepted his presence easily.

Not Adamo. He stood across from Royce, a children's table held between them despite Adamo's limp arm. He made up for his infirmity by using his chest to brace the furniture and gripped the side in his uninjured hand, muscles bulging.

No way to carry a table.

Royce sensed Adamo wouldn't appreciate anyone pointing that out, or telling him that he wasn't man enough to help. To make things easier on him, Royce took most of the weight on himself.

Rowdy laughter and conversation surrounded them. They were silent. Mindful of the mushy ground, Royce sidestepped the mud. Adamo stepped in it. His foot slid backward, knee bending, the table careening his way.

"Hold on, I have it!" Royce reared back and dropped the table to the side. The blasted thing was heavy enough to break a rib or two if it fell on someone.

He offered Adamo his hand. "You all right?"

"Oui."

"Good. Now, aren't you glad you didn't shoot me in the back?"

Adamo sniffed. "I had to stop you. You refused to stay put. Even little ones are better at obeying orders."

"I agree. I put you through a lot when this is your home, not mine, and I'm glad you're here to protect it and me." He offered his hand in friendship.

Adamo accepted, grip firm, his crooked smile faint at first, then wide. "Your strength is like an islander's."

"It will never match yours, I can assure you. What say we get this table to its proper place and then work on the benches?"

"I can carry each by myself."

"Excellent. I'll sit by the palms and relax while you do everything. You are a good man."

"Zola tells me I boast too much. She may be right if you sit as I work."

They laughed.

"Is Zola your woman?"

"She wants to be." He flushed. "I like her. She's sweeter than honey and smells better than any flower. I should have chosen her instead of Canela." His smile faded. "You know about her?"

"Simone told me a little. Zola sounds wonderful, exactly what a good man needs. I wish you two great happiness."

"This time I trust what I know is right. I'll protect Tristan and this island to my death if I must."

Royce prayed matters didn't come to that.

Simone waved from the birthing chamber. He returned her smile. "Is everything all right in there?"

Adamo bumped his shoulder. "Never ask a woman that. They will tell you and tell you and tell you."

"I know. It's bloody difficult to get a word in edgewise sometimes. Do you mind that they talk so much?"

He chuckled. "No. Do you?"

"With the right woman, never."

Simone called out, "The infant wants to come. Baylee wants to wait." A shriek tore from the room. "We will have to see who wins."

"I'm wagering on the infant."

"Me too." On the next screech, she ducked back inside.

Royce helped Adamo set up benches. Together they spread banana leaves and palm fronds over the dampened ground, as the men had done in other areas, then brought out more tables, emptying a room that stored the furniture.

Sweaty and winded, Royce plopped on a bench. "I need to rest."

Adamo sat. "We did much but will do more once you can. Rest as long as you want."

"We both should."

They shared a glance and smiled.

High-pitched laughter rang from behind. Royce looked over and stood. "What are you doing?"

Four young boys stopped, his cages held between them. The tallest one smiled. He was possibly six or seven like the others. "While we celebrate, the creatures should too."

"Put those down. Now."

They dropped the cages. The birds beat their wings. Hens squawked.

Tristan crossed the courtyard and stopped at Royce's side. "Best not to use a sharp tone with the children. They're not used to our English ways. The islanders are far more tolerant with their offspring. What's the matter?"

Royce pointed. "The boys brought Edward's pets out here. They should be in the storage room."

"Why? Creatures need fresh air and sunlight, the same as we do."

"Yes, of course. But the children will get curious and may open the cages. What then?"

"The things will be free as they were meant to be, rather than caged. I would think they'd be healthier that way."

"They could escape."

"To where? The hens will surely stay in the courtyard near their food. I'd wager the birds will do the same."

Not likely when their true home was in Mozambique, their memories urging them to wing back there for a meal. "I don't mind the hens going loose. You're right, they won't fly away, but I can't take a chance on the birds. Edward babied them. They'd have no chance in the trees with falcons, eagles, and buzzards about. I need to keep them safe, and have, by only setting them loose in the storage room while I clean their cage. Will you please tell the children not to fool with them?"

Tristan related the message firmly but kindly.

The boys grew solemn and nodded.

Tristan ruffled the shortest lad's hair, then regarded Royce. "Is it all right if they free the hens or would you rather do it?"

"They can. I'll return the birds and the empty cage to where they should be."

Younger children chased the chickens around their new home.

Royce put the cages where they belonged and sagged against the doorframe, his lies and panic about discovery draining him more than the physical work he'd done. He envied how easily the islanders interacted. No guile or subterfuge. Simply decent people living their lives.

The English could learn much from them. He already had.

This island was more home to him than London could ever be.

* * * *

Diana embraced Simone. *"Vous êtes une merveille. Nous ne pouvions pas faire sans vous."* You are a wonder. We couldn't do without you.

Given how easily the words had glided off Diana's tongue, Simone suspected Tristan had told her what to say to keep from struggling as she usually did. "Merci. You should tell Baylee the same thing. She did all the work to birth such a beautiful daughter."

Diana's smile faltered as it always did when she didn't understand what an islander said. "Ah, oui."

Laure placed the infant in Diana's arms for her to present to the others. An island custom.

She stepped out of the room. Men cheered. Women smiled and wept.

Simone leaned against the jamb, legs unsteady from too much joy. She'd delivered a perfect new child to a healthy mother and had Royce waiting for her. He stood next to Tristan, James, and Adamo, belonging there. As much a part of this island as she'd always been.

Catching her eye, Royce winked.

She blushed hotly and looked back into the room.

Gavra avoided Simone's gaze.

She hurt from their bickering, but also had her own life to live. "If Baylee needs me, will you call?"

"You should stay here and tend her."

Baylee slept, mouth open, perspiration dampening her face. "She needs no healing."

Gavra dropped soiled towels into a basket.

Simone joined Royce. Women rushed into and out of the kitchen carrying baskets of rice bread, bananas, grapes, and pineapples. Men handled trays laden with roasted beef, bacon, and fish.

Peter ran up to Tristan. "Time for the spirits? Or is it too early?"

The sun hadn't dipped to the trees.

"Go on. The infant didn't wait and neither will we."

James sighed. "I best pace myself. Last time that I imbibed nearly did me in."

"I recall that." Tristan bumped James's arm. "I doubt any of us will forget it."

Royce leaned down to Simone. "What happened?"

"Most had too many spirits and slept late the next day. Pirates attacked." She lowered her voice further to keep Adamo from overhearing. "The ones Canela brought. Come. Time to feast."

Adamo and Zola sat to the left of Simone and Royce, James on the right, saving a place for Gavra. Tristan, Diana, Peter, and Laure faced them.

"Royce." Tristan held up a squat brown bottle. "Care for some fine brandy?"

"No, thank you." He spoke French as Tristan had. "I'm not much of a drinker. I prefer water."

James shook his head. "Odd."

"Never say that. He is not." Simone leaned past Royce and frowned at James. "Water is good. I drink it."

Peter snickered. "That's because you're a woman. You can't take what a man can."

Tristan elbowed him.

Peter threw up his hands. "What did I say this time?"

"Too much."

Diana glanced from one to the other.

"Best we eat." Royce speared a beef slice but didn't slide it on his plate. "If that's acceptable."

Tristan took bacon, bread, fish, and a grape cluster. "It is if you don't plan to starve. None of us are going to serve or feed you."

James and Peter laughed.

Simone put her lips to Royce's ear. "I will."

His breath glided hot against her cheek. "Not here. Later."

"Where?"

"Do you know another place besides the birthing room? One that's rarely used?"

"Oui. When the world goes dark, I will take you there."

* * * *

Even without drink stealing his good intentions, Royce couldn't manage a saintly demeanor for long. He slid his toes over Simone's.

She slipped her hand beneath his napkin and fondled his cock.

He swallowed the wrong way and coughed violently.

James pounded his back. "Easy. We don't want to interrupt our fun to have to bury you."

"We wouldn't." Tristan popped a grape into his mouth. "We'd simply throw him in the sea." Tristan translated for Diana.

She laughed, her dark blue gown fluttering around her breasts. "He would do that, you know."

"I would save you." Simone squeezed Royce's fingers.

He rested their hands on her thigh to keep her from any more mischief.

The islanders brought out their reeds, drums, and lutes. Torchlight consumed the coming darkness, the breeze balmy, moon and the brightest stars already winking down on the gathering.

Simone tapped her toes against his, matching the beat.

The pleasant tune, soft night, and her touch took years off Royce, allowing him to feel like the young man he'd been before his father's betrayal. "Does anyone dance here?"

He'd spoken English.

Diana glanced at him, eyes and diamonds sparkling. "The islanders have their ceremonies, of course. We don't intrude and we certainly wouldn't ask them to perform."

"That's not what I mean. Have any of you tried the minuet?"

Peter made a face. "The what?"

Diana threw him a weary look. "It's a dance between men and women. Would you like Royce to explain?"

"No."

"Good." She faced Royce. "I've heard of it, but never engaged in anything like that. Our father considered dancing scandalous."

Tristan finished his ale. "He was a reverend. Quite dour. Right, my love?"

"Indeed. No one was more so."

And she'd ended up wed to a pirate. It appeared miracles did happen. "I can assure you the minuet is quite respectful and fun. What say we try?"

James waved his hands. "Not me."

"Then Simone and I will." He spoke French, telling her what they'd said.

"Oui. I would love to try this dance."

Tristan and Diana joined them. With Laure's gentle prodding, Peter shuffled over. Adamo and Zola were next. After a quiet but heated discussion, James and Gavra followed.

Royce directed half the couples to one side and the other half several feet away, facing them. He spoke French. "Relax. This is supposed to be fun."

The musicians had stopped playing and exchanged glances.

Diana waved her hand. "What did you say?"

Peter spoke first. "He said if we were armed, we could shoot each other easily this way."

Tristan laughed. "Stop it."

Royce translated his original comment for Diana. "Watch what I do and follow. That should be sufficient." He slipped back into French. "The first thing everyone does is turn toward their partner." Royce faced Simone, her hand in his. "The ladies curtsy, the men bow."

Simone shook her head. "What is this curtsy?"

"You lift your cloth like I'm lifting my shirt and you do this." He bent his knees.

James and Peter howled.

Simone ignored them and practiced her curtsies. She smiled. "I like this."

"Everyone will. Let me go through the steps." Once he'd finished the men and women's parts, using hand signals for Diana, everyone said they understood the basics. "If you can't recall what I did, simply follow what I do."

Simone squeezed his hand. "The women too? Or only the men?"

"No. You—just do your best. The point is to have a good time."

Peter huffed. "I've had less trouble learning Greek. I say we go back to the table."

"Go ahead." Royce shooed him away. "The adults will manage, I'm sure."

Scowling, Peter grabbed Laure's hand and remained.

The musicians didn't have a tune that matched a proper minuet, making it difficult for the steps to match what they played. James kept choosing the wrong foot. Diana stepped on Tristan's toes repeatedly. Adamo went in the opposite direction Zola had. Gavra bobbed in place, breasts bouncing. Peter and Laure ran into each other. Simone matched Royce's steps rather than doing her own. Children wove in and out of the mess.

Royce laughed harder than he had in years, tears filling his eyes.

The islanders joined in.

Tristan clamped his shoulder. "Thank you for the lesson, but I've had enough. You're an abominable teacher."

"And you, sir, are a dreadful student."

"I should run you through or shoot you for that. Perhaps after I eat."

They retired to the table, filling their bellies, laughing freely, imbibing the ale and spirits.

Royce needed no drink. The night, these people, and Simone were enough.

She leaned into him. "Teach me the steps again."

"Now?"

"Oui. Then I can show the others how easy it is and what a good teacher you are."

Peter laughed. "Won't take much for you to outshine us. We were frightful."

"Come with me." She took Royce's hand. "We can go into the forest, so no one sees and laughs at what I do."

Gavra frowned.

Royce wasn't certain anything he said would change her distrust.

Certainly not the truth that he'd want Simone till time ended.

With the others occupied by their own conversation or laughter, he followed her away from the crowd and into the shadows.

Chapter 10

Past the courtyard walls, Royce held back, forcing Simone to stop. He presumed she'd said what she had for Gavra's benefit. Given that she wasn't a concern any longer, he'd hoped Simone would lead him to another room near the birthing chamber. Ill-advised, considering the celebrants' proximity. However, the forest wasn't an adequate substitute for a soft bed and clean room.

If her intent had been their coupling.

Moonlight reflected in her eyes, her dark hair lustrous in the diaphanous rays. "Come." She tugged his hand.

He weighed too much for her to budge. "You actually want to learn how to dance?"

"Do you want me to?"

"Not tonight. I thought we'd have other fun."

"We will."

"Here? The ground is wet." Leaves and debris carpeted the area, mud oozing in between. "This won't be comfortable for you."

"The beach was wet. Did you enjoy that so little?"

The moment had changed his life, and he wagered hers too. However, he'd had no choice except to lead her there, since he'd needed to dig up his pouch. Another lie he'd told that he prayed she'd never discover or could somehow forgive.

"Oh no. How sad you are." She cupped his face and grinned.

"Are you making light of me?"

"I am. Follow me back to the stone house."

They circled the wall and sidled between an opening that faced a door he'd never seen. "Where are we? What's inside there?"

"A secret hall to Tristan and Diana's chamber."

"Wait." He held her arm. "You want us to use their room?"

She laughed softly. "No. Tristan would shoot you. Me, he would scold. Come."

The door opened to a narrow passage so dark he might have been blind. With one hand clasped tightly around hers, he slid his other on the polished stone to maintain his bearing. Their feet tapped the floor, the noise outrageously loud in the confined space.

She slowed and stopped.

A slight creak sounded. The black in front turned gray, revealing a chamber.

What had seemed a wall was the back of a large armoire set on small wheels to move it easily for entry into the room. "Did Tristan make this?"

"My people did. The cruel capitaine told them what he wanted."

An escape route both clever and necessary given the blackguard's occupation.

Royce checked the floor to see if their feet left any tracks. Shadows made it impossible to tell.

Laughter, music, and song sounded from the courtyard. However, the noise came from everywhere, the passage disorienting him from knowing which direction the gathering might be. Despite his and Simone's whispers, the closed shutters, and little available light, he felt horribly exposed, worried Tristan or Diana would push through the door at any time. "We best leave here."

In the hall, Simone trotted to the right, pulling him with her.

"Are we going to your chamber?"

"No. Here." Panting, she opened a door and pushed him inside the room.

He stumbled and flailed his arms to right himself.

She opened the shutters.

"Wait. You shouldn't do that."

"Why? The moon is big and fat."

Ashy light streamed across the space, showing a room not unlike his, and nearly as regal as Tristan's. A crucifix hung above the bed. "Is this where the priest stays when he's here?"

"Oui. No one would dare come inside or be near the windows. This is a divine space."

He sensed she meant sacred. "If this is off-limits to the less than righteous, aren't you worried about us using it for…"

"Our love? No. What god would be angry that a man and a woman did what they must to show how they adore each other?"

He couldn't think of any, but he wasn't a pious man. The long-ago missionaries who'd come here to change Simone's people, including their culture, language, and beliefs hadn't fully accomplished their goal with her.

He grinned.

"I see you like what I did." She untied her cloth. The silk floated to her feet. "Why are your breeches and shirt on you and not the floor? Why are you waiting to undress?"

He tore at his clothes and stood nude before her. She before him.

Rays illuminated her curves, the moon designed to shine on no one except her.

She crossed to him and touched his healed wound, the scab mostly gone, then took his hand and placed it on her scar. Delight registered on her face, rather than sorrow. "Both of us are marked."

They were and on the same leg. What were the odds of that happening randomly?

She stroked his thigh. "We match."

In more ways than he could voice. They were from different worlds, cultures, and beliefs, yet they fit perfectly. Or had.

She'd stepped away, her breasts bobbing gently, hips swaying. Eve tempting Adam all over again.

He followed. "Where do you think you're going?"

She regarded his fully erect cock and plump balls. "To bed." She crawled onto the wide mattress and stopped in the center, arms at her sides, legs parted, hiding nothing.

No man deserved her seduction, certainly not him.

Her sultry smile encouraged Royce to be playful. He rested his knee on the cool white silk. "Come here."

"Catch me."

"What?"

"If you can. I think you may not be able to."

He pounced faster than any rutting buck. Simone rolled away, escaping him easily. His chin hit the mattress. The bedframe creaked.

Her giggles filled the room, giving him a reason to live. He propped his head in his hand. "Are you going to make me work at this? Do you honestly want me to wear myself out running after you when we could be enjoying ourselves instead?"

"You hate my game?"

Anything she did was all right with him, even pretending insult or hurt to prolong the pretext. "I didn't say that. But I toiled hard and long today, hauling countless tables to the courtyard. Twice—no, three times,

I pulled a muscle in my back. My toes hurt so badly I can scarcely stand. My arms are too tired to lift more than an inch." He raised his hand and let it plop to the mattress. "See? Yet, we will play your game if that's what you want. Anything to please you."

She sat on the mattress and eased his hair off his shoulder. "Anything?"

His laughter drowned out hers. He pulled her down to him and rolled them over.

She fought to go the other way. They ended up in the middle, facing each other, breaths colliding.

He rubbed his nose against hers. "What fun I have with you."

"Me too. But it can be better."

"How? Tell me. I have no idea."

She looked skeptical. "Do you make light of what I say now?"

"Me? Never."

"I should shoot you." She pushed him to his back, straddled his hips, and took his rigid length fully within her.

Their curls touched. Her snug channel imprisoned and sheltered.

Heat whipped through him with cyclone strength. "I like this better."

She leaned down, her hair veiling them, her mouth touching his. "Than what?"

"You shooting me."

"Never would I point a pistol at you." She ran her tongue over the seam between his lips, stopping before he could coax her more deeply inside for a much-needed kiss. "I would have Tristan do it for me. Perhaps Gavra."

He laughed quietly. "In that case, I had better behave."

"Love me. I ask no more than that."

Such an easy task and possibly an unreachable dream with time and circumstances against them. Tonight, though, fantasy ruled, the moonlit room bewitching, her warmth and weight persuading him to believe they'd have a future, home, and children on this isle. An ideal life he'd already constructed when he knew better than to yield to preposterous wishes. He was an adult, not a child.

His own sorrow didn't frighten Royce. Hurting her would kill him.

Their tongues dueled to see whose mouth they'd fill. He let her win, wanting to give her everything she desired. Steadily, Simone tightened her cunt around his rod. Each squeeze firm, though too slow to deliver release, yet too fast for him to ignore.

Carnal need enticed, drawing him into its web, refusing to let go.

He plucked her nipples, loving the sounds she made, a woman burning with passion. Caressing her supple globes proved insufficient. He wanted raw lust, not tenderness, her soft flesh coaxing him to forget restraint, to take her more as an animal than a man.

She pressed into his touch, wordlessly saying she wanted whatever he offered, then pushed to her knees and released his shaft except for his crown. Her moisture coated his rigid column, a thrilling sight. She slid down, her channel consuming him.

Blood pounded in his ears.

She touched her chin to her chest, her hair gliding over his belly.

"More." He'd pleaded as he never had with another woman, needing Simone to give him everything she could. "Squeeze harder. Pump faster."

Her descents and ascents jiggled the mattress, the intensity she created shockingly good.

She lifted her face to the ceiling and gulped air.

Royce stroked her nub, keeping time with her steadily contracting channel. He and she matched here too, synchronized in their lovers' dance. "Again." He snatched air. "Faster. Don't stop."

She rode him as he would have done with her, giving no quarter when it came to pleasure, liberating delight, encouraging awe. They reached joy together, her voice raised in a timeless cry a woman gives a man she loves, her channel quivering around his shaft, his seed filling her.

Weakened and panting, he eased Simone to him, their skin slick, chests heaving. "Merci."

She kissed his shoulder. "I'm a good student at last, doing what you wished?"

"Trust me. You couldn't have been better." Her lovemaking had nearly killed him.

"I can try to be even more."

Royce prayed not now. Exhaustion pressed in, chasing away the glow she'd produced.

She twisted his hair around her finger. "Are you asleep?"

He was too weary to answer.

"Will you wake soon and do this again?"

He hoped so. There wasn't a point in being alive if a man denied himself what he'd found here.

* * * *

Once Simone shook Royce awake, they made love twice. After the acts, he dropped to the mattress, arms and legs flung out, too tired to play. She traced the veins in his shaft, but couldn't stir him. She licked his sac. He smacked his lips and stilled.

She drank him in. His complexion was more golden now than bronze from too many days spent indoors, his hair longer than when he'd first washed up on the beach.

He needed a shave.

She required every moment that he could give her, even if it meant bringing him to this room. The one place that would remain unoccupied and free from anyone's presence.

Except the priest's God.

She'd lied earlier when she'd made light about coming inside. Deliberately angering any creator wasn't wise, especially the priest's, who was far sterner than the one her people believed in. *Mère de l'homme*, the greatest goddess of all, loved her children and wanted them to be happy on this isle before she cradled them in her arms and brought them home. Surely, such a kind being would look down on this room tonight and protect a man as worthy as Royce, along with a lowly subject like Simone, from the white god's wrath.

If only matters for her and Royce were how Diana and Tristan lived. Or James and Gavra, Zola and Adamo. Each man slept next to his woman every night. They never had to explain themselves to anyone or hide what their hearts demanded.

No wonder Peter argued when Diana tried to keep him from Laure, preferring that he spend time studying his books. Not even an educated Englishwoman could believe words on paper were as wonderful as a lover in bed.

Simone curled next to Royce, her hand on his tired shaft, his heat unable to brighten her mood. They couldn't spend the night here or share the morning and rising sun. They had to hide their growing bond and steal away to be alone.

When he left the isle, the others would pity her. Some would accuse, saying she gave herself to the wrong man. That would be her easiest burden because they'd be wrong.

If Royce had no choice except to stay, he'd never forgive himself for not helping his mother and sisters. His guilt and grief would change him, keeping her from his heart.

She squeezed her eyes. Their love had seemed simple when their lips first met. Now though…

Simone prayed to every god she knew for a solution that would serve all, begging forgiveness for her sins from the white god, pleading with her people's deity to grant her hope.

Wind rushed inside, ruffling the silk sheet. A good omen. Someone had heard her.

Content, she lost herself in Royce's warmth, his quiet breathing lulling her to sleep.

* * * *

"Simone."

Her eyes flew open. Royce loomed above her, his face shadowed like the room. She clutched his arm. "Is someone in the hall? Do they want to come in?"

"No. But we best go to our own rooms before anyone does show up here or peeks into the windows."

"My people would never do that. They would knock down the door first." He laughed.

She couldn't, missing him already. "How can we leave now? We barely enjoyed each other. You sleep too much."

His smile disappeared, a slight frown forming. "That's hardly the proper way to make a man feel worthy."

"You are. If you were less than that, I would never want you to wake. Since you're far more, I feel sad when you close your eyes."

"Forgive me for doing so, but I can't keep them open or find enough strength to speak when you wear me out. Not that I'm complaining about your zeal, but we must leave this room at once. I don't want anyone cross with you."

"What is zeal?"

"What you do in bed with me."

She hugged him. "I will do it again. I like this zeal."

"As I do, but we have the islanders to think of."

"Why? They have their own beds."

He pulled her hands away. "This is the priest's chamber. You and I don't care about being here, but others will if they knew." Royce left the bed. "We need to go."

"And hide what we do."

He tossed her cloth. "This is your home. You have to live with these people. It's not wise to push them into a confrontation or fuel what anger they already have."

"After we leave here, when will we be together as we are now? When the sun rises? When it sets? Do you ever want to see me?"

"You know I do." He pointed. "Never ask that or pretend you don't know my feelings."

"I love you too." She knotted the silk. "When will you help me with the potion books again and teach me to read?"

"Not right away, even though I want to. When Adamo and I worked together, he asked me to help rebuild his house. I promised I would. While the weather holds, the men need to do whatever they can to repair what the storm damaged."

She lowered her face, hiding her sadness.

He lifted her chin and kissed her lightly. "It won't be long before we'll be spending our days together as we have. For now though, I'll read to you after sundown, and show you the alphabet. Those are the letters that form words, which create sentences, then paragraphs and chapters, then books, or letters, the kind people send to each other."

He knew too much. "I want to understand what you say, but your words confuse me."

"My fault, not yours. What I said is I'll teach you everything. I promise your reading lessons will be a great improvement over the dancing ones. Does that make you feel better?"

"I want to do the dancing again."

"We shall." He lifted her into his arms and turned in quick circles.

Simone pressed her face against his hair to quiet her laughter, her joy renewed.

Once she settled, Royce kissed her as a man would when he wanted more dancing and love, but also put her down. "Go." He turned her to the door and pushed gently. "I'll leave after you."

She padded backward down the hall, bumping into walls and doors, hoping to see him leave the chamber. Disappointed, she rounded a corner and ran into Gavra.

Simone jumped back.

Gavra grabbed her arm and pulled her toward the room where she and James slept.

"Let me go."

She tightened her grip. "We must talk."

"When the sun rises. Not now. I want to sleep."

Gavra reached the chamber and pushed Simone inside. She pivoted and tried to get past. Gavra shut the door, blocking it. "I will never forgive myself for taking the pirate to your hiding place after your family died."

They'd never talked about that day. Simone hadn't pressed, not wanting to bring up terrible memories. "He forced you. He raped you."

Tears spilled over Gavra's lids. "I was your friend. I should have protected you."

Simone pulled her close. "You are my friend. You did everything you could. I should have been there for you and killed him and the others who…" Her throat tightened, not letting her speak.

Gavra held Simone's face. "Listen to me, please. From that day on, I promised to look after you so no harm would come. The Englishman—"

"No." Simone pulled away. "Never say anything unkind about him. Royce is a good man."

"He's English."

"So are James and Tristan."

"Both are here for life. They can never leave. Royce can and will."

Simone turned away, arms wrapped around herself, the chill in her soul making her tremble. "I know. But he's here today and tomorrow. The storms will return. He has to stay until they leave for good."

"And when he does? Will you go with him?"

She'd never fit in his world. One look at Diana would tell any islander what England and London were like. Women covered themselves. They had pale skin and spoke a language Simone couldn't hope to understand. "This is my home. I stay here."

"Alone. Unless he puts a child in your belly."

She shrugged.

"Simone." Gavra embraced her. "You're more sister to me than the ones I have, especially Laure. She never listens to me about Peter. She keeps promising to make him a man."

"Oh, poor Laure. Poor Peter."

They giggled and hugged. Simone wept as Gavra did, happy to make their friendship strong again. Gavra smelled of cinnamon and the bread she made, comforting scents that reminded Simone of when there hadn't been any walls between them. "I never planned to fall in love with Royce. It happened before I had a choice. Like you and James."

"He's always been good to me and the islanders."

"Royce has done nothing wrong. Well, maybe tonight. You have to forgive him for trying to teach us his foolish dance."

Gavra laughed so hard her face turned scarlet. "You kept tripping over your feet."

"Me? You jumped up and down like you were trying to get away from a snake."

"I was doing the curtsy." She bounced on her heels.

"No. You bend one knee and then the other." Simone showed her.

They fell against each other, struggling for breath from their newest laughter.

Simone quieted first and smoothed Gavra's hair. "We must never argue again. Promise me. I missed you."

"I wept every day. James told me to talk to you. I was too proud."

"We both were." She kissed Gavra's hand. "I promise not to be too sad when Royce goes away. Until then, please be happy for me."

"I want to. But..."

"He'll never hurt me or anyone else on this island. I promise."

* * * *

Given the simple construction, Royce had no trouble helping to rebuild Adamo's house. The task took him and another man two days. With only occasional sprinkles or gentle showers, they repaired three others over the following week. Tristan, James, and Peter tended the animals. The men who worked the fields harvested what they could and looked to the future rather than worrying about ruined crops.

After their lovemaking, Royce kept falling asleep on Simone, their passion keeping him from teaching her anything except how to please them carnally. Tristan's words proved true. Royce was an abominable teacher, forgetting everything except pleasure.

The returning storms would change that. A dark and menacing cloudbank rolled past the horizon, on its way toward the isle. In the opposite direction, blue sky stretched endlessly, sun blazing above the turquoise water. If he'd had the power, Royce would have captured the scene in a bottle for him and Simone to gaze at during the coming days.

At least the priest's chamber remained free, no one chasing them from there. Even Gavra had stopped frowning at him, though her rigid civility wasn't much better. When he'd asked Simone if they'd spoken, she'd laughed. "About your dance."

Pity he hadn't introduced Gavra to the steps earlier. She might actually smile by now.

Finished with thatching Phillipe's roof, Royce bid the man farewell and ran to the mansion. Wind picked up, scooping dead leaves into the air, rustling branches. Butterflies scattered. Lemurs settled more deeply into the trees, seeking shelter.

The clouds rolled in faster than he could run, half the sky already darkened and bruised. A fine shower sprayed his face. Sun beat against his back.

In the courtyard, mothers grabbed their children and hurried them into the building. Clutching his side, Royce slumped against the storeroom doorway. Rays shone on his face. Plump raindrops fell. Something dropped at his feet.

He flinched and backed up.

A bird traipsed right and left in front of him, its head bobbing, a metal container on its leg.

Stunned, he held the creature to his chest and rushed into the room. The blasted thing couldn't have returned after all this time without delivering his message. Bishop would be enraged at no contact. Days or weeks might pass before Royce had a chance to send another bird.

He checked the tube. Its top was askew. A paper inside. Not the quality he'd used but thinner.

He'd heard of birds homing between two points, as long as they were fed at each, but hadn't believed it until now. His hands shook, making it difficult for him to remove the cylinder.

Once he put the creature in its cage, he unrolled the paper.

R. H.

Secure the chart. Send location immediately. Your mother and sisters are depending upon this.
Fail me and I will see to their fates.

B. B.

Chapter 11

Rain beat softly against the glass above the dining table, the storm lulled to a shower.

Royce didn't hope for a clear day tomorrow or in the near future. Even if the weather grew fair, he had no idea how to access the bloody charts. Diana and Peter were usually in the library on pleasant days, more so when they couldn't go outside.

"Do you want this or not?" Tristan shook the tray holding the roasted beef.

"Yes, of course." Royce speared two slices and dropped them on his plate. He had no stomach for food or this evening ritual but had little choice except to endure. "Thank you."

James filled and lit another oil lamp. Gavra winked at him, poured his tea, then saw to everyone else's.

Royce emptied his cup. The pleasant brew didn't comfort him in the least. His mouth remained dry, swallowing difficult.

"Something wrong with your beef?"

At Tristan's question, Royce shook his head. "It's quite good."

"You've yet to taste it."

"It looks juicy and tender, the same as always." He cut a piece and slipped it into his mouth. "Excellent."

Tristan exchanged a glance with James. "One would think you'd have a heartier appetite considering the labor you did today. How did things go at Philippe's?"

"I finished his roof before the clouds arrived. Hopefully, the thatch will hold during the next storm. Are you predicting this newest one will last as long as the other?"

"I have no idea. Nature does what she wants without consulting me."

Peter chuckled.

Diana passed the bread to Tristan. "Perhaps you should leave Royce to his meal and ask my brother about his studies today."

"Fine with me. What happened?"

Peter straightened, shoulders squared. "Nothing. Once the rain started, I stayed in the library without pause. If tomorrow proves to be the same as today, I shan't budge from my chair in there. I'll stay clear through the night and read every book on the shelves."

Royce gripped his fork, nails dug into his palm.

"Capital, Peter, and bravo to you." Tristan raised his teacup in a toast. "To what do we owe your admirable, yet sudden, dedication to your lessons?"

"Laure." Diana selected a banana. "She insists Peter follow your lead in learning everything he can so she can boast about him to the other women."

"Smart girl. I hope you've thanked her as you should, Peter."

"How could I?" He rubbed his neck, the skin as red as his face. "I've been stuck in the library looking at books, not her. Even if I was free to roam about, Gavra is keeping her busy in the kitchen."

James scooped fish onto his plate. "Putting together a meal is quite a chore. You should try it sometime. On second thought, stay far away from there and don't let Gavra hear you complain about Laure's new tasks. She's needed in the kitchen. I'm quite sure she'll appear at your side at midnight or so."

Tristan and Diana struggled not to laugh.

Royce prayed they were only teasing Peter. Surely, he stopped at a reasonable hour given his hatred for books. "How long into the night do you usually study?"

"Until I finish my work. Those are the new rules I must abide by."

"Perhaps I can assist if you have questions. Speed things up."

Interest registered on Peter's face. "That would help. Once it's dark, Tristan's never around. Diana keeps him in their chamber."

Her face and throat went as red as Peter's had, matching her silk gown.

Royce turned to Tristan. "Do you mind me helping out?"

"Shouldn't you be doing so with Simone?"

He'd forgotten mentioning his plan to teach her. "I will. I can do both."

"Why would you want to?" James asked. "Haven't we given you enough work repairing and rebuilding the islanders' homes?"

"Those tasks are at an end until the weather clears."

James clucked his tongue. "The storm doesn't allow anyone to remain idle. You can work in here. The storage area needs a good scrubbing. So does the room where we keep the excess furniture."

Royce fought frustration and panic. "Surely those projects aren't as important as expanding one's mind. I can begin with Peter this evening. Do you agree, Tristan?"

"Do what you must. But he completes his assignments, not you for him."

"Understood." Royce pushed out of his chair. "We can start now."

Peter scrunched his face. "I've yet to finish my meal. You've barely touched yours."

He sank back down.

James watched the scene. "Odd."

Diana glanced up. "What is?"

He held Royce's gaze. "Many things."

* * * *

James's comment unsettled Royce as much as having the man's pistol aimed at his heart. Either James had been teasing good-naturedly or his suspicion had mounted as to Royce's true purpose here.

He welcomed his escape to the library until he and Peter sat down to work.

Peter was a horrible pupil, unable to keep still for a moment. He drummed his fingers, squirmed, bounced his legs, and glanced at the hall every time footfalls sounded.

Royce stood.

Peter's face brightened. "Are we through?"

"No." At this pace, they'd never be. The charts were maddeningly close yet out of reach as long as anyone was in here with him, curious as to why he'd want to see the damn things. He shut the door. "Fewer distractions will hurry things along."

Peter shoved his book away. "I hate Latin. Can't use it for anything on this isle. It's completely useless."

"Until you need to read Tristan's books on agriculture and animal health. What's going to happen once he's gone and you need that information to keep this island prosperous and the people fed?"

"That's not going to happen for at least a few years."

Peter already had Royce and Tristan in their graves. "Do you want to still be doing these lessons when you're my age? You know, ancient."

"Hell no. Can't you hurry things along for me as you promised at the table?"

"How? By opening your head and pouring the information inside?" He pushed the book back and lit another lamp. "You have two more sheets on Latin conjugation before you can see Laure. Pout and delay if you like, but you'll be in here even longer rather than where you'd prefer to be."

"Bloody stupid books." He glared at the tome.

Light rapping sounded. Royce twisted around. "Who is it?"

"Me." Simone opened the door a crack. "How long will you stay in here?"

"That's up to Peter."

She slouched worse than the boy did. "Can I come in?"

"Sorry, no. I'll see you later, all right?"

"No, but it has to be." She left.

Peter muttered obscenities, flipped a page so hard he tore the paper, and repeatedly slammed his fist against his chair.

Royce wanted to scream that things would be far worse if Bishop and his men came here. Which they would, without notice, if he didn't access the charts and send a blasted message.

"There." Peter pushed his papers away and stood.

Royce grabbed his arm and yanked him down. "I need to review and correct your work before you can leave. This could take a while."

Peter rested his head on the table.

Surprisingly, much had gotten through his thick skull. Only two minor mistakes. "You did well."

"Can I leave?"

"Go."

Peter raced to the door and stopped short before running into Diana. "What are you doing here?"

"This is where the books and my lessons are." She eyed him. "Have you finished yours?"

"Yes. Only got two exercises wrong out of thirty. I must leave."

Diana rounded the table and selected a chair.

Royce stood and helped her with it, striving to act natural. "If you don't mind, I thought I'd stay in here and set up another lesson plan for Peter. When Tristan joins you, I'll show it to him."

"He's settling a dispute between the men and may be a while. Tempers flare with so many cooped up here rather than being in their own homes."

"Of course." There'd be no getting the charts tonight. He crossed the room.

"You're leaving? What about Peter's next lesson?"

"I'll work on it in the morning long before he needs the exercises. I didn't realize how fatigued I am. Have a good evening."

"You as well."

Once in the hall, he slammed his fist into his palm and reeled from too many worries. He'd been a fool for behaving so strangely during the meal. James might have spoken to Tristan, then sent Diana into the library to see if Royce snooped where he shouldn't.

Tristan might guess what he couldn't yet prove and then hide the charts, forcing Royce to speculate on the island location in order to send some information to Bishop. Hoping for Bishop to set sail and die in a shipwreck was madness. More likely, he'd find his way here, enslave the islanders, and capture or kill Tristan, James, and Peter. Royce sensed Bishop would spare him for torture, forcing him to witness his mother and sisters' fate.

He stormed into his bedchamber, paced until his legs wouldn't hold him, and dropped to the bed.

Simone came inside. "I waited in the priest's room for you to come to me. Why are you here?"

He'd forgotten to join her. "Sorry. I…" He didn't have the will to speak.

She sank to her knees at his side. "Gavra told me you helped Peter with his lessons tonight. Was he such a bad student?"

Royce embraced her.

Simone pressed her cheek to his. "He was. Your sad face tells me so. I promise to be better and not cause you any trouble."

"Hold me."

"I am."

"Tighter."

She squeezed his shoulders.

He pulled her onto the bed. "Stay here with me tonight. Promise you will."

"I do."

"Don't let me go."

"Never." She pressed her length to his, wrapping him in her soft, fragrant embrace.

Apprehension wouldn't allow him to relax, draining him further. Depleted, he succumbed to weariness and sleep.

* * * *

Royce dreamed he was in the library. Books reached beyond the ceiling to the heavens. Peter had Latin lessons in his hands, Diana French. Both failed his easy questions, forcing him to repeat himself endlessly. When they glanced at their work, rather than him, he crept toward the charts.

The marble floor cracked, the fissures filled with mud. The gooey substance sucked at his feet, not allowing him to reach the maps.

Simone appeared at his side and handed him the medical book. "You forgot to teach me. I want to learn. Show me how to write tambavy as you did here." She held up a paper with Tristan's name scrawled on it. Royce's message to Bishop was below her thumb.

He tried to snatch the script before the others saw it.

She held the paper out of reach. "You promised to teach me. Did you forget? Did you lie?"

Royce woke, gasping for air.

Simone pushed up and clasped his shoulders. "Did you see your family or Edward in your dream?"

"I can't recall. Neither probably. I have no bad feeling."

Excitement pulsed through him, his nightmare providing the answer he'd sought. "I need to get up and begin my day." Watery light bled around the shutters, relentless rain hammering them.

Simone scooted to the mattress edge. "I should go too and see how Gavra feels. Morning is the worst time for her because of the infant."

"Go then. Wait." He hugged her.

"When will we see each other again? Tonight? In here?"

"No. I'll meet you in the priest's chamber for the midday meal."

"I'll bring you a feast."

"I only need you."

She kissed him soundly and bolted away.

As Royce washed, he rehearsed what he planned to say to Tristan. He needed to use few words and behave naturally, rather than as if their lives depended upon a positive answer. If he spoke too much or pleaded his case, Tristan might grow wary. As Shakespeare had written, "Methinks thou dost protest too much."

Prepared but apprehensive, Royce strode into the dining area. "Good morning, everyone. Mind if I join you?"

Diana, James, and Peter looked at Tristan.

"Not at all." He gestured to a chair next to him. "I wondered how long you'd last in the kitchen."

"Simone's been bringing me my meals for days. However, I don't think Gavra dislikes me as much as she did. Does she, James?"

"I have no idea how she feels. We don't discuss you when we're together."

"Then all's right with everyone's world." Tristan twisted in his chair to face the kitchen. "I'll have her bring a cup, plate, and utensils for you."

"Wait a moment. There's a matter I'd like to discuss first. I noticed something last night while I was in the library with Peter."

"What are you saying?" Peter slapped the table. "I did my work. I only got one exercise wrong."

"Two. I didn't say I noticed something about you or that it was bad, now did I?"

James licked honey from his spoon. "He never gave you a chance. What did you notice in there besides countless books?"

"Charts."

Tristan glanced at James. "What about them?"

Last night's dream had shown Royce how to access the maps without stealing into the library while everyone slept. Or arousing suspicion by asking Peter too many questions about them during his lessons. "Simone's already eager to learn medical procedures and whatever other knowledge I can depart. I thought it would delight her to see where this isle is located in relation to Madagascar and the African coast. I doubt she realizes what's beyond these shores." He smiled. "I'd like her to know there is a boundless world out there. If you have charts of England, I could point out where we hail from."

Diana beamed. "That is a splendid idea. While you're at it, you can show me what the markings on the charts mean."

"I'd be happy too."

"Hold on now." Tristan turned his frown on her. "I can teach you everything there is to know about what's on them. I wrote the information."

"Indeed, but you failed to explain anything when you, James, Peter, and I were in the library. You poked fun at my questions and they laughed. It's time to let another party handle my education in this matter. You don't mind, do you, Royce?"

"Whatever you two decide." Getting between them might risk his access to the blasted things.

Tristan cupped her chin. "I promise to promptly answer anything you ask and to do so without the smallest smile. I'll be more somber than your dearly departed father. Your education is mine to see to. Royce can handle Simone's."

He stood. "Do you mind if I collect them now?"

"Peter will. He'll leave them in your room. I want to have a word about you helping Adamo with his house."

"He asked me to. I didn't mind."

James smiled. "Yes, we know. He told us."

"He had complaints about my work?"

"On the contrary." Tristan looked at Peter. "Why are you still here? Those charts won't walk themselves into his room. Go."

Peter sighed loudly and left.

Tristan eyed Royce as he might a creature he'd never seen before, uncertain whether to be pleased or vigilant. "Where did you learn carpentry and how to construct buildings? You said you were a merchant broker."

"I am. However, I've always liked working with my hands. I told you, physical labor doesn't frighten me."

"Good. When the storms stop, I want you to help the islanders rebuild. Adamo said you're quick, patient, skilled, and you never complain. Exactly what a man wants and deserves in a wife, but few get."

Diana elbowed him.

"Only joking, my love." He kissed her cheek. "Do you mind, Royce? We could use you."

"I'll do whatever you want."

Peter ran into the room. "Charts are on your bed. Take care you don't mess them up."

"I won't. I feel foolish asking, but where is this isle in relation to the other land masses?"

Peter gave him the coordinates. "If you can't find it for Simone, simply point to the first speck you see. She won't know the difference. No woman would. Except for my sister, of course, since she loves to learn." He gave Diana a stiff smile.

Royce marveled that she hadn't killed the boy yet. "That's why I want to show Simone precisely where we are, so she does know. Thank you all. I'll take a look at the charts and prepare for her questions."

"Shouldn't you be tending the birds now?" James cut his beef. "You always do at this hour."

They'd been observing him. Royce should have expected as much. "You're right. Thanks for reminding me."

"Surprised I had to. You may be good at repairing homes, but we had better not let you near the pigs or hens given how easily you'd forget to feed the poor things."

Royce laughed with the others, wishing he could tell them the truth. A bullet in his brain would stop that fantasy.

He made fast work of feeding the birds and cleaning their cage.

With oil lamps lighting his chamber, he spread the charts over his bed. Mozambique and Madagascar were easy to spot. This island, however...

Neither Tristan nor James had corrected Peter on what he'd blurted, which meant one of two things. He'd stated the accurate position or he hadn't, and they didn't want anyone else to know.

For their sakes and everyone's on this island, Royce hoped the spot he'd just pinpointed was the proper one. He ran his finger over the chart, selecting another island of similar size, though farther north and having even less access than this one. He wasn't a mariner, but knew enough to avoid areas such as that given trade winds and currents. A ship unfortunate enough to sail into those waters wasn't likely to come out.

Bishop's couldn't.

Not if Royce had a hand in it, his plan formed.

Bishop was arrogant and foolish enough to insist upon the journey no matter how hazardous. Knowing him, he'd entice a captain and crew to risk their lives for gold, recruiting the most ruthless who'd sell their own mothers and daughters for a few guineas.

All Royce had to do was play to Bishop's weaknesses, coaxing him to his grave, pointing him there with the message he'd send.

In a perfect world, once the storm season ended, news would come from the other islands about shipwrecks. Bishop's bloated corpse found. Everyone here would be safe and hidden from the outside world. Royce would find another way to gain the capital he needed to bring his mother and sisters home.

After that...

He'd be older than even he could imagine, needing years to accomplish his goals and would have to leave here to do so. The babe he and Simone might have already created would be a young woman or man when he returned. An islander would have made Simone his. Royce couldn't ask her to wait for him. That would be too cruel. She deserved more happiness than he could give.

Wind rattled the shutters. The door opened.

Simone padded inside. "Why are you here?"

"Where should I be?"

"The priest's chamber for the midday meal with me."

"I didn't realize so much time had passed."

"What are these?" She touched the chart nearest him. "What do they say?"

"They tell us where this isle is located in relation to other land masses."

"You know too much. You confuse me again."

He pulled her onto his lap. "I'm a brute. I promise to be better. See these small circles here?"

"They look like a hen's egg. Larger at one end, narrow on the other."

"How right you are. Those represent the islands Tristan trades with during fair weather. One of them is where the priest is staying."

Color drained from her face. She pushed the map aside. "Put it away. Never show it to me again."

"Why? Don't you want to see where you live and how vast the ocean is that separates this land from England?"

"What is this vast? Why do you use words I can never understand?" She stood. "No, I never want to see this. One day you hope to leave. These things show you how. You can look at them without me."

He caught her at the door. "I don't have them in here because I long for England or I'm desperate to return there. I wanted to show you that even though this isle is far smaller than where I grew up, it's a million times more beautiful. A true home, not simply a place to live. Paradise any man would be mad to leave."

She turned into him. "You have to for your sisters and mother. I know that, no matter what you say. If you were sad being here, I would die."

"You want me to leave?"

"You have no choice."

"Why in the hell can't I have you and my family's safety?"

"You mean bring them to this isle?"

"No… I don't know. I have to figure things out. Fix everything I've messed up."

"You did nothing. Your father did."

He gathered her in his arms. Her perfumed flesh clouded his thoughts and made him dream when he shouldn't. "I want to find a way to make everything right for my family and us. What that may be, I have no idea, but there has to be a way. Please say you believe me."

She hugged him. "Never have I doubted you. Show me this island again and your England home. We can solve your problem together."

"No. The charts upset you. I want the blasted things out of here and the medical books inside so I can tell you about new potions and poultices you can make. I want to show you how to write tambavy, and teach you the alphabet, and how to read, and—"

She touched his lips, stopping him. "So much in one day? I may fall asleep before you do."

He laughed. "It will take years to teach you everything I know. Are you with me on that?"

"Oui. I never wanted anything else. But your family…"

"I'll see to them and to you."

Happy tears glistened in her eyes. "So much work. You should eat to keep up your strength. I can bring the food in here."

"I'll tend the charts while you're gone." He gave her a fast kiss. "Don't make me wait for you." He'd done so for a lifetime. "Don't be long."

"Never." She opened the door. "I'll bring you a feast. We can stay in here until your meal with Tristan."

"Perhaps beyond. Well into tonight. Go."

She disappeared down the hall. He closed the door.

After reviewing the chart and matching it to what he recalled when he'd first arrived here, he rolled up the papers and dropped them on the chair. Heavier rain fell. He filled and lit another lamp.

Naked feet slapped the hallway floor.

Smiling, he threw open the door.

Tristan advanced, eyes icy, pistol in hand, its muzzle pressed to Royce's forehead.

He staggered back.

Tristan followed. "One more move and you're dead, you bloody bastard."

Chapter 12

Blood roared in Royce's ears. He gripped the chair to keep from moving or falling.

Charts rolled off the cushion.

James advanced, pistol in hand, his eyes cold and hard. Peter followed and stood beside him, weapon raised.

This was no jest that would end with them laughing at him, then James calling him odd. Nor did it have anything to do with an islander's complaint about what Royce might have done. Tristan and the others' faces revealed the truth… They'd unmasked his deception.

Royce couldn't imagine how this happened. Even with his missteps, he'd been careful, taking pains to undo any damage and regain trust. If he'd said anything in his sleep, Simone would have asked what he meant and accepted his lie as she had the others. She couldn't have betrayed him.

Tristan shoved Royce into the chair. He fell hard onto the seat, his weight making the wood creak. The legs tapped the marble floor.

A crash sounded in the hall.

Simone. Her tray and their food lay scattered.

Gavra ran up to her.

Eyes wide, Simone rushed into the chamber. "What are you doing? Stop." She tugged Tristan's arm, forcing the weapon away from Royce.

"Simone, don't." Royce pled as he never had. "Please, you must leave."

Tristan lifted his weapon. "Not another word." Gently, he pushed Simone away. "Gavra, get her out of here."

"No!" Simone slapped Gavra's hands.

She grabbed Simone around the waist and pulled her from the room.

Diana darted into the scene. "What is going on?"

Tristan trained his pistol on Royce's heart. "I'll tell you later. For now, I want you to leave this to me and James. Peter, return the charts to the library and stay there. No arguments, do you hear me?"

"Aye, Captain." He gathered the maps and shut the door behind himself.

Simone's cries grew fainter, the others' footfalls fading. An eerie quiet enveloped the chamber, wind and rain pausing, seeming to wait for what would come next.

Royce prepared for death. He had no prayers to save himself. Failing his family and Simone was his greatest regret. Once he drew his last breath, Tristan and James would likely toss him into the sea, letting it take care of his remains, rather than allowing him a proper burial here. His passing and distance from this land would forever separate him and Simone.

He seethed at the injustice and destiny he hadn't been able to change. Didn't matter that he'd tried to amend his plan and see to Bishop's demise. That bastard was safe. Everything for Royce had ended, and so quickly too, without a reasonable explanation. Other than the most likely. The islanders had alerted Tristan to longboats approaching, launched from a ship.

In the rain.

The men didn't keep watch during storms. No sane crew would sail or row in one, except for a fanatic like Bishop and his legendary riches. However, not enough time had passed between the bird returning with his message and him reaching these shores. Even if such a swift journey were possible, Bishop's arrival wouldn't give away Royce's scheme or that they knew each other.

Tristan was a shrewd and intelligent man, but not even he could have deduced so much without any clues.

Hope sparked, urging Royce to question this. His instinct to survive kept him quiet and focused on Tristan. Any change in his expression could mean the difference between life and death.

Tristan pulled a paper from his waistband and tossed it on Royce's thigh. "Read that."

He didn't want to even though Bishop couldn't have sent it. The paper was too large to fit in a cylinder. If Bishop had attached it to the bird's back, the sheet would be soaked through.

This couldn't be something damning that Royce had scribbled during Peter's lesson. Royce had been annoyed and distracted, wanting the charts, but hadn't lost his composure.

Warily, he unfolded the sheet and went cold at his scratched out sentences, then Tristan's name that he'd lied about to Simone, telling her the letters spelled tambavy. Bishop's name was there too, not merely his initials that could have represented anything. In a cruel twist, Fate had made Royce's dream real, turning it into a living nightmare.

Tristan breathed hard. "Care to guess where we found that?"

In the birthing room where Royce had written it. When Simone had left to get the chick and medical stopper, the wind had blown his papers. He'd slapped them down. This one had escaped his notice, most likely hiding beneath the bed. He supposed an islander had found it while cleaning the room for the next woman, who would deliver a babe in hours or days. Not knowing what the sheet said, she'd given it to Tristan.

He pointed his pistol at Royce's face. "How many birds did you send with messages?"

Lying now was ludicrous. Even a trusting soul like Simone wouldn't have believed him. "Only one."

"You're sure? Think hard or your answer may be the last words you speak."

"There was no way to send more than one. I had no writing instrument or paper when I first came here. Adamo, Phillipe, and other islanders guarded my room constantly, making certain I stayed inside. Once I secured what I needed to write the note, the weather was against me. Think back to when I asked if I could write medical passages from your books for Simone. That didn't happen straight away. Nor could any bird survive the lightning and winds that battered the island."

"When did you release the one bird?"

"The morning Baylee gave birth. I went into the forest away from the beach and the man keeping watch. Once the creature took flight, I returned. You and James were outside the storage room looking for me to help the islanders set up tables."

James's mouth twisted, disgust filling his eyes.

Tristan showed no emotion. Men prepared to kill looked as he did now, hardening themselves against taking a life, making certain they'd feel no regret. "What did your message to Bishop say?"

Royce repeated it verbatim. Words he'd never forget.

James growled. "He's lying."

"No. I had to delay Bishop from asking for more information or taking action."

Tristan pushed his pistol closer. "Why?"

"Because of Simone. Because of Diana and you and the others here."

"What have they to do with this?"

Royce told him about Bishop's plan to give away Tristan and Diana's coming child, to see him and Peter hang, and to put the islanders on the auction block. "I couldn't do that to any of you."

"Yet you're here."

"Not by choice. Between my mattress and a slat is the message Bishop wrote me that explains why I agreed to do this. The bird I sent to him returned here with his note before the newest storm began."

James growled. "What do you take us for? Damn fools? No bird homes between two locations."

"If they're fed at each, they do. I don't expect you to believe me, but why would I lie about Bishop's message when I told you where to locate it?"

Tristan edged closer. "Perhaps you're worried we'd find you out and needed an excuse for what you did."

"How could I have guessed you'd discover the paper in the birthing room unless I planted it there, which is lunacy? If I wanted you to know what I was doing, I would have told you upfront and saved everyone this encounter, particularly me. Should you still need proof that I'm not lying now, check Bishop's writing against mine. They are not the same."

James groped beneath the bed and pulled out Bishop's note and the pouch. He checked inside and hurled it across the room. Together, he and Tristan read the note.

Tristan spoke first. "What has Bishop to do with your mother and sisters?"

"If I fail him, he'll see that the owner they're indentured to sells their contracts to an even crueler man Bishop's acquainted with. Vermin travel in the same circles, you know. This new master also beats his servants, though he does so for sport, along with raping the prettiest and youngest girls who haven't a chance against him. Without my help, my loved ones face horrors I don't want to imagine. They'll never return from the Colonies. When Bishop sent for me to find your island, he knew I'd do anything for money. I made certain everyone knew I could be bought by the highest bidder."

"And that reputation was your mother and sisters' downfall."

"My father saw to that. He's an earl who gambled, slept with high-priced whores, and drank away the family fortune before he swindled everyone. Currently, he resides in Newgate. My mother's father was a marquess. Clearly, she married down when she chose my father."

James's reddish eyebrows lifted. "You're saying you're a peer?"

"Yes. I'm also a barrister, or was one before my father's crimes destroyed my profession and any chance to work at a career that paid well. After he cheated too many nobles, things came crashing down. My youngest sister is still a child, the other a few years older than Peter. I tried my best to support them and Mother with physical labor. That's where I learned carpentry and how to fix things. No matter how many hours I toiled, it wasn't enough. While Father languished in prison, where he damn well belongs, we were homeless with little to eat."

James sneered. "You're telling us none of your family or high-and-mighty friends offered to help? I thought your kind stuck together against the likes of us."

"Your kind is far better than mine will ever be. Father was an only child, his parents deceased. The same holds true for my mother. Second cousins, great aunts, and great uncles abound but they were my father's first victims, easily duped. You can understand them turning their backs on us as they scrambled to survive. As far as friends go, common thieves have nothing on nobles. Loyalty for their peers doesn't exist. When it comes to how they view commoners, matters are even worse, as I'm sure you know. They use the laws they write to take everything from the weak to give to themselves and then expect gratitude along with a 'Thank you, sir' in return. Privilege and appearances matter more than honor. People are there to use or discard, especially those who have fallen from grace and might taint a peer by association. If my family and I had dropped dead on the street, our former friends and acquaintances would have stepped around our bodies and gone on their way, satisfied in their righteous superiority."

Tristan crushed the note and threw it aside. "What did you plan to do with the charts?"

"Find this island to keep its location from Bishop."

"That doesn't make sense."

"If you'll allow me to explain—"

Tristan shoved his pistol closer. "You'll speak when I tell you to and answer my questions quickly. If you want to continue living, you had better tell naught but the truth. How did you discover us?"

"Bishop heard rumors about an isle off Madagascar with a white man and woman on it. I spoke to natives who'd heard you were here. They couldn't tell me your exact location. I questioned others. None could point me to this spot. After eliminating where each group came from, I determined what island would meet a pirate's need for security, including impossible access from a ship, and was bountiful enough to support life for years, perhaps decades. My deductions led me to your shore."

"The natives brought you here?"

Perspiration ran into Royce's eyes. He blinked it away. "I brought myself in a skiff, transporting the birds, hens, and enough pieces of wood to resemble wreckage. I chose the hens to throw you off so you wouldn't consider how I'd be using the birds. The storm quieted enough times for me to inch my way here. During the worst weather, I hid on the other side of your island that's inaccessible to ships. I suspected that if you kept watch, it wouldn't be from that location. Nor would you check the shore during a squall that no mariner would sail in. Once on your beach, the pounding surf destroyed my boat. I ripped my clothes, cut my forehead, and gouged my thigh so you'd believe I'd been shipwrecked."

"In the Sea Sprite, a phantom ship."

"No, it exists."

Tristan lifted his weapon from Royce's heart to his head. "Why not tell Bishop you'd found me and leave him to do the rest?"

He stared at the barrel. "I feared you'd easily kill him and the crew given that you're far more skilled in battle and surprise attacks than he or they will ever be. With him dead, I wouldn't have the funds to rescue my family. He won't pay me until I deliver you and the others. I had hoped to do so, collect the money, then murder him myself, and free everyone."

James laughed disdainfully. "If that was your plan, you're as crazy as he is. You and he would have been dead before your first hour on this land."

"I realize that. Which is why I had to find another way."

Tristan glanced at the pouch. The cylinders had spilled out. "Was it your intent not to send any more messages?"

Royce explained his idea to direct Bishop to a similar isle, farther north, hoping he'd sail there and die, battered by the rocks and pounding surf. "I want him dead as much as you do."

"Your new plan would have him gone before he paid your fee. Wouldn't that leave your sisters and mother at risk?"

"Until I found another way to help them."

"Why the change in his and your original plan?"

"Simone. I love her."

* * * *

"How could you do this to me?" Simone pushed Gavra away and crossed the kitchen to get as far from her as she could. The other women had already fled. "Everything you say about Royce is a dirty lie. You want to keep us apart."

"He wants white men to come here and hurt us."

"Liar." She threw a pot.

Steaming soup arced, barely missing Gavra. She reared against the table, her face white.

Simone trembled, shock warring with anger. "Did I burn you?"

"Did you want to?"

"No!" She opened her arms, wanting to hug Gavra, beg for forgiveness, bring the morning back when they'd laughed and talked.

Gavra backed away. "If you refuse to believe me about Royce, ask Tristan. He has the paper with the writing on it."

"Because you gave it to James. You should have given it to me. I would have shown you that Royce wrote tambavy, not Tristan's name. That he copied words from the medicine book so I could help our people."

"He wrote to Benedict Bishop, the man who wants James, Tristan, and Peter to hang."

"No." Simone couldn't believe anything so evil. "Royce is a kind and gentle man. He loves me. He would never hurt my friends."

"He already has. After Tristan shoots him—"

"No."

Gavra stopped Simone from leaving the kitchen. "He has to kill him to save us. You should have let him die on the beach."

Simone punched Gavra's hands, but she wouldn't let go. "Please, I have to save him from Tristan. I can explain that Royce made the mistake. He sees terrible things in his dreams. He barely sleeps or eats. His soul is sick and made him write those awful things. He could never mean them."

"You want Tristan to take that chance so white men can come here and murder us like the pirates did our families? Or fill you with a child, then leave the infant to starve in the forest?"

She wept too hard to speak.

Gavra cried too, her damp cheek against Simone's. "This is the only way. You won't be alone for long. Many of our men want to claim you as their woman. Open your eyes and see them. Let one into your heart. He'll make you forget Royce."

Never.

Gavra stroked Simone's hair. "Let Tristan do what he must."

Wrenching sobs shook her.

The sounds competed with the rain and wind, but weren't loud enough to mask a shot if Tristan fired.

* * * *

Despite Tristan's piracy, he'd never killed a man in cold blood. He'd make an exception for Bishop. Shooting him in the back wouldn't prove difficult. Letting him believe that pleading for his life would make a difference was a game Tristan would enjoy playing. He'd murder him slowly, as painfully as possible, to punish him for his greed and the monstrous captains he employed who loved whipping men to death or abusing young boys carnally. He'd drag out the torment for the agony Bishop had caused Diana and what he would have done to her and Tristan's child if given the chance.

Royce was another matter.

Tristan had grown to like him. His ready wit, tolerant nature, and intelligence made him a worthwhile friend. Or so Tristan had thought. No other man had fooled him as easily and completely. For that, Royce deserved a bullet through his heart and one through his skull.

Hard raps hit the door. "What's going on in there?"

Diana.

Tristan loved her beyond anything reasonable and understood her need to know what affected them, but he bloody well didn't want to deal with her now. "I'll tell you later."

"Now. Simone's collapsed."

"What?" Royce stood.

Tristan shoved him back into the chair. "Move again and you'll regret it. James, guard him so he stays put."

Tristan opened the door.

Diana tried to see around him.

He advanced, forcing her to retreat. "What do you mean Simone collapsed? From what?"

"Gavra said she was crying uncontrollably, swooned, and fell to the floor."

"Then you best tell Peter to carry her to her chamber. Give her whatever one does in a situation like this."

Diana gestured frantically. "That would be salts. I don't have any. Simone might, since she's a healer, but I can't ask until she regains consciousness, which eliminates the need. Peter refused to tell me what's going on, surely because you told him not to. What happened with Royce?"

Tristan pulled her down the hall, sidestepping the food Simone had dropped. "I wanted to share this later, when we'd have time to discuss it and I could soothe you, but—"

"Soothe me why? How?" She gripped his arms. "What happened?"

He explained Bishop's plan in broad strokes, leaving out the parts about hanging and having their infant torn from them.

She clutched her throat and staggered back. "Dear God, what are we going to do? We need to prepare."

"We shall. However, right now, the weather is on our side. Not even Bishop can sail here in a storm."

"He can during a lull. The last one lasted more than a week. The coming dry season goes on for months. Mozambique isn't that far away."

"I'm aware of that and I'm handling the situation. Once I've made my plans, I'll share them with you. Until then, you can help by seeing to Simone so she feels better."

"You mean perform a miracle? The man she fancies is a vile…" Diana shook her head. "I can't find a word in any language to describe one who'd do something like this to people who offered nothing but kindness. What are you going to do with him?"

"My first thought was to put a bullet through his heart and one in his head."

She went gray. "When you left piracy you promised not to spill more blood."

"Only as long as you, our coming children, Peter, James, and the islanders weren't attacked. That said, I'm not going to murder Royce. He does have a reason for what he did. I didn't want to believe him, but there is the note Bishop sent here."

Her eyes rounded. "Bishop knows where we are?"

"No. The tale's long and I need to get back to question Royce. You must trust that I'll see to everyone's welfare, especially yours." He backed away.

She followed. "I have no doubt you'll do your best for us. But I insist on being in there with you and him. We promised to share everything, good and bad. It was in our marriage ceremony."

"How would you know? The priest spoke Portuguese. You stared at him as you do when the islanders speak French too quickly for you to understand."

She clenched her jaw. "This is no time to make light of things."

Tristan couldn't have disagreed more. He wanted to see her smile. Since spiriting her to this island, she'd faced one crisis after the other, forcing him to fight even harder for her understanding and love. After he'd banished Canela, Tristan had hoped he and Diana would have a new beginning of quiet days and sensuous nights. Not likely now. "Forgive me. Let's go inside."

James held his pistol to Royce's temple.

Despite the threat, Royce jumped to his feet. "Is Simone all right?"

Tristan pulled the chair over, giving it to Diana. "Are you deliberately trying to get shot? Can't you see James is eager to do so?"

"I don't care about me. Please tell me what happened to Simone."

"When she found out what you'd done, she swooned. Ruthless lies and betrayal will do that to a woman."

"I never lied about how I feel toward her or you people."

"Yes, we know." James pressed the muzzle to Royce's throat. "You had no choice in this matter. This is your mother and sisters' fault."

"Wait." Diana stared at Royce. "You have family?"

Tristan retrieved the crumpled message and handed it to her.

Royce glared at James. "The fault lies with me alone. I don't care if you kill me, but you will not say anything against my sisters or mother."

"None of us should or will." Diana held up the paper. "This is precisely how Bishop ensnares others, finding their vulnerabilities and exploiting them. He'll stop at nothing to get what he wants, even if that means harming innocents. I believe he prefers when that happens. He's holding Royce's family over his head. Royce had no choice in what he did."

James rolled his eyes. "Feel sorry for him if you must, but we're the ones who would have paid if Gavra hadn't given me the sheet he'd practiced his note on. If not for that, when do you think he would have told us what he and Bishop had planned?"

Royce rubbed his forehead. "I never would have if I could have gotten away with it."

"Finally." James extended his arm in a grand gesture to Royce, then Diana. "The truth comes out."

Royce spoke to her. "I explained to James and Tristan that I wanted the chart so I could send Bishop in another direction, away from here. I hoped he'd die in a shipwreck."

"But Bishop hasn't, has he?" James aimed his gun at Royce's groin.

Diana sighed. "Royce is unarmed. Must you point your weapon to either kill him or maim him so badly he wishes he were dead?"

"James." Tristan gestured to his pistol. "Put it away. We need to discuss this calmly and rationally."

"What I've done is contemptible," Royce said. "I want to make this right anyway I can if you'll allow—Simone."

She leaned against the doorway, face damp, eyes swollen.

James held Royce's arm, keeping him from going to her.

"Is it true?" She stared at Royce. "Did you write Tristan's name but told me it was tambavy?"

Shame flashed in his eyes. He nodded.

Simone whimpered. "No. You never lied to me, except now, because of the pistol. It makes you say these things." Tears dripped from her lashes. "You needed to practice Tristan's name so you could write things to him. When you looked at what you wrote, you thought it said something else."

"Simone—"

"Did you write on the paper telling a white man how to come here, or did you put what I needed from the medicine books? You told me that. You read it back to me. It was about a potion, I know. Tell Tristan that."

"I can't." Royce's voice shook. "I lied to you. I practiced my message to the white man."

"No."

"I'm sorry, but it's the truth."

She covered her mouth and turned away.

Chapter 13

Royce had never been as weary.

During his darkest days in London, he'd maintained hope that he could make things right, even with creditors hounding him for money to pay his father's debts and his mother and sisters out of reach physically and financially. All he had to do was sell his services and soul to Benedict Bishop.

Past that, he hadn't considered what his life would be like. Hadn't really cared.

Simone had been an unknown entity then, a faceless person he'd use to reach his goal. Destroying her trust, or anyone else's here, wasn't something he'd pondered. Murdering Bishop, then gaining Diana's freedom would surely be enough.

What a bloody fool he'd been.

He craned his neck for a better view of the kitchen and the women working there. None appeared in the doorway. They spoke softly, no voice distinct enough to be Simone's.

Tristan had gathered everyone in the dining area to discuss options and to plan. Charts lay across the table. Peter had joined the group and remained uncharacteristically quiet.

"No, no, no." Gavra's voice rose above the other females. "*Nettoie le sol. La soupe est partout.*" Clean the floor. The soup is everywhere.

She entered the dining area, tea service in hand.

Royce tried to catch her eye. She rounded the table and filled Tristan's cup. He and James studied the maps. Diana touched her diamonds, her gaze haunted and turned inward. Gavra poured Peter's tea. He stared at the steaming liquid.

She gave Royce his serving.

"Thank you. How is Simone?"

"You stay away from her."

"I just want to know how she is."

"How do you think? You killed her with your lies. You made her the fool, the same as all of us. Make him stay away, James. Tell him he's hurt her enough."

Gavra's mouth quivered. Her eyes shone.

James left his chair. With his arm around her shoulders, he led her into the kitchen.

Tristan faced Royce. "Best you don't push your luck with James. He's a fair man, the finest I know, but if you make Gavra cry again, I can't promise he won't beat you to a bloody pulp."

"He can kill me for all I care. I still want to know if Simone's all right. At least physically. I know what I've done to her faith in a world that should be sane, kind, and honest but isn't. If I could give my life in exchange for her renewed belief in men, me in particular, I would."

"Don't be so quick to offer something you may regret." Tristan regarded the chart.

Royce touched the paper. "There."

Tristan knocked his hand away. "What?"

"The island I told you and James about in my chamber. Close enough to this one not to raise Bishop's suspicions. Ideally located to lure him to his end in a shipwreck."

Diana lowered her teacup. "What about his crew? You'd be sending those men to their deaths along with him."

Royce shrugged. "No need to fret where they're concerned. He hires the vilest people imaginable."

Peter snorted. "Like you."

"Yes, exactly. I'm as monstrous as they are. Perhaps worse." Royce tapped the chart. "I say we draw Bishop here and be done with him forever."

Tristan shook his head. "No way to ensure everything will turn out as you want. I don't like having to depend upon the weather or circumstances aligning themselves to solve problems. We'd have no source to tell us what happened to him. He could redouble his efforts to find this isle."

"It's our only option unless you intend to sail to Mozambique and kill him yourself."

"No. Absolutely not." Diana gripped the table. "I'll allow no talk like that. Tristan, I forbid you to do anything so dangerous."

He straightened. "You forbid me?"

"Indeed I do. Our child needs you and so do I. If you can't see the folly in this, then you had better listen to me, or I'll sail to Bishop's hellhole and see to the matter myself. Don't forget, I pursued and waylaid you in Madagascar, pulling you from sleep with my rapier at your throat. I can do the same with that bloody beast."

"As I recall, I then escaped and captured you for all time."

Her face reddened.

Tristan smiled. "Ah, so you remember too. I made fast work of turning things in my favor and will do the same with Bishop."

"As he's a man, he's immune to your charm."

"You're not."

"Indeed." She screwed up her mouth. "That's my downfall. Whenever you're around, I can't think clearly. With him, I shan't have that problem."

"How right you are, because I forbid you to even consider such a thing." He held up his hand. "Before you rail at me, I have no intention of leaving the island. I'll kill Bishop on the beach. Or, if he's able to steal closer, in the forest."

Royce leaned in. "What? You want him to come here?"

"What better way to know that he's dead?"

"No." Diana pressed into her chair, shoulders to her ears. "That would be madness to have him discover this isle."

Tristan patted her arm. "It's the only way, my love. I don't want to spend the rest of our days worrying that he'll arrive for a surprise attack. We both know he's not going to give up. I've taken too many of his ships. You escaped his grasp. He's used to winning. His pride demands it. That's his fatal flaw and we can use it to settle this."

"What of his crew? You intend to murder them after you're finished with him?"

"Why not?" Peter lowered his cup. "Won't bother me. I'll help."

"You will not." Diana turned to Royce. "Talk some sense into them."

"Gladly. I'll kill Bishop. He's mine. No one else's."

"What?" Diana stood. "Are you as mad as they are?"

"He doesn't deserve to live after what he'd threatened to do to my mother and sisters. Some people must die to spare others who are more deserving. The blood will be on my hands. Not Tristan's or Peter's."

"What about the crew?" Peter glanced around the table. "Who gets to do them in?"

Diana sank to her chair. "We're now contemplating deliberate murder for men we've never met."

"Of course." Peter smiled as one would when explaining a universal truth to a slow child. "Happens in war all the time. You've studied history. You already know that."

"Indeed I do. But those are battles fought by forces loyal to their countries. Those on both sides are aware of the situation. It's not an ambush on unsuspecting mariners. The men aren't even pirates. No matter what Royce said about them being vile, I'd wager some went to sea for the same reason Tristan did. To eat and survive. How can we kill them so casually?"

"We can't let them leave." Tristan took her hand. "They'll know where we are. They'd tell others. We'd never see an end to this."

"They could always join you here," Royce said. "At least those who are as Diana described, impoverished and wanting to make a decent life for themselves. I can't imagine them finding this isle less pleasant than being at sea."

"Whether they stay would be up to the islanders." Tristan pushed his saucer aside. "It's their land, not ours. Whatever they decide, we have to respect their wishes. Right now, we're getting ahead of ourselves. You need to pen a message to Bishop that will bring him here without arousing suspicion. The moment the weather improves, the note must go out."

"What about our countrymen?" Diana gripped her cup. "Bishop has connections in government. What if he uses the information Royce sends him to pull the fleet into this? Warships and hundreds of men may show up, prepared to attack."

Tristan held her chin. "For us? The Royal Navy has better things to do than run down a former pirate who thwarted a corrupt merchant. However, to be certain, let's ask Royce. He's a peer."

"He is?" Diana looked at him skeptically. "You are?"

"I am. But a disgraced one, thanks to my father's crimes. The last I heard, Russia and Sweden has the navy occupied in events at those locations. Doubtful they'd pull together a crew to help Bishop on what they'd consider a minor excursion. He would also risk you telling the authorities everything you know about him once they arrived. Like a cockroach, he prefers to hide and operate unseen."

"Does that mean we're doing this?" She moaned. "An ambush, murder, possibly a slaughter?"

"I understand your concern, but as Tristan said, this is the only sure way to break Bishop's hold." Royce pulled the map over. "Are the coordinates Peter offered this morning correct?"

Peter crossed his arms. "Of course they are."

"I'm afraid not." Tristan pointed to an island. "This is where we are."

Slightly south of the location Peter had stated. "We should compose the message together. Make certain it's precisely what you want and to assure you that I'm not keeping anymore secrets."

"I'd already planned on that. Peter, fetch what we need."

Diana pushed to her feet slowly.

Tristan looked up. "Are you all right?"

"Tired. I'm going to rest for a bit."

"I hate to ask..." Royce measured his words. "Will you check on Simone? See if she's feeling well or at least better? When you have a chance, will you tell me what you know? I never wanted to hurt her. I hoped to avoid that with my newest plan."

Diana gestured helplessly. "I can't. It's not that I don't want to, but my French is too poor. I wouldn't be able to translate what she said accurately or convey my thoughts to her."

He'd forgotten she wasn't fluent. "Tristan, can you take a moment to speak with Simone?"

"I'd rather not. I'm not good at handling problems with women."

Diana touched his shoulder. "You do splendidly with me. However, if it makes you feel more competent, we could do this together. I'll tell you what to say and you could translate."

"No. At least for now. We need to write the message first. It has to be perfect and ready when the sky clears."

She brushed back his hair. "Do what you must. After I rest, we'll have a word with her. Won't we?"

"Yes, of course."

Once Diana's footfalls had faded, Tristan gave Royce a hard look. "Consider this a warning—don't ask Diana to act as an intermediary between you and Simone. As far as Simone goes, stay away from her. Never say her name or let her enter your thoughts."

"You don't think I've tried? I love her, as you do Diana. How many warned you not to pursue her, but did you listen? I think not."

Tristan chuckled. "You're correct. I was a besotted fool as you are, and still am. However, I wed Diana and made a home here with her. I don't see you doing the same with Simone."

"My current situation is too unsettled."

"Exactly. Once you resolve matters, you can then make your plans. That is, if you're still interested in doing so. In the interim, as long as you don't bother Simone, I promise to keep Gavra from stabbing you and James from putting a bullet in your head."

"Why would you want to do that?" James took his seat. "I'd rather like to shoot him."

"Be my guest." Royce threw out his arms. "There, I'm the perfect target."

"Don't tempt me."

Royce relaxed. "How's Gavra?"

"Calmer, thanks to my tender care. Don't speak to her again. She doesn't like you."

"Did she say anything about Simone?"

Tristan held his head. "Is there no end to this?"

Royce spoke first. "Convince me Simone's all right and I promise never to ask again, until I grow worried, which will probably be always. So no, it won't end."

James bumped Tristan's arm. "He reminds me of when you were having problems with Diana. Worried you weren't good enough for her. Remember?"

"I do now. Thank you for bringing it up and in front of an audience."

"It's just him."

"My name is Royce."

"Here's everything you need." Peter put the paper, ink, and quills on the table. "Can I stay to help write it?"

"No." Tristan took a sheet and quill. "Do your studies. We'll show you the note we decide on when we're finished."

James lit additional lamps. The lengthening day and dismal weather made it seem more like night than late afternoon.

"First, we need to determine what the note should contain." Tristan dipped his tip into the ink. "Bishop must come here on our schedule, not his, so we have surprise on our side. Next, we need his immediate response and date he plans to set sail. He must believe Royce requires the information to get us into a vulnerable position. Let him think the more forewarning Royce has, the easier it will be for Bishop to best us."

"I agree." Royce took his quill. "To get him here as quickly as possible, I should tell him that you and the pirates I manufactured have discussed going after a new prize. You heard of a ship passing this area and plan to take her. If Bishop doesn't arrive at the time he says, he will have missed the opportunity to capture you and Peter. We can also tell him Diana is on the journey, serving in the crew. She did say she intercepted you in Madagascar. I'd like to hear that story someday."

Tristan colored. "It's quite a tale and not for your ears. Your idea's excellent. Bishop believing we'll slip from his grasp yet again will certainly compel him to act. What else should we include?"

"The coordinates." Peter had spoken from the hall, an open volume in his hand. "The correct ones this time."

Royce would wager Peter's book was upside down. Trying not to smile, he spoke to Tristan. "Another mind focused on this couldn't hurt. What say we ask him to join us?"

Tristan gestured Peter inside.

They deliberated for hours, adding and discarding ideas. Royce wrote so much his hand cramped.

Tristan sagged in his chair. "What do we have?"

"The final version, I hope." Royce slid it to Tristan and gathered near as James and Peter did, the lot of them reading quietly.

B. B.

Coordinates on other side of sheet. Your action required now.

T. and pirates preparing to take a prize. May be away for months. D. joining them. Their departure date next to coordinates. Most vulnerable times here, when I keep watch (alone), also there.

Must act before he departs. Need your immediate response and when you'll set sail.

Miss this chance and there may not be another. T. has spoken of locating to another isle.

R. H.

* * * *

Royce's papers surrounded Simone on the chamber floor. He'd written them the first day he'd read her the medicine book. She kept the sheets without telling him, wanting something of his to keep close.

She pressed them to her face. They didn't bear his musky scent. She ran her finger over the symbols, not knowing what they said. A tear splashed on one, smearing the ink. She blew hurriedly to dry the drop. Whether his words were bad or good, a lie or truth, she couldn't part with them.

It was wrong to love him more than she did her people, but Simone couldn't stop. If she'd been able to read and had seen these before James did, she couldn't have betrayed Royce. She would have talked to the priest's god and her own to make things right. They would have helped her and never let the white men come here as Gavra warned.

And Royce wanted.

Simone held the paper to her chest, longing and hopelessness tearing her apart, the pain worse than the pirate's sword slashing her leg. When she'd been with Royce, her scar hadn't looked ugly. The mark proved they matched and were born for each other. Not even death could separate them.

He did love her, even if it was only a little. His face and eyes couldn't lie about that.

A light rap hit her door.

She gathered the papers and pushed them under her bed. "Gavra?" Simone didn't want to see her, but did, confused as to what she should do.

The door opened a crack. Tristan smiled. "Diana and I wanted to see how you are. May we come in?"

"Oui." She stood and offered Diana the chair.

"Perhaps you should sit." Tristan gestured Simone to the bed. "We heard you collapsed before. Are you all right now?"

"What happened to Royce?"

"Nothing. We spoke. He's in his chamber."

Good news. Perhaps. Simone wrung her hands. "As your prisoner? Will you send him to the same island you did Canela? He needs to help his family. If he goes to the other isle, he may never find his way home. Please, you have to stop hurting him and help him as he needs."

"I haven't done anything, nor do I plan to. We settled things between us."

"How?"

"He's going to take care of the white man we're worried about. Make certain he doesn't harm anyone here."

"How can he do that from this isle when the white man is on his own land? How can Royce win by himself without a pistol or sword?"

"All the men here will fight at his side when Bishop comes with his crew."

She jumped up. "The devil comes here? Royce will be in a battle with him and pirates?"

"Not pirates. Mariners."

"What does it matter? He could die."

Diana tugged Tristan's shirt and spoke English. He answered her. Their conversation grew heated.

Simone could scarcely keep still. When Tristan and James were still pirates, Gavra had cried herself to sleep every night James wasn't here, terrified he wouldn't return. That he'd die without them seeing each other a final time. Simone had comforted Gavra, but never understood her stark terror.

"I have to see Royce." She padded around Tristan. "We must talk." She had to convince him not to do this.

"Wait." Tristan held her arm lightly. "It's best you not go to his room. Diana and I also came here to talk to you about that."

"We can use mine. Or do you want us to go your library?"

He blew out a breath and released her. "It's best you don't speak to him at all. Diana and I—"

"Why? You said he fixed things with you. Did you lie?"

"Of course not. But Diana feels, that is, we both feel it's best you not get too involved with him, as a friend or anything else. Once we see to Bishop, Royce will leave to help his family. He can't stay here forever. Didn't he tell you that?"

Simone squared her shoulders. "I told him. He said he wanted to help them and be with me and would fix everything. He has with you, why not with us?"

"That's different. Diana, please." Tristan brushed her hand away and spoke English.

She slumped back and sighed.

He faced Simone. "I wish I could give you what you want. I'm certain Diana would also love to do that. Royce can't, no matter what he said. He has obligations elsewhere that will take him away, surely for years, possibly forever. I don't want you getting hurt."

"Do you think your cruel words stop that?"

His eyes widened. "They're not cruel. They're the truth."

"Are you forbidding me to talk to him?"

"I haven't the right. You're free to do whatever you want. However, consider what prolonging this will do to him. He can't think of anyone but you. He doesn't even care about his own safety anymore. Repeatedly, James threatened to shoot him for talking out of turn and Royce kept doing so, wanting to know if you were all right. Give the man some peace. He knows what he must do. He simply can't face it yet, so he engages in this dream about you and him being together. It won't happen. It can't if he wants to bring his loved ones home. They come first. I'm sorry, but that's the way it has to be. To let him believe otherwise is only going to increase his suffering when you do part."

The room swayed around her. A terrible taste rose to her mouth. She forced it down.

"Do you need to sit again?" Tristan reached for her.

Simone backed away. "I will never speak to or look at Royce, as you want. I'll make him forget me so he can go to England with a lighter heart. I only wanted him to be happy. It would kill me to bring him pain."

"I know you didn't mean to. And I'm terribly sorry this hasn't worked out."

"Me too. Please leave. I want to be alone."

"Of course." Tristan led Diana from the room and closed the door gently.

Simone covered her face, but wouldn't allow herself to cry.

* * * *

Two doors from Simone's room, Diana tugged Tristan's hand. He pretended not to notice and fled down the hall, away from female tears, heartache, and problems he had no idea how to fix.

"Tristan, will you stop?"

"Once I get to the dining area. I'm famished. Forgot to eat the evening meal." He'd been dealing with Royce's troubles instead. Now they were his problems, forcing Tristan to compose missives and plan an attack that might see him, James, Peter, or the island men killed.

That should have been enough to give Royce nightmares, yet nothing except Simone engaged his thoughts. Their grand love that was far more hopeless than Tristan's had ever been for Diana. He didn't have a family to go back to. Staying here wasn't only easy for him, he had no other choice if he wanted to live another day. As far as Diana's family, she only had Peter to worry about.

Even with those obstacles absent, their problems never ceased.

She crowded him at the table, arms crossed. "What did you say to Simone? She looked worse than she did in the kitchen. Why didn't you wait for me to talk so you could translate as we'd planned?"

"I had no chance. She hounded me with questions as you're doing. How do women ever converse with each other? You never stop speaking."

"Men kill each other without blinking an eye. There. It's your turn to insult my sex. Then it will be my turn to slander yours."

He dropped to his chair and pulled her onto his lap. "I refuse to argue with you. You smell too good." He pressed his face to her hair.

She pulled back. "I love you too. But right now, I want to talk. Please tell me what you said."

"The unvarnished truth. She shouldn't be around Royce at all because it isn't fair to him. When it comes to her, he's obviously lost whatever good sense he had. He can't think of anything except Simone. She needs to accept that he's going to leave as soon as we deal with Bishop and she'll never see Royce again. No matter what he wants, nothing will change his responsibilities to his mother and sisters. They come first. Simone's an afterthought in his existence."

Diana rubbed her forehead.

Not a good sign. "What?"

"Please tell me you didn't use those words."

"I can't recall what I said exactly. She was so upset I merely tried to reason with her by using logic instead of emotion."

"That's usually what starts and intensifies our disagreements."

He pulled her closer. "I like to get you worked up for later when we forgive each other in bed."

"Be serious."

"Very well. Adding honey to the awful truth won't delay the inevitable. Simone's here for life. Royce and his family will return to England where they belong. Best they accept it and move on rather than killing each other slowly with love that isn't possible."

Chapter 14

The following morning, it was time to alert and to prepare the islanders for Bishop's expected arrival.

Men gathered in the courtyard beneath a gentle shower and worsening clouds. Tristan stood on a table so everyone could see him. On the ground, James flanked his right. Peter and Royce his left. Those in front regarded Royce curiously, rather than with malice. He hoped their peaceful natures wouldn't deteriorate into anger for the danger he'd brought them. Tristan had promised to word his speech carefully to avoid anyone knowing Royce's role in this.

These people were no fools.

"We have a situation." Tristan's shout was a harsh contrast to the lightly tapping rain. "Benedict Bishop, the white man who caused Yellow Scarf and the other pirates to invade here, will come himself this time. We expect him and a large crew to arrive before the next full moon. Perhaps longer if the storms return. These men will attack. We must be prepared to fight them and win."

The islanders exchanged glances. Alarmed murmurs rose.

Adamo stepped forward. "How can you know such a thing?"

Another man called out, "Did you dream this?"

Tristan held up his hands for silence. "No, I didn't learn this from a dream. We have information on what Bishop plans to do."

"What is this information you speak of?" Water dripped from Adamo's nose and hair. "Where did it come from?"

Royce gripped Tristan's wrist and spoke English. "Let me tell them. It's my fault. They need to know the truth."

"Take care with what you say. James, Peter, and I are no match for so many men."

If they tore Royce apart, he'd bloody well deserve it. However, he wanted them to save their rage for Bishop.

He climbed on the table and spoke French. "I came here from the white man's ship. He lost valuable cargo when it sank. His men will be looking for it."

Adamo frowned. "And you wait until now to tell us?"

Mutters and heated conversation rippled through the crowd.

Tristan gestured for quiet. "Please. Let Royce speak and he will explain." Tristan leaned in. "You had better tell them something acceptable."

"I shall." He faced the men. "The weather has been too foul for Bishop to sail this far. He comes from a land where the sun sets across water so wide no man can reach here for days. The storms won't last. When there's a lengthy lull, he will set sail. He's a greedy and cruel man like the pirate who once ruled this isle. He won't rest until he has his valuables back."

A man in the front spoke. "How does he know to look here?"

"He doesn't for certain. However, he knows the water as Tristan does and what route his ship took. Along that course, which includes this isle, is where he'll search for wreckage. Some is still on the shore where you found me. His men will scour every island before this one to see if it has his belongings and other wealth they want. And then they'll come here."

Adamo shook his good fist. "Again, I ask the same thing. Why did you wait until now to say this?"

"I'm a coward." Royce pointed at the men behind Adamo. "I see many of you nod. You're right to agree with me. I should have been concerned about everyone here, but I worried for myself, what I should or could say to Tristan, fearing it would mean my death for bringing trouble. I knew you could kill me at any time and feared you would."

Protests rose from the islanders, many saying they were peaceful unlike the white men who'd come here.

Royce lifted his hands. "I had no idea what anyone here would or wouldn't do when I first arrived. At that time and well after I started to heal from my injuries, I held my tongue as there were too many pistols pointed at me." He gestured to Adamo. "Yours included."

He straightened. "I never would have shot you when you had no weapon."

"I didn't know that. I'm not making excuses for what I did, but haven't you ever been in a situation where you knew the right thing to do but chose another path? The wrong one? Even though you may have regretted your decision, it was too late. Circumstances got out of control without you wanting them to and you paid the price for not acting in everyone's best interest. You thought only of your own."

Those surrounding Adamo stared at him.

Royce hated bringing up how Adamo had helped Canela betray their people in a futile attempt to gain her love, but too much was on the line for compassion.

Adamo hit his chest. "I admit it. I'm a coward like you. I will never forgive myself for what I did to help Canela."

"You made a mistake. We all do. You're one of the finest men I've ever known and you'll fight bravely beside your people. I will too. To the death, if necessary. This isle belongs to all of you, your women, and children, not Bishop or any others who dare come to the shore. I know Bishop's ways and told Tristan what to expect. We need to keep a constant watch on the sea. One man at the point, as always, with the glass. Others on those parts where the land touches water deep enough for a skiff or longboat to use. If anyone sees something unusual, Tristan must know immediately."

Royce told them the time Bishop would likely strike. The same hours he put in his message when he lied about keeping watch.

Philippe pushed through the group and stood next to Adamo. "When do we start to do these things?"

"Immediately," Tristan said. "We haven't anything to worry about until the sun returns over several days. However, we do need to prepare and make this new security part of our daily tasks."

James lifted the papers he held. "I've prepared a list for who will keep watch and in which location. Before you leave the courtyard, I'll tell each man where he'll be and when. Even when you're not on duty, you must always be alert, your pistols ready to fire at any moment."

"What about our women?" A man with a long scar on his chest came forward. "What do we tell them?"

"You don't. We will." James shouted loud enough for everyone to hear. "Gavra is gathering the women in the stone house so Tristan can speak to them next. Females and children stay within those walls, protected from harm while we men fight. Are you with us on that?"

They shouted their agreement, one oui blending into the other, creating an impressive roar.

Time for the women to know what trouble headed this way.

* * * *

Royce dreaded this meeting more than the one with the men.

Females filled the kitchen and dining area. Many crowded the hall. Some had babes nursing at their breasts. Others had slipped their arms around older children who sat beside them on the floor. The boys and girls fidgeted, chattered endlessly, or sang to themselves.

Peter held Laure's hand. James embraced Gavra. Fear registered on the young women's faces, worry in their eyes.

Royce's fault. He'd brought this horror on these good people and Simone. Unable to find her, he twisted and craned his neck, desperate for one look. She leaned to the left of a woman in the hall and peered around her.

His heart paused.

Simone's gaze met his.

Overpowering tenderness and desire welled within, urging him to gather her into his arms and never let go. He couldn't move or draw a full breath, helpless to do anything except feast on her. Less than a day had passed since he'd last seen Simone, yet those few hours had been longer than the rest of his life.

Yearning filled her eyes. Love softened her beautiful features.

He smiled gently.

She lowered her face.

Tristan and Diana entered the room. Her wan complexion and the dark circles beneath her eyes confirmed her distress at who might die in the attack. Tristan pressed his mouth to her ear. She nodded at whatever he said, but held on to his hand, forcing him to break free.

He joined Royce. "Best we begin. Do you want to explain things here as you did to the men?"

"No."

"Don't blame you. Women refuse to believe our tall tales about glorious conflict. They have to live with the enormous loss."

"You should have killed me on the beach to keep things from coming to this."

"Too late for that now. Besides, your family needs you. Never forget that. Your responsibility toward them will help you survive the battle."

Tristan held up his hands to the women.

They quieted their children and bounced their infants. Several cried, their shrieks piercing.

Royce welcomed the noise, envying men who returned home after a long day to their wives, sons, and daughters. Such a small thing to expect and currently out of reach for him and Simone.

She peeked at him. He couldn't look anywhere except her.

Tristan explained the coming problem to the women.

Gasps filled the room.

He spoke gently and confidently, promising the isle would remain in the islanders' hands. He never touched upon the price for success, the possible gore and death.

Women murmured to each other. Children grew restless, pestering their mothers for attention.

The young woman next to Simone wept. Simone hugged her but didn't cry.

Royce wagered she'd already known about the coming assault. She certainly understood his part in bringing it here.

A heavily pregnant woman slapped her hands together, drawing Tristan's notice. "Will all the men fight or only some? My Étienne has trouble walking. He hurt his leg when he worked on Adamo's home."

Zola stood. "Adamo's arm is weak. He has trouble seeing out of one eye, but he will fight to protect this isle and us. All men will, except those who are cowards."

"You dare accuse my man of such a thing?" She shook her fist. "You should save your words for Adamo. He helped Canela bring Yellow Scarf here. Adamo deserved what he got."

"Ladies." Royce stood between the women. "Be careful not to say what you can't take back. We're preparing your men so they don't get hurt. I'm the only one who's going to face danger when Bishop and his men arrive. I'll be the first one they come upon and I will be alone."

"No!"

Everyone turned to Simone.

She ran from view.

Tristan clamped Royce's arm. "Leave her be. There's nothing you can do to make this better. We stand, fight, and die if we must."

* * * *

Unspoken dread settled over the mansion, the women quiet, men tense, children more boisterous than normal, testing everyone's patience.

Royce didn't have to avoid Simone. He never saw her. Whenever he had a free moment, he passed her chamber. The door was always ajar, the area deserted. She wasn't in the priest's room either. Royce might have checked every space in the building if Tristan hadn't kept him so blasted busy.

His tasks included making certain the islanders' pistols were in good working order. Some also had cutlasses they'd taken from pirates. For good measure, Royce had them make spears.

Each evening, he, James, Peter, and Tristan debated strategies, arguing which might work best and finally settled on one that included suggestions from all involved.

"Are we agreed?" Tristan glanced around the table.

Everyone nodded.

"Then we stick with this unless Bishop surprises us with something that renders the plan useless."

Royce rubbed his eyes. "What might that be?"

"I have no idea. No one could. But we have to be ready to change course on a moment's notice. He and his crew certainly aren't going to wait for us to decide." Tristan slapped what they'd written into Royce's hand. "Gather the islanders in the morning and tell them what we plan to do."

He held the meeting in the courtyard as Tristan had with his. Puddles and mud covered the ground. Water dripped from the mansion and trees. The sky cleared, weak rays trying to burn through clouds.

At another time, the increasingly pleasant weather would have been something to celebrate. Now, it simply ushered the inevitable closer.

Royce read the papers aloud and paused frequently, waiting for questions.

Phillipe clapped his hands, pulling attention to him. "Will this rid us of the white man and his crew for good?"

A lie would have been easy to voice. Unfortunately, they deserved the truth. "There's no way to tell until they arrive and we strike. However, we do have surprise on our side. We know they're coming, while they have no idea we'll be waiting for them. As I said before, I'll be the first they spot." He swept the crowd, including everyone in his answer. "Should something happen to me, you can..."

Royce forgot what he'd meant to say.

Simone stood to the far left, away from the men.

She edged behind a trunk but only partially hid herself. Her dark hair and green cloth fluttered in the breeze, painting the perfect picture of an angel he wanted.

Or a ghost he couldn't have. She disappeared within the vegetation.

Someone tugged his sleeve.

Phillipe looked up at him. "We can what?"

"What? I don't understand." Royce hunkered down to leave the table. "Where are you going?"

He'd planned to follow Simone and neglect these men for his selfish needs. "Nowhere. Where was I?"

"What should we do if Bishop harms you?"

"Leave and go to Tristan and James. Don't try to save me. Spare yourselves."

Phillipe nodded.

"No." Adamo shoved Phillipe aside and faced Royce. "We save everyone. We fight together. We survive together."

Royce shook his head. "Think of the women and children. You want to come back for them. I don't matter. Let's get on with this."

He read the sheets and answered the men's questions, repeatedly emphasizing their safety. "How are the spears coming, Gérard?"

"We have thirty."

"That's good. However, we need one or more for each man."

"My brothers and I will work hard until we have them."

"Merci." He addressed the crowd. "Let Tristan know if you have any concerns. That's all for now."

They dispersed to their usual jobs.

Royce ran to where Simone had been. Gone. She wasn't near the palms or the other courtyard trees either. Outside the wall, he stepped in muddy water and on rocks, unmindful where he trod.

Green flashed to the side. He rounded a tree and stopped.

She lingered by the periwinkle, silk bag in hand to gather her healing leaves, her face down, shoulders trembling.

Her tears sapped his hope. By all that was sacred, he should leave her in peace as Tristan had warned.

Royce pushed forward, stepping on a fallen branch.

At the rustle, she flinched and looked over.

He prayed she wouldn't run. He wasn't sure what he'd do if she stayed. Only a few yards separated them, and insurmountable difficulties. They never should have met. He held out his hands. "I love you."

Simone ran to him.

He lifted her into his arms, their mouths melding, tongues dancing.

Her tears were salty, lips strikingly soft, her desire as untamed as his. He couldn't fill her deeply enough. She wrapped her legs around him and tightened her arms on his shoulders.

Men's voices sounded from behind, near the courtyard wall.

Royce pulled his mouth free and carried her behind a trunk. "Will the birthing room be free today?"

She shook her head.

"We can go to the priest's room then."

"No." She cupped his face. "You have to forget me. Your family needs you. You have to leave. I cannot bring you sadness."

"Without, you I have no joy, no reason to live. I'd be better off dead."

"No, no, no." She touched his mouth. "Never say that. You cannot go to Bishop first and alone. The other men need to help."

"I don't want them killed for the trouble I've caused."

"You did this for your family."

"How do you know that? Did someone tell you?"

"You told me by what you say, how you look, the way you touch, and your sad smile. You could never be an evil man and hurt me or the islanders because it pleases you. If you die, I die. If you go to Bishop alone, I'll follow you and will kill him with my hands."

Royce kissed her so hard his lips tingled. She struggled for air. He did too. "I want you safe. You'll obey me in this."

"Let me go." Tears fell from her chin. "Never look at or speak to me again. I make you want things that are bad and will see you hurt. I am poison to you."

"You're my life. Did Diana tell you to say this?"

"She tells me nothing. She understands nothing I say."

"Tristan talked to you then."

"He wants you to do what you must."

"I know, but he damn well better mind his own business when it comes to you and me. Can we use the birthing room?"

"Jacqueline's infant may come today or may wait until tomorrow or longer. I have no way to know."

"The priest's room it is." He gave her another kiss, this deeper than the last. "Are you with me?"

She pressed her cheek to his. "My heart belongs to you. I can never say no."

Royce loved her even more. "Don't ever change, please. Always want me."

She hugged him.

He carried her to the courtyard walls and put her on her feet. "Do you want to go in first or shall I?"

"Me. I'll be in the priest's room. You too. No matter how wrong this is."

Them being apart was the bigger crime. "I give you my word, we'll make our love right someday."

"We have now." She gave him a quick kiss and tore across the grounds.

Two island men looked over at her, then resumed cleaning up the downed vegetation.

The sky cleared quickly, warm wind tearing the clouds apart, the sun poking through. If the weather held, the bird would be in the air soon, winging its way to Bishop who would hopefully be dead before a fortnight had passed.

Royce waited as long as he could before entering the courtyard, not wanting to draw attention to himself and Simone. The men's backs were to him. He strode past as any islander might, accepted by the others, allowed to move about as he pleased without anyone querying him.

Except for Tristan. He might question the route Royce intended to take, guess the purpose, then lecture him as he would a schoolboy on avoiding lust.

"Peter." Royce grabbed his arm before he could pass. "Where's Tristan?"

"Seeing to the cattle, the fields, the horses, and no end of other tasks. The trouble you've caused won't change that."

"I didn't get involved with Bishop to deliberately hurt you or anyone else here."

"I know that. Your family comes first. So does mine. I don't want anything happening to Tristan. Promise you'll protect him."

"We both will. Wouldn't have it any other way."

Peter offered a small smile and took off.

In the priest's room, Simone stood on the bed, touching the cross and speaking softly.

Royce closed the door. "What are you doing?"

She started and blushed. "Talking to your god. I already talked to mine."

In the nude no less. Her soul was more innocent than the most devout parishioner. No god could ever find fault with her. "About what?"

"Taking away our troubles. Keeping you safe. That more than anything."

He tossed the papers and his clothes aside and padded to the mattress. "Come here before I perish waiting for you."

She slipped her arms over his shoulders, her legs around his hips, her damp slit to his cock. "I like this. Will you take me standing?"

"The bed's softer."

"I like that too."

Laughing, he dropped them to the mattress, keeping her beneath him, captive to his view, touch, and unquenchable love. "I missed you."

"Every night I saw you in my dreams." She eased his hair back. "I wanted morning to never come. I stayed away to give you peace."

"It was more like Hell. But it's over. Swear it is."

"Love me so it will be…and promise not to sleep after you do."

He chuckled. "You drive a hard bargain, but I won't close my eyes for hours."

"If you do, I'll shoot you."

"I believe you would."

She brought his mouth to hers, their smiles touching.

Her passion fed his but Royce couldn't rush. Each second was too sacred to do anything except savor and explore. She felt warmer than he recalled, smelling of flowers and musk. No one on earth could have softer skin. She loved him.

He shouldn't be this lucky but didn't question his good fortune. Fighting lust, he entered Simone gently to prove how much he honored her, then sank into her heated depths. His scalp tingled. Their bodies touched.

She pulled her mouth from his and made a pleased sound he'd always hold dear. He kissed her chin, then pumped, an easy slide meant to arouse.

Her color rose. She couldn't keep her eyes open. Her breathing hitched.

She was almost as far gone as him. Wanting her to surpass his passion, he touched her nub.

"Ah... I like that."

He adored everything about her. "What say I do it again?"

"For always."

And beyond. Their first look, touch, and kiss had sealed their fates, precluding anything else. He tended her with more zeal than the most licentious rake, except that Royce gave, rather than taking, and delivered release. Her unrestrained cries stirred him as much as his own relief would when he allowed it. Maybe in an hour or two. Or at the end of today. Perhaps tomorrow.

He had to hold off and keep this dream alive.

She breathed noisily and looked at him through hooded lids.

He kissed her lashes. "Are you falling asleep on me?"

"Only a little."

"I'll have to wake you." He straightened, pumped, and stroked between her legs.

Simone clutched the sheet. "More. Never stop."

He pushed her over the edge a second time and thrust as she descended, dooming himself to surrender. His carnal craving demanded its due. He shuddered unable to pump any longer. No need. Her pulsing sheath pulled him deeper.

Perspiration dampened her face. She matched his smile. "You stare."

"You do too."

They gazed at each other until he couldn't support himself any longer and sank to his elbows.

She caressed him. "Are you all right?"

He fought to keep his eyes open and suppressed a yawn. "I'm not tired. I won't sleep."

"Maybe we both will."

"Merci." He rolled them over so she could lie on him. "Only a few minutes. Wake me."

She kissed his throat. "Rest."

Royce wanted to tell her he would, but he floated instead, soothed by her weight and quiet breathing. Darkness descended.

A loud knock sounded.

Startled, he sat up.

Simone lay on the other side of the mattress, still slumbering. He had no idea how she'd gotten there or how long he'd been out.

A fist or foot hit the door. "Royce, are you in there?"

Tristan.

Simone lifted her head and blinked sleepily. "Why is he here?"

"I don't know."

She sank back to the mattress. "He told me I could do whatever I want. I want to do this."

Royce wasn't certain whether to laugh or moan. "Put on your cloth." He looked over and called. "Yes, I'm in here. Give me a moment."

He dressed hurriedly and opened the door a crack. Tristan showed no emotion. "The sky is clear. We need to begin our plan."

Chapter 15

Simone rolled off the mattress. The bedframe creaked.

Without looking at her, Royce motioned her back.

She stayed where she was, uncertain where he wanted her.

He faced the door, not opening it more than he had and spoke English.

"No," Tristan said. "*Utilisez le français. Je ne veux pas de Diane entende et s'inquiète.*" Use French. I don't want Diana to overhear and worry.

"You want to work on our plan now? Not in the morning? Another storm may come."

"That's always possible. But we need to be ready."

"Understood." Royce joined him in the hall and closed the door.

He couldn't meet Bishop alone. If that devil hurt or killed Royce... Simone knotted her cloth and sped from the room.

He and Tristan were already far ahead, conversing quietly in French, their backs to her. They turned a corner.

She followed as closely as possible, her steps light to avoid making too much noise. The house was quieter than it had been, the good weather bringing everyone outside. Sun shone around shutters.

The warm light had once promised good fortune, pleasant days, celebrations for new life. Now it would bring danger and death. Her stomach twisted.

Royce and Tristan entered the library. The door closed.

Pressed against the wall, she waited to make certain no one else worked or lingered nearby. Women's voices floated from the courtyard. Children hollered and laughed. Simone crept to the library and pressed her ear against the wood.

Chair legs scraped. Royce spoke. "*Toujours en français?*" Still French?

"Oui. Diana *peut passer.*" Yes. Diana might pass by.

"Very well," Royce said. "Although the sky is clear, I don't know if there's enough light left today for the journey. The last time I did this, I chose morning for the additional time."

"Once it gets dark, there are islands for shelter between here and Mozambique."

"Yes, I know. But the message will get there faster if there are no delays. God only knows what could happen during a long night on another isle. We'll lose precious time if we have to send an additional bird because a predator hunted and killed the first one the moment it entered its territory."

"Why not use two then, or more, to make certain one gets through?"

Royce cleared his throat. "If it were up to me, I'd send them all to get this bloody matter finished and to prove to Bishop he must act with great haste or lose his chance to take over the isle."

Simone covered her mouth.

"However, if I were to let every bird loose and none returned for one reason or another, then where would we be?" Royce signed loudly. "Even if I keep a few here for later use, the creatures could fall ill or die, leaving us no way to communicate with Bishop. This has to be done correctly."

"Morning it shall be. First light. James and Peter will want to be there when you release the bird."

"Agreed. We'll gather in the storage area. James should make certain Gavra and the other women who work beside her don't fetch grain or fruit at that time and happen upon us. After what you and I have said to the islanders, we wouldn't want to alarm them with what we're doing now. I don't want to consider what will happen if we lose their trust in us and this."

"I'll have him handle her and the rest."

Simone bolted toward the courtyard to warn the men. They had to stop Tristan and Royce from this madness. For reasons she didn't understand, they were sick in their minds and hearts, lying to and betraying her people. The islanders had to capture them to keep everyone else safe. They'd also have to take James and Peter, since they'd side with Tristan. Diana too. She couldn't remain free even though she was with child.

Simone stopped.

The men might be so outraged and frightened by this, they could accidentally harm Diana and possibly kill Tristan, James, and Peter.

And Royce.

She doubled back, not knowing where to go, what to do. At last, she ran to the kitchen and stopped in the doorway.

Gavra looked up from the bread she was slicing. Her face went slack. "What happened? Is something wrong with James?"

Simone grabbed Gavra's arm to keep her from leaving. The other women watched them.

Gavra bared her teeth. "Tell me what happened. Is James hurt?"

"No. I saw him last after the morning meal. He should be tending the horses or cattle as he always does."

"Then why do you look so worried? Did Royce say something? Has he lied to you again?"

He'd lied about everything. Tristan had too. And possibly James. None of it made sense to Simone. They were good men.

They were also white. The same as Bishop and the pirates who'd come here. James loved Gavra, but she was brown, not pale like Diana. Tristan ruled fairly but he would do anything to save her. His loyalty belonged to his wife, Peter, and James, not the islanders.

Gavra broke free and shook Simone. "Tell me."

She couldn't. Royce had promised her his love. She'd seen truth then, not lies. She didn't know what to believe or if she'd heard his and Tristan's conversation correctly. Maybe the sickness was in her, not them. "I fell asleep and had a bad dream. I ran here without thinking, not to make you worry."

"Then you should answer me when I ask a question." Gavra collapsed on the bench and laughed weakly. The other women joined in. "Sit down. A cup of tea will make you feel better."

"No. I need to work on my potions for Jacqueline. Forgive me for frightening you." She hugged Gavra, wishing she could share what she knew, but couldn't. At least not yet. "We can speak more during the evening meal."

Simone ran from the kitchen.

* * * *

Royce copied his message several times. During each effort, he reduced his script to avoid taking up too much paper so it would fit more easily into a tube. He checked the cylinders, all in good working order. The birds were healthy, the largest one prepared for tomorrow's flight.

Edgy, he returned to the mansion and paced its quiet halls, worried over the bird dying midflight. Any delay would anger Bishop. Given his desire for Diana and his distrust, he may have already written Royce off and contacted another man to handle the scheme. That rogue might have spoken to islanders to determine where the island was. With Bishop at his side, they could be on their way with no one here knowing when they'd arrive or what they'd planned.

Perspiration ran down Royce's face, a drop stinging his eye. His shoulders burned, stomach rolled. He would have offered his soul for Tristan's brandy. Not a sip, though. The full bottle so he'd sleep and escape coming doom.

He slammed his fist into his hand, tired of this. In the past years, he'd had a bellyful of inescapable problems that only grew worse, affording him less and less time to solve them with certain success always unknown.

If only tomorrow would never come. With today frozen in time, he could breathe in the fresh air. Sun could warm his face. The children's laughter would bring a smile. The priest's chamber would become his and Simone's home. They'd never have to leave. Making love would fill their days and nights.

Somehow, his family would be safely in England and would welcome the woman he adored.

He needed Simone now, more desperately than he ever had.

She wasn't in the priest's room.

Royce knocked on her door next. No answer, nor was she inside.

He shouldn't have left her without making plans to meet up later, but he hadn't wanted Tristan to know for certain they were together. Another lecture from Tristan and she'd weep anew, leaving Royce to deal with her unhappiness, then restate his promise that he would have her at his side. Somehow.

Another problem yet unsolved.

Too worn to face it, he entered his chamber.

Simone turned from the window, her eyes puffy and red.

Tristan had gotten to her already.

Royce closed his door and crossed the room to comfort her.

She stepped back. "More lies. Always lies. Why?"

"Tristan's? What did he say to you this time? No, wait. Whatever it was, pay no attention. He means well, but what you and I do is none of his business. I will see to our future, please believe that." He smiled. "Let me hold you and make you feel better."

She put up her hand, stopping him from touching her. "Tristan said nothing to me. He spoke to you."

"When? You mean at the door to the priest's chamber? I didn't tell him you were inside. That's why I left quickly. So he wouldn't find out and bother you again about leaving me alone."

"He told you to send the bird today, as you did before, so Bishop could take over the isle."

Royce went hot, then cold. "You listened at the library door?"

"I ran from there to tell the men what you planned, but I couldn't. I worried too much for you and the others. I went to the kitchen and still kept my tongue, not telling Gavra anything. I want to heal the sickness you have. You gave it to Tristan and James. Maybe Peter. Why do you want to hurt us? We did nothing bad to you."

"I don't and we're not. Please listen to me." He wanted to embrace her but didn't dare. "We have to bring Bishop here, on purpose, to have surprise on our side."

"No." She clenched her jaw. "Another lie. You told Adamo that Bishop knows the water and would look for what belongs to him here. That is surprise enough."

"That was a lie. But—"

"If he never knows where we are, he'll never come here, unless you send for him. Why would you do that?" She flapped her hands. "If you try, I'll have to tell my people to stop you."

"You don't know what you're saying. What you overheard isn't the entire story. I thought the best course was to send Bishop to another isle in the hopes he'd die in a shipwreck. Tristan argued that we'd have no way to know if that ever happened. He's right. Bishop might die or could survive. What's more, if we don't lure him here and take care of him ourselves, Tristan and Diana will never be safe. Bishop wants Tristan and Peter to hang. He means to take Diana for his own, forcing her to lie with him. He's threatened to give her babe away when it's born. He will hound them forever to get what he wants, which means you and the other islanders will face another invasion. This one will be far worse than the last you survived. Bishop intends to imprison your people and sell you as slaves. You'll end up in a land far from here, separated from Gavra, sold to a cruel master who will work you to death, beat you as he pleases, and rape you whenever he sees fit. When you birth his children, he'll give those innocents to the highest bidders. To save you and the others from that, Tristan and I came up with this plan. We have to make certain Bishop comes here and that he dies."

She sank to the floor.

Royce joined her. He lowered his hand, uncertain whether she'd accept his touch. "I promise to protect you with my life. Nothing will happen to you or the others."

"Why did you lie? Why not tell everyone this?"

"Tristan wanted to protect me. He feared if your people knew the danger I caused by coming here, they'd want me dead. I can't blame them for that."

She covered her face.

"I'm sorry I didn't tell you everything." He touched her knee. "I thought it best you not know. I was wrong. No more secrets or lies. All right?"

Simone slipped into his arms. "No one here would ever hurt you."

"Because you'd shoot them first?"

She laughed softly, then moaned. "What you said to Tristan frightened and hurt me, but I was ready to betray my people for you. Never tell Gavra that."

"She and I don't speak. I doubt we ever will."

"I should talk to her."

"No." He eased Simone away so she had to look at him. "You can't tell Gavra or anyone else what I've confessed to you. If the islanders know Tristan lied to them, even if he did so to spare me, they won't trust him. Nothing he or I said to them changes what's going to happen. The only difference is that by drawing Bishop here, rather than waiting for him to show on his own, we can control the situation and outcome. You must keep quiet. Promise me."

"No one will ever know this secret. I want to watch when you let the bird go."

"Why?"

"I want to protect you."

"From what?"

She grabbed his shoulders and shook him. "You must listen. I'll tell Gavra not to look for me. That I need to work on my potions. She'll never know we're together with the bird. I'll lie to her for you."

"For us and the islanders. We're all in this."

"As one people."

A family. He nodded.

* * * *

Dawn arrived soft and fair.

In the past, Simone had welcomed a beautiful morning as the goddess's sign that the coming hours would see pleasure unfold, trouble hide. Today, the coming sun and gentle breeze taunted her. She wanted black clouds, flashes of light, booming thunder, rain pouring down in sheets. That would keep the bird from its journey and Bishop away for a little longer.

Maybe forever if he died while waiting to sail.

"How old is this Bishop?"

Royce scrubbed a towel over his face. Water clung to his dark chest hair. "Nearly thirty years past my age. Why?"

"Is he sick?"

"In his soul? Most definitely."

"No. Does his throat or limbs or any other part have the illness?"

"He's fat and quite ugly. Other than that, I don't know. I hope you're not asking because you want to be able to recognize him when he arrives. Women and children will stay in this building. Under no circumstances are you to give him one of your potions or poultices."

She planted her hands on her hips. "I can do what I want, but I would never help someone so evil. I thought if you wait to send the bird, he might die from being old or sick."

"Can't count on that, love. This is the best way. Ready?" He offered his hand.

She gripped him so hard her fingers hurt.

He kissed her forehead. "Everything's going to be all right."

Simone held back. "Will Gavra be in the kitchen? Should we leave through the window to keep her from seeing us go to the storage room?"

"Diana said she'd ask the women to come to the library to discuss recipes she wants them to try. Her poor French should keep everyone busy and gesturing to each other for hours."

Simone couldn't return his smile. "What about the men? Will they see you take the bird out?"

"Tristan said he'd send them to work in areas away from us. The women and children will be in the courtyard. No way to change that. However, it's not fully light outside. We'll wait until no one's looking in our direction, then keep to the shadows and head into the forest. You'll leave last, behind the men."

"Because I'm female, less than you?"

"Absolutely not." He pulled her into him. "You're a better person than I'll ever be. Most women are. However, I don't want anyone questioning why you're going with us. Once we're deep enough within the trees, we'll stop and wait for you to catch up. Do take care no one sees you."

"I did when I waited for you in the priest's room."

"Then this should go well and the bird will leave here in no time."

Simone wished he'd find another way.

James, Tristan, and Peter were already in the storage area, waiting. They stared at Simone, then frowned at Royce.

She took his hand and faced the others without fear. "Say nothing bad to him. Be angry with me. I listened at the library door and heard everything. I thought you were betraying my people. When I asked why, Royce told me the truth about Bishop. Why we need him to come here. Royce said I could watch him let the bird go. I will not return to the stone house."

Tristan rubbed his neck. "Let's get this over with. I need some bloody peace."

Royce attached the cylinder to the bird's leg, his note already inside, then cradled the creature to his chest. James and Peter left first. Royce and Tristan followed. He blocked Royce from the women's view.

Simone waited for her turn. She paced restlessly, palms sweaty, heart racing.

Something flew by the doorway. Four-year-old Henri darted past.

She retreated into the shadows.

He squealed. "*Je l'ai.*" I have it. He held up a ball Tristan had made and scurried back to the courtyard.

Other children shouted, wanting to play with the toy. Women hauled out washtubs.

Simone took off into the forest and ran into Royce.

He grabbed her arm, keeping her from falling. "There you are. Let's go."

She trotted to keep up. They stopped where the cliff dipped into the sea. Water sprayed against rocks. Breaking surf replaced the children's shrill laughter. Sun left its hiding place, its rays streaming over the land.

Royce lifted his arms and released the bird.

Simone talked to the goddess, begging her to make things right and to protect Royce. She grasped his shirt. "What do we do now?"

"We wait."

James sighed. "And hope."

The men watched the bird grow too small to see.

Tristan pivoted and led the group back to the stone house.

* * * *

Simone picked at her midday meal, unable to stomach more than a bite. The women's chatter annoyed her when she'd never noticed the noise before.

She had too many questions about what to expect in the coming days so she could keep Royce safe. She needed to talk to him, but he'd left with the other men to work on their houses and wouldn't return until dark.

"Is something wrong with that?" Gavra sniffed Simone's fish. "Smells like mine, yet you barely taste it."

Follie pointed her fork. "You should give her what Diana wants us to cook."

Gavra made a mocking noise. "First, I'd have to know what that is. She talked. I listened. When she said 'horse' and smiled, I knew we were in trouble."

They laughed.

Simone rubbed her forehead.

"Are you sick?" Gavra regarded her closely, then sucked in a breath. "Are you with child?"

The women leaned close, staring.

Simone swung her legs over the bench and stood. "I worry for you, Gavra, and my potions, hoping they'll be strong enough to help when your child comes. And when Diana's does. And all of yours." Simone jabbed her finger, taking everyone in. "My task is to see that each woman survives her infant's arrival and that every babe is perfect."

Gavra shrugged. "You have never failed us. Why would you do so now?"

"Anything could go wrong. Someone might die."

The women exchanged glances. Gavra frowned. "Why would that happen?"

"Because I cannot stop this. I spoke to the goddess but she no longer listens to me. She sent the sun when I begged for rain."

"What are you talking about?"

Simone wanted to run but couldn't move. "I worry about the clear sky bringing Bishop here."

"No." Gavra waved her hands. "Never say his name again or mention the battle. I want to forget what Tristan said. I need to hope."

Follie wrapped her arm around her. "Tristan could be mistaken. Bishop may not come. Then when one full moon follows the other, we can laugh and continue our lives."

Simone left before she told Follie how wrong she was. The bird had flown away despite Simone's pleas to the goddess. Bishop would soon set sail intent on slavery, rape, and murder.

* * * *

Upon his return to the mansion, Royce could barely keep his eyes open, tired from physical labor he'd deliberately sought to keep from thinking and worrying.

Before his head hit his pillow, Simone peppered him with questions on strategy, what success they'd have, and failure they'd endure. His promise not to lie kept Royce too honest, stealing any chance for tranquility. She clung to him throughout the night. He held her tightly.

One day passed, then two.

Rain returned. Gentle and soothing.

Simone brightened and hugged him at the basin. "I talked to the goddess last night. She listened this time. Do you hear the storm?"

"It's a shower. Ships sail in this weather all the time."

"It comes before the gale, showing the dark clouds the way to this isle. The priest told us about Noah. For him, it rained forty days and nights. The sky can do the same for us."

He lifted her chin. "Do you want me to answer honestly or lie?"

She bit her lip. "Not one or the other. Hold me."

He did until they had to go to their respective tasks, him to check the islanders' security, Simone to her patients. Children had coughs. Men needed treatment for their scrapes and cuts.

The third day ended and turned into the fourth, then the fifth. Soon enough for the bird to have reached Bishop, rested, and for him to have sent a message back, if he intended to do so.

At the evening meal, Tristan drummed his fingers on the table. "Why hasn't he responded yet? The weather's been mostly clear, the rain mild and brief."

"I don't know his reasoning." Royce lifted his cup. "Could be he worries that someone here might intercept the bird before I can get to it, read the message, and destroy his plan. Whatever that may be."

Peter paced. "I say we send another bird."

"Not yet." Royce forced down his cold tea. Eating wasn't possible given the knot in his stomach. "I can't let Bishop think I'm too eager to get him here."

"Why not?"

"Exactly." Diana put down her fork. "Given that his arrival will mean you met his terms and can free your family, you wouldn't be casual about this. You'd want him here."

"I agree. However, if I send him frequent messages, that indicates I can move about as I please, attach tubes to birds' legs, and put them in the air at will. My first message told him the isle has over eighty armed men on patrol. He'll wonder how I can keep communicating with him without anyone seeing or questioning what I'm doing. He may then consider that this is a pretense meant to trap him. I don't think we should take that chance. I say the islanders should maintain a constant lookout, as we decided, and be at the ready. Especially during those times I'm supposed to be keeping watch. If anyone has a better idea, I welcome it."

Diana slouched. Peter slumped against the wall. Tristan and James rapped their fists on the table.

Royce stood. "I want this to be over as quickly as possible, the same as everyone here. If nothing happens by week's end, I'll word another message, making certain to keep Bishop's suspicions at bay, and will send a new bird. If you'll excuse me."

He returned to his chamber, worry gnawing at him. Bishop might have guessed their game and had already planned a new one, those rules in his favor. Or the bird never reached its destination because a hawk enjoyed it for breakfast. Or the message had fallen into the wrong hands, say a pirate or a Mozambique official, one wanting to storm this isle for plunder and the other delighted to have new victims to hang.

The possibilities were endless.

He lay across his mattress, grateful Simone helped an island woman birth her baby rather than being in here with him. Royce didn't have the strength to pretend everything was all right and they'd have their golden future. This torturous wait might go on for weeks or months.

Or it could end quickly and unexpectedly, Bishop somehow taking them by surprise.

Royce wanted to howl. He rolled onto his belly, praying for sleep, darkness, peace.

Someone grabbed his shoulder.

Bishop.

Royce flung out his arm, ready to fight. Tristan and Simone stared. Light poured through the unshuttered window, the angle telling him it was late morning. "Why didn't you wake me?"

"I just did. The bird returned." Tristan handed Royce Bishop's note.

R. H.

Departing immediately. Will arrive during your watch. Expect four longboats. Twenty men will remain on the ship. If needed, they will join me in taking T.

Find an excuse to fill him and the others with spirits to lessen their fight. Additional funds available if you succeed.

Light one torch for your location.

D.'s future and those on the isle are in my hands now.

B. B.

Chapter 16

Simone couldn't stop trembling. She joined the other woman in the dining area for Tristan and Royce's talk about the coming trouble. Mothers held their children more closely than normal. The tiny girls and boys squirmed. Weeping, Jacqueline cradled her new infant to her breast.

Men filled the courtyard to hear the news regarding Bishop. After Tristan spoke, the islanders lined up on two sides. James and Peter went to each man, telling him what he had to do.

Simone collected healing leaves and herbs to treat the expected injuries. She had no preparation for death. Dizzy, she leaned against a trunk, offering her life to whatever god would listen and spare Royce.

"He cannot die, please. His mother and sisters need him. Take me."

The islanders could always find another healer. Six-year-old Isabelle had already taken to following Simone at times, showing interest in plants that cured. Simone's passing would affect Gavra the most. However, her love for James and their coming infant would give her a reason to live.

Royce would return to England with his family and find a white woman to love.

Men hurried past Simone to the point, reminding each other what steps to take so they'd survive.

She filled her bag with what she'd need and returned to the stone house to prepare and to wait.

* * * *

Royce, Tristan, James, and Peter huddled around a chart on the dining table.

"Bishop's ship will most likely anchor here." Tristan pointed.

Royce leaned in. "This is the only possible location? We have to be certain."

"I'm aware of that. There are more spots, but his captain would be a fool not to use this. It's ideal."

"How far is the Lady Lark anchored from there?"

"Close but hidden in a cove. If they look hard enough with their glass, they should be able to spot it even in the dark. I wager they will. It will prove to them that they reached the correct isle."

James had already drawn a larger version of the island on paper. His image bore crude depictions that represented trees and large rocks. "Where do I put the X to show the islanders where to go?"

Tristan made the mark for him and looked at Royce. "Can we believe Bishop's note that he'll leave no more than twenty men on his ship?"

"There's no reason for him to lie unless he suspects something. However, he could change his plans during the voyage for reasons unknown to us."

"We can't send too many men there to take the ship. We need them here for those in the longboats."

"Why?" Peter rested his elbows on the table. "Here, we have surprise. We can shoot them before they step foot on the beach, eliminating their numbers quickly as we would when hunting animals."

Royce frowned. "Except they're not that. They're men. I know I said Bishop employs only the most vicious and they deserve to go down with him. Those were words said in haste and anger. Facing reality is far different, especially when it comes to murder. I didn't become what I am because I enjoy this life. Nor did you, Tristan. As Diana pointed out, some in the crew could be as you and I are. What if they want to surrender?"

Tristan fingered the map. "They'd have to prove their loyalty to me and those on this island to remain here. Those who don't will have to go to the isle where we sent Canela and the pirates. It's the fairest solution I can offer."

James held up his drawing. "Is this settled, Tristan? Nothing will change about it?'

"We stay with that. You and Peter choose the islanders who'll mount an attack on the ship. I'd like to send more than twenty men, but we need an impervious force here to protect the women and children. Tell those you select to haul the longboats and skiffs to the location they need and ready them for the night in question. When the islanders strike, every man must have a pistol and spear. Those who have cutlasses must bring them. If the crew surrenders, the islanders can take prisoners. We'll deal with them later. About Adamo. He'll surely hear from his friends what they're going to do. Under no circumstance do you allow him to join them. Although he's eager to prove his loyalty to this isle, his infirmities will hold him back.

I don't want his death on my hands. He stays at the point so no can get past it to here. Tell him Zola needs his protection more than anyone else."

"Laure too," Peter said. "I'd like to stay behind and protect her, but my place is at your side, fighting to the death if need be."

"You'll go where I put you. No argument." He pulled the chart closer. "From now until Bishop arrives, we do the same thing each day and evening, preparing for him, making our actions second nature. This attack must unfold flawlessly. The islanders, our women, and coming children are depending upon us. We can't fail them."

* * * *

Simone ate little that evening, Royce even less. They held each other in bed, neither of them sleeping. Days ago, she'd wanted nothing except truth. Lies seemed kinder now. Daydreams too. Imagining a full life, love, wearing a marriage collar, having his children.

A future without him meant nothing. She'd die willingly to see him safe and back home where he always should have been. "Tell me about England."

"In what way?"

"Is there more than one to talk about?"

He laughed gently. "There certainly is. You have its history, what it looks like, the weather, the government, people, buildings, culture, amusements, wealth, poverty, laws, crime, no end of things."

"Before your father hurt everyone, did you like this London where you lived?"

He eased her to the mattress beneath him. "If you're asking if I regret coming here, then no, except for the trouble I've caused. Meeting you changed my life, including how I see things. Although England was my home and I liked it well enough, that was before I knew this isle existed. Bishop won't best me. There isn't a god that would allow such a horrible outcome. You're not going to protect me either. If I have to, I'll have Gavra tie you to your bed to keep you in this building."

"She will never listen to you."

"Then I'll have Diana do it."

"I'll fight her and win."

"Very well. If you show up on the beach to help me, I'll be so worried about you I won't be able to fight properly. While I'm keeping you safe, I'll forget to protect myself, which will leave an opening for Bishop or his men to shoot, stab, or knock me down with a blow. Is that what you want?"

"You know it isn't." She punched the mattress. "I promise to stay here."

"Merci." He embraced her tenderly.

Her frustration drained away, replaced by desire.

Their searching kiss lasted until they both needed air. He pressed his cheek to hers. "Are you too tired for us to enjoy each other?"

"Never."

He entered her lazily, as he would if they had endless time, not a few short days. He left his scent on her. She did the same with him. They joined in every possible way: their bodies, minds, hearts, souls. Hope shone in his eyes.

She masked her lingering doubt and surrendered to his warmth, the wonder of being his.

* * * *

The hours and days dragged by, driving Royce close to madness. He couldn't sit still or think coherently, his mind going in too many directions.

The islanders' tempers were short, everyone unsettled.

Each morning brought weather fairer than the last with intermittent showers and brief gusts during the afternoons.

Not enough to delay Bishop's ship.

When Royce wasn't on watch or helping the men prepare, he secluded himself and Simone in the library.

She regarded the passages he'd recorded from the medical texts on proper methods to stop bleeding, avoid infection, dress wounds, use tourniquets, remove bullets, save limbs. "What do these say?"

"I'll be through in a moment and will read them to you. When you have the skill, you'll be able to do so on your own."

She lowered her face.

"Damnation, Simone. I will have the time to teach you. Don't argue with me."

"I said nothing."

Didn't matter. Her face told him she didn't believe a word he uttered. He wrote furiously, taking his tension out on the paper and pen. "Done. While I'm speaking, stop me if you have any questions. If I can, I'll find answers in the volumes."

She nodded.

He read.

Her color drained. She held herself as one would when cold.

Royce didn't stop. To save the injured, she had to know what to do. At last, he came to the final word. "Events may not come to this many injuries. The crew might surrender when they see our force. Bishop isn't the sort anyone would willingly die for. We have that in our favor."

She tightened her arms. "Read the words to me again. I want to be ready."

* * * *

During their earlier preparations, Royce, Tristan, and James had determined how long Bishop would need to reach here.

That night had come, his arrival pressing close.

A crescent moon did nothing to chase away shadows in Royce's chamber. Stars illuminated the sky, though nothing else. Inky dark ruled, perfect for an ambush from those here and for Bishop from a longboat.

Although Royce had been anxious for this moment, he didn't leave his room just yet. He had ample time to reach his vantage point before Bishop's ship arrived. Right now, Simone needed him more.

She paced ceaselessly.

Before she passed him again, he caught her and forced a smile. "I adore you."

She held him tightly. "Be safe."

"I shall. We'll have tonight and many others to look forward to. Please believe me on—"

"Royce!"

Tristan.

Royce opened the door. "What is it?"

"Philippe just rode in from the longboats. Bishop's ship approaches. He'll anchor soon."

"This early? Are they certain it's his?"

"It damn well better be. We haven't the means to fight two crews and battles. Get to your post. Don't forget your torch. James and Peter are moving the men into position now."

Royce embraced Simone a final time and flew down the hall.

* * * *

Never had Royce longed for darkness as he did now. The torchlight made him feel horribly exposed. A target. Once Bishop confirmed this was the correct isle, he only needed to know if the fabricated pirates had collapsed from drink, then where to find them, Tristan, and Diana. If Bishop didn't have the patience for more conversation, he might order a crewmember to execute Royce immediately.

With him dead, there'd be no fee to pay. A good business decision.

He put the torch well away from his post, then crouched in the vegetation and gripped his pistol. The only weapon he allowed himself. He had to put on a good show for his guests, convincing them of his welcome, luring them more deeply into a trap.

Around him, foliage rustled from the damp breeze and men reaching their destinations.

Chirping insects competed with the rolling surf, both dreadfully loud. Something crawled on his calf. He flicked it off.

His pulse couldn't have beat harder without bursting a vessel. He wiped sweat from his eyes and rolled his shoulders.

In the distance, something interrupted the scant light that shone on the water. He squinted.

An oblong shape neared. Others followed behind it.

He guessed each longboat held ten oarsmen, forty in all. Forty-one with Bishop. Counting the crew left on the ship, the men on this isle outnumbered them.

Either Bishop was a bloody fool for bringing a small force to fight eighty plus pirates, or his arrogance had convinced him he'd win against inebriated marauders. Given his greed, he might not have wanted to waste funds on a larger crew.

The boats reached shore.

Bishop sat in the rear of the first one, a seat reserved for a frightened little girl. Like Katie. Too young to understand what brutal men had done to her. Too innocent to realize what the future held. Intense loathing whipped through Royce for cruel men who didn't deserve to draw another breath. Tonight, he'd balance the ledger in his favor or die trying.

Bishop struggled to his feet, giving Royce a clean shot.

The closest mariner glanced up, then pointed to where Royce stood.

He cursed himself for losing his chance. Shooting Bishop now and surviving the men's return fire wasn't likely. He fetched the torch and padded down the path.

Bishop lumbered forward, his belly leading the way, his full wig and clothing regal. Silk, velvet, and brocade in this clime. Sweat ran down his corpulent face. "Are all asleep?"

"Every last one." Royce kept his voice as quiet as Bishop had.

"Did they imbibe?"

Royce smiled. "We had a celebration. They won't recall anything tomorrow."

"Dead men never do. Where are they?"

Royce pointed in the direction away from the mansion. Anyone unfamiliar with the terrain would run straight off a cliff in the dark.

"Very good." Bishop gestured to the crew.

They raised their pistols at Royce. The man nearest him seized his gun and shoved it beneath his belt.

Bishop's eyes narrowed. "Pity you won't be joining us. I'll send my condolences on your death to your mother and—"

"Damnation." A mariner pointed his pistol. "There. In the bushes." He fired.

An islander dove for cover.

Bishop's men shot into the blackness. Screams rose. Someone hit? Dying?

A deafening screech followed, the islanders' voices joined in a battle call demanding blood, retribution, justice.

Everyone seemed to shoot at once, the explosions deafening.

Bishop pivoted to the longboat.

Royce slammed him with the torch, igniting his shirt.

He bellowed and swatted the flames.

A bullet whizzed past.

Royce ducked and groped for Bishop's pistol. The bastard fought him for it. The weapon flew out of reach.

"Royce, here!" Tristan tossed a gun.

He caught it and advanced on Bishop.

The swine lurched back.

Royce followed. "This is for Simone, my family, and Diana."

Bishop dropped to the sand and crouched like the coward he was. "Shoot him, you bloody fools!"

"They can't. They're busy dying." Royce shot Bishop square in his forehead.

He dropped back.

Natives felled the intruders nearest them. More islanders swarmed from the vegetation, pressing in on the crewmembers. Several dropped their pistols and sank to their knees, arms raised.

Others fought.

James shot one. Adamo raced down the path and fired on another, hitting him. Peter wrapped his arm around a man's throat and wrestled him to the sand.

"James!" Tristan pointed at the path. An escaping crewmember pushed past Adamo and raced to the point.

Simone shot out from the trees and swung a large branch, hitting the man's belly. He doubled over. She pummeled his head and back.

Royce tore up the path and pulled the limb from her. He pointed his pistol at the mariner. The man didn't move.

"I felled him." She smiled.

Royce wanted to scream. "What are you doing here?"

"Protecting you. You're bleeding."

Blood covered his left arm. He didn't recall getting shot nor did he feel any pain. "Hide in the forest until I return. I must go back."

She grabbed him around his middle and held on. "Tristan and my people have the others."

Several men were on their knees, hands raised. Some lay dead. Island men surrounded the injured, their pistols, cutlasses, or spears lifted to keep the mariners from trying anything.

Tristan looked over. "Peter."

"Aye."

"Come with James and me."

They ran up the path. Tristan stopped at Royce's side and frowned at the blood. "How badly are you injured?"

"Not much. I can move my arm and fingers."

"Go back to the house and tell Diana we had success here. We'll ride to the ship now to help the other men."

"I'll go with you."

"No. Stay there. Take Peter with you."

"What? Me? Why? I'm going with you."

Tristan clamped Peter's shoulder. "You faced the worst and came through unscathed. That's only because I shot the bloody bastard who was getting ready to kill you while you were on the sand with the other mariner, acting like you two were the only ones on God's earth. I can't watch you and save my own hide in the bargain, so don't press your luck. I'm certainly not doing so with mine. Anything happens to you, Diana will never forgive me. You know how she is. I'd rather face a pistol than her wrath. Go." He shoved him. "Where's Adamo?"

Simone pointed to the beach.

Tristan shouted, "Adamo, you're in charge. Please have the men fetter the prisoners and bring them to the courtyard."

"What do we do with the dead ones?"

"Put them in the sea. Bishop first."

"May he rot in Hell." Royce wrapped his arm around Simone's shoulders and led her to the mansion.

* * * *

Simone treated Royce's injury in the dining area. The wound was shallow and stopped bleeding quickly. Nevertheless, she trembled. "You keep getting hurt here. You have to stop doing that."

He laughed.

Diana and Gavra glared at him. Their men were still outside, facing danger. Both women circled the table. Round and round they went, making Simone dizzy. "There were only twenty white men on the ship. Far less than those who came to the beach. Tristan and James will not get hurt."

Royce frowned at Simone. "How do you know that?"

"I talked to my goddess. She saved you. She listens to me again."

"No. I meant, how did you know how many men would be on the ship?"

Simone shrugged. "I listened to you and Tristan."

"You eavesdropped."

"What is this eavesdrop?"

"You damn well know. You also disobeyed me and came to the point."

"I stopped the man who ran away. I protected you." She gave him a stern look. "I can do what I want."

He sagged in his chair.

Gérard rushed into the room, dark hair flying. "Tristan sent me."

"Why?" Peter stood. "Does he want me to join him?"

Diana shoved Peter back down. "What did Gérard say about Tristan?" Royce translated.

Gavra ran up. "Is James all right?"

Gérard nodded. "No one is hurt. Once they see to the white man's ship, they'll return here."

* * * *

In the courtyard, Simone treated the injured islanders and crewmembers by torchlight. Royce stood guard, protecting her. When it came to healing, she proved a stronger person than he'd ever be. She didn't flinch at blood or hesitate to dig bullets from arms, legs, or shoulders.

Gavra and Follie offered the men food and water.

When given the option of staying on this isle or lifelong service to natives on another, seven prisoners chose to remain here. Of those, Heath Garrison was the most civilized, a strapping young Englishman. After thanking Follie for the food, he asked if he could help his mates in any way.

"Stay put." Royce pointed his pistol. "You and the others have to prove yourselves before you can move freely."

Heath lifted his hands. "Understood." He ate quietly, his gaze averted from the females.

Many of the unwed ones peeked at him.

Royce sensed trouble. The same he'd faced when Simone had stolen his good sense and heart with little effort.

Tristan joined him. "We need to have a word. James, Peter, and the other men will keep Simone safe while you're inside. Come on."

They went into the library. Tristan closed the door. "Thank you for killing Bishop."

"I wouldn't have been able to if not for you. Why didn't you take the shot?"

"You'd earned it by being a good man and friend. I've been speaking to Diana…or rather she's been speaking to me." Tristan moved a bookcase away from the wall as Simone had done with the armoire. He pulled out a red silk bag and tossed it on the table. "That's yours."

"What is it?"

"Open it and see."

Rubies, emeralds, diamonds, and pearls as big as birds' eggs spilled out, along with gold and silver jewelry. A fortune. "Is this for killing Bishop?"

"It's to free your family and bring them back to England. That should easily support your mother for life and allow your sisters to move in the right circles so eligible gentleman will offer marriage."

"Where did you get this?"

"Where do you think?"

The gems were larger than any Royce had seen. "This is too much."

"I have far more. I hoped to give everything to Diana. She only wants the diamond marriage collar and me. About Simone."

Royce straightened, prepared to fight if need be. "I love her. Not that it's any of your business. Don't try to talk me out of it. You can't."

"I came to that conclusion when I discovered you were using the priest's room for your trysts. What do you plan to do about her?"

Royce touched an emerald the size of a baby's fist, a plan forming. "I want to take her with me."

"To England? You'd expose her to ridicule from those who'll never be half the person she is. I doubt she'd want to endure that or leave Gavra, even for you."

"I know and that's not what I meant. You've given me a way out of my dilemma."

"Which is?"

Royce dropped into a chair. "Sit down and I'll tell you."

Epilogue

The storms had retreated for another season, the surf calm, morning bright, sun warming Simone's shoulders.

Diana and Gavra hugged her, their swollen bellies getting in the way. She laughed as they did.

Tristan and Royce spoke to islanders who traded here. Today, their boats held prisoners who would spend their lives in service to natives they'd wanted to harm, as Bishop did.

Diana stroked Simone's cheek. "*Soyez bien.*" Be well.

She nodded.

Gavra blinked back tears. "Come back to us soon."

"What else? This is my home. Royce's too. You will grow to love him."

"Are you giving me a choice?"

"No." When the priest had returned to this isle, Simone and Royce stood before him, promising their futures to each other. Royce slipped the marriage collar around her throat. Their child grew inside her. "Gavra, you must make certain not to have your infant until we return."

"How long will you be away?"

"Royce said weeks."

With the islanders' help, they were sailing to Mozambique in Bishop's ship. There, Royce knew an agent he trusted who could get money to Nell, Katie, and his mother to free them. A banker would handle the arrangements for their return to England.

Simone hadn't understood much of what Royce had said. What mattered was that he wanted her to come with him on this voyage, unable to spend a night apart, and that his loved ones would finally be safe.

Someday they might come here to see him.

He crossed the sand to her, faced shaved, hair tied back, shirt and breeches clean. "Do you ladies need more time to say your farewells?" He spoke in French, then English.

Gavra and Diana hugged Simone again.

At last, they parted. Royce led her to a longboat and swept her into his arms.

She touched her nose to his. "Am I to sit on your lap while the other men row to the ship?"

"I can't think of a better way to travel."

"You want them to do all the work?"

"I'll do some. I have it—I'll take care of you. That's my job from now on."

"And I'll protect you."

He laughed, then kissed her deeply, warming her more than the sun, making her his.

Simone melted into him and the world faded away.

Be sure not to miss Book 3 in Tina Donahue's Pirate's Prize series

FORBIDDEN DESIRE

Heath Garrison had known only hardship and danger until his capture then liberation on a tropical isle. The days are balmy, food plentiful, and the twins, Netta and Aimee, irresistible. Bare-breasted and guileless, they celebrate life and sexuality in a way Heath has never known. Choosing one over the other won't be easy. Or necessary.

Sharing is the sisterly thing to do. Enchanted with the virile Englishman, the twins won't rest until they win his attention and heart, delivering all of them to ecstasy. Too bad pirates have a different idea with the island their intended prize and murder their goal.

A Lyrical Originals novel on sale December, 2017

Learn more about Tina at
http://www.kensingtonbooks.com/author.aspx/24772

Chapter 1

Tristan Kent's island—1718

Heath Garrison swept his spyglass northwest past the Mozambique Channel. Thousands of miles in the distance lay England. Home. Odd word for a place where he'd faced unending struggle and barely survived. Still, a man couldn't easily dismiss his birthplace, even when compared to this island paradise.

A balmy breeze grazed his naked chest and tugged his hair. Sun poured down. Lush vegetation, the sea's tang, and flowers perfumed the air.

Or perhaps the sweet fragrance came from elsewhere.

Despite his captors' innumerable warnings, he inched his glass to Netta and Aimee, island women no more than twenty. Born identical twins, a cruel pirate's rule had put an end to their exact resemblance.

To Heath, they couldn't have been more perfect.

He settled the glass on them.

His pulse quickened.

Their backs were to him, their focus on the leaves and flowers they gathered. Wind stirred their dark brown hair that hung straight and long to their waists. Both women wore silk tied low on their lush hips, one's cloth a deep rose shade, the other's bright blue. The fabric fluttered above their bare feet.

They abandoned the bush in favor of another.

He edged to the side, careful not to snap a twig that would disturb them. An insect buzzed near his ear. He brushed it away.

White petals overflowed Aimee's palms. She dropped them into the silk sack Netta held. The difference in their hands gave away their identities.

He edged closer for a better view of Netta's old wound.

A lemur cackled on its perch. Its companions jumped from tree to tree, rustling branches and leaves.

At the sound, Aimee and Netta turned. Their naked breasts quivered. The enticing nipples pebbled, ideal for a man's mouth.

Heath's watered.

Previous warnings rang in his head. He wasn't to approach, talk to, or even look at the island women. Didn't matter. Weakened with desire, he couldn't back away or flee even though they spotted him.

Their lips parted.

Their softened gazes and heightened color showed their approval at seeing him. Willing surrender registered in their dark eyes. Rose bloomed in their light brown cheeks, their skin satiny, flawless with youth, and surely scented with musk. An invitation no sane man could resist. If he didn't mind being beaten or possibly set adrift from this isle located a week or more from even the most primitive civilization.

Heath lowered his glass. Face down, he called himself a bloody fool for entertaining the idea of enjoying two women at once, much less sisters. This place certainly wasn't London, but that hardly meant he could behave like a rutting animal.

Dead leaves crackled beneath feet.

He didn't dare acknowledge Netta and Aimee's approach or retreat. Wasn't his business what they did. He pivoted and froze.

Royce Hastings glared. The expression he always reserved for Heath and the other captured mariners. Months before, Heath, his mates, and Benedict Bishop had landed here to take Tristan prisoner. Royce promptly put a bullet in Bishop's head and the fear of God into most of the crew.

"What are you doing here?" Royce stormed closer and put out his hand. "Give me the glass."

Heath gripped the instrument. If need be, he'd fight for it. He'd done nothing wrong, except in his thoughts. "It's mine, as you well know. Tristan allowed me to keep it to watch for intruders."

"That would be ruthless pirates or worthless mariners like you and those bastards you sailed with. Not Aimee and Netta. What did I tell you about bothering the women?"

Too much. Despite Heath's background, he wasn't a schoolboy who needed daily lectures on how a proper gentleman should behave. Good sense told him nothing would come of his attraction. He'd have more chance to woo King George's wife Sophia than he would either twin. "I haven't said a word to them or any woman here, not even to thank the ones who bring me food and drink in exchange for my work. Most think I'm addled or mute."

"Keep it that way. Leave the islanders to their own people."

"As you did with Simone?" She was the island's healer and several months pregnant with Royce's child.

He rested his palm on the pistol shoved in his breeches waistband. "You dare mention my wife's name? Do you want to die?"

Heath held up his hands. "I'm not the enemy. I've stated repeatedly, I'm with you and everyone else here. Bishop only told us Tristan needed hanging for his piracy. Not once did the swine mention his intent to claim Diana and the treasure here. He certainly didn't disclose his plan to sell the islanders as slaves. At least not to me. Given what I escaped as a boy, I wouldn't have signed on for that."

"So you say. Why should anyone believe you, considering your attack?"

A strange argument coming from a man who'd posed as a shipwrecked merchant to infiltrate the isle for Bishop and help him bring Tristan down. How convenient Royce had forgotten his misstep. "We both came here for less than honorable purposes. Or have you forgotten your role in Bishop's unending plot to see Tristan dead?"

"I had good reason for what I did."

According to gossip, to save his mother and sisters servitude and worse in the Colonies. "Indeed. And I sailed to this isle solely because a man must work to eat. My employment was on ships. Unfortunately, I wasn't born a noble like you."

"You didn't have a wastrel father either who lost every farthing to drink, whores, and wagering."

"How right you are." Heath smiled pleasantly. "I had no father at all, good or bad. If you find me so distasteful and untrustworthy, allow me to leave when the other islanders come here to trade or we go there."

The only solution. Heath couldn't be an outcast for life. His early years proved hopeless enough. To witness other men building their lives and families while he remained alone was inconceivable, especially with Netta and Aimee tempting him. He didn't think he'd survive their union with men they'd someday love. There wasn't a thing he could do to change their futures, nor would he approach them in any way. But that didn't make him a blasted saint without human need. "I must leave during the next visit."

"Impossible." The wind blew Royce's dark hair. He pulled it back. "Tristan can't risk you telling the world about this island."

"As you told Bishop, bringing him, me, and the rest here?"

"Tristan spared your hide, which means you're here for life. You're lucky we feed you."

Heath tightened his fists. "I labor for each morsel, same as everyone else."

"Not today you haven't. We need you in the courtyard to set up tables for the celebration. Come on."

"Wait. Diana's already had the child?" Her and Tristan's first in an unlikely union. Despite being a reverend's daughter, she'd waylaid Tristan to rescue her younger brother from a pirate's life. Tristan captured her instead and made her his.

"She's begun the ordeal. Simone said it shouldn't take long. Follow me."

Some distance past his original spot, Heath lost his resolve not to glance back.

Surprise crossed Netta and Aimee's faces. The look women wear when caught doing something they shouldn't, or when a man gazes into their hearts and souls to uncover their secrets.

Netta returned to her work first, her movements forced, unsettled. Aimee blinked slowly as one would when drugged.

Rumfustian had never intoxicated Heath as they did.

He lumbered forward and bumped into something.

"Watch where you're going." Royce shoved him.

Heath twisted to regain his balance and reined in irritation. Better to earn Royce's trust than to trounce him and get a bullet in his brain or heart for the affront.

They passed through the forest and an opening in the courtyard walls. A sprawling stone mansion, white as snow, surrounded the vegetation.

Naked island children of varying ages scurried past palms and plants. Their laughter rang in the heated air. Men set up plank benches and tables. Squawking chickens flapped their wings in an effort to avoid too many feet.

Tristan's blond hair stood out like a beacon. So did his heavily scarred back, courtesy of a cruel captain who'd nearly whipped him to death. He paced to and fro, his usual bronze complexion pasty, features haggard, a pistol in his waistband. Diana's silver-and-diamond marriage collar dangled from his fist.

James, his friend and former quartermaster, watched from the side, red locks flapping in the breeze. Also armed, he caressed his two-week-old son to his heavily freckled chest. The infant's complexion was islander brown, like his mother's, not a spot in sight. James spoke to Tristan. "You've nothing to worry about. Simone's taking good care of Diana. Gavra is too when she should be here tending to our Willy. He's hungry."

The babe squirmed and wailed.

James simultaneously bounced his son and followed Tristan. Both wore a path in the dirt.

Heath quelled laughter at the once fierce pirates. If their enemies and those whose ships they'd taken could see them now…

A screech tore from a side room.

Tristan whirled around and reared back before he ran into James. "Bloody hell. That was worse than the last one. I thought having Diana take off the collar would allow her to breathe more easily, not scream like the Devil's after her. What in damnation is going on in there?" He pushed past.

James grabbed his arm. "You don't want to go into the birthing room. Trust me. What you'll see is for no man's eyes. It could stop your heart."

"Don't be daft. I have to help her."

"How? Was you who got her into this or have you forgotten?"

Tristan yanked his arm away. "If Diana survives the birthing, I will never lie with her again."

James howled. "No bloody chance of that happening. If you don't take her, she'll do that to you, at the point of her rapier if need be. The same as when she captured you at the Quest before I saved your hide."

"Must you keep reminding me of—"

Diana's prolonged moan cut through the other noise.

James gestured Royce over. Heath followed. They surrounded Tristan, keeping him from the room.

He glowered. "I know Gavra will try her best. Simone too. However, that doesn't address all eventualities."

James transferred Willy from his right shoulder to his left. The infant spit up. Yellow liquid oozed down James's back. He groaned. "You speak of events that will never be. My mother birthed eight children and survived each ordeal. If not for her advanced age, she would have had ten more."

"That's you—her. A farmer's daughter used to hard labor, sturdy to a fault. Diana's father did nothing except preach and rail at her for everything she did. Her days with him never prepared her for life on this isle."

Royce chuckled. "I would think not."

Tristan shot him a look.

He lost his smile. "I'm only saying with the woman going about as they are—not Diana of course. She's always fully clothed—that is, her gowns are quite nice. They suit her, because she's English, not—I'm not sure what I meant. James is right. Since time began, woman have birthed with few problems. My mother thrives in England with my two sisters."

Diana swore in English then even louder in French, the islander's language Heath understood.

Once his goal had been to better himself, learn all he could, and become more than what he'd been born as. Being a lifelong celibate on this isle hadn't been in his plan. He should plead his case to Tristan and James.

Tristan scowled at him. "What have you to say?"

"Nothing." Surely he hadn't spoken his thoughts aloud. "I'm here to work." He backed away.

Tristan gripped his forearm. "What of your mother? How many infants did she have and survive through?"

"I don't know. I never saw her."

"Because she died giving you life?" Tristan dug his fingers into Heath.

Pain shot up his arm. He suppressed a wince. "No. The workhouse beadle told me I wasn't an orphan like the rest, which annoyed him greatly. My mother left me there because she couldn't feed herself, much less me. After that, I have no idea what happened to her."

James gestured dismissively. "Probably married some willing fellow and had half a dozen more children. Isn't that right?"

For Heath to say otherwise might get him killed. Even pirates hunting a prize weren't as ruthless as a future father worried about his wife and coming child. "I'm certain she had the largest family she could and is with them as we speak."

"There you have it." James smacked Tristan's shoulder. "You can calm down. To make certain you do, I'll have Aimee and Netta check on Diana." He motioned them over.

They approached gracefully, more a glide than walk, their breasts bouncing with each step. Aimee held the bag in front. Netta hid her left hand. Both peeked at Heath.

His legs weakened, cock stiffened.

"*Bonjour.*" James smiled. "*Voulez-vous vérifier* Diana*? Voir comment elle va?*" Will you check on Diana? See how she's doing?

She wailed.

Tristan covered his eyes.

"Now." James shooed them away.

"*Oui.*" Aimee grabbed Netta's wrist and hurried to the birthing room.

Meet the Author

Tina Donahue is an Amazon and international bestselling novelist in erotic, paranormal, contemporary, and historical romance for traditional publishers and indie. Booklist, Publishers Weekly, Romantic Times and numerous online sites have praised her work. Three of her erotic novels (Freeing the Beast, Come and Get Your Love, and Wicked Takeover) were Readers' Choice Award winners. Another three of her erotic novels (Adored; Deep, Dark, Delicious; Lush Velvet Nights) were named finalists in the 2011 EPIC competition. Sensual Stranger, her erotic romance, was chosen Book of the Year 2010 (erotic category) at the French review site, Blue Moon reviews. The Golden Nib Award at Miz Love Loves Books was created specifically for her erotic romance Lush Velvet Nights. Deep, Dark, Delicious received an Award of Merit in the RWA Holt Medallion competition. Take Me Away captured second place in the NEC-RWA contest. And The Yearning was honored with an Award of Merit in the RWA Holt Medallion competition. She's featured in the 2012 Novel and Writer's Market. Before penning romances, she worked in Story Direction for a Hollywood production company. You can find her online at http://tinadonahuebooks.blogspot.com/, twitter.com/tinadonahue and https://www.facebook.com/DonahueTina1/.